M000201534

BLOOD AND MONEY

MCBRIDE AND TANNER, BOOK 1

RACHEL MCLEAN

ACKROYD
PUBLISHING

BLOOD AND MONEY

CHAPTER ONE

PHINEAS MONTAGUE, Silicon Valley's newest internet billionaire, stood with his hands on his hips and gazed out across the loch. He liked to do this walk every night: two miles along its bank, to the spot where his house disappeared from view, then back again via a circuitous route that took him through woods and across moorland.

He turned to check on his house, a low, modern structure nestled in amongst trees a couple of hundred yards back from the water. It was ideally placed: the perfect view combined with the ultimate in privacy. Here on the eastern side of Loch Lomond there was little passing traffic to disturb his concentration. The lights of the main living room shone out towards the loch, awaiting his return.

He leaned back, stretching each vertebra in his spine one by one, and drew in the deepest breath he'd taken all day. If he could live here 365 days a year, he'd be a happy man. But Phineas was on his annual 'deep thought' week, during which he could escape the rigours of running the world's most exciting internet startup and hide out in the beauty of the Scottish countryside.

The house didn't have WiFi. There wasn't even a road this far up; he had to come in by helicopter. Here, he could breathe. He could stare at the sky, its inky blackness hardly tainted by even the faintest of light pollution, and imagine himself hurtling through space on the rock that was Planet Earth.

He relaxed his back and shook himself out, preparing his muscles for the walk back home.

He heard a sound behind him and turned. In the distance, possibly half a mile away, there was movement. The sun was setting behind him, and he could see the shapes of the trees against the golden light. He knew why people came here: taking photographs, painting, absorbing the scenery. He hated it when they tramped past his house, but there wasn't much he could do about it, what with Scotland's irritating insistence on the right to roam.

Phineas squinted, trying to see what it was that had moved, and then it reared its head. A deer, nostrils flaring, breathing in the smells of the forest. Phineas grabbed his camera from the pocket of his hiking trousers.

He took a few steps towards it, swallowed immediately by the trees, where the creature wouldn't see him. He leaned against the trunk of a huge larch to steady himself, and brought his phone up.

He zoomed in. He had the latest optical lens, of course; this camera wasn't even on the market yet. He could see the deer clearly on the screen.

He stared at it, wondering what was going through its mind. Had it not noticed him? Did it care that he was trespassing on its land? He cast around, wondering which way the wind was blowing. Could the creature smell him?

Suddenly, onscreen, the creature's head shot up. Phineas frowned.

He'd heard something, too. Not just the movement of the animal. Something sharper.

The deer jerked into life and ran off. Phineas looked up from his phone as it disappeared into the trees.

Was that a gunshot he'd heard?

His breathing picked up as he turned and scanned the shore opposite. Dim lights shone through the trees; the A82 snaking its way up the western shore.

To the south was the town of Balloch, beyond it the filthy hulk of Glasgow. Those poor bastards who had to live in the city.

It had been: the crack of a bullet. Hunting season wouldn't start for months. And besides, he was too far south.

"Some bastard after that deer?" Phineas muttered under his breath.

He stopped and waited. The deer was gone, hopefully uninjured. Swallowing, he turned back to look at his house. Still shining into the dark, still serene in its modernity.

It's nothing. He was being paranoid.

He raised his arms above his head and prepared to start moving again. The next section was marshy in places, especially when it had been raining, which it had for ten days straight before finally drying up today. If he fell and sprained an ankle out here, he might not be missed for a couple of hours, and the air was starting to turn chilly.

He took in a breath, swung his arms, and prepared to move.

He was about to turn when he heard another crack, and felt a sharp pain in his leg.

He cried out.

He looked down. In the dim evening light he could see darkness spreading across his leg. He gasped and swayed, suddenly dizzy.

He closed his eyes.

You'll be fine, it's just your leg. He blinked and turned back towards the house. He could get back quicker that way. He could feel his heart pounding in his ears.

He couldn't see the house. He'd gone further into the woods than he thought. Still, he could see the water, and the banks opposite. He could navigate that way.

He felt a wave of nausea roll through him. He put out a hand and stumbled, then crashed to the ground.

Shit, it hurts.

He hit the ground, his head slamming into a tree.

The pain in his leg seemed to have grown tentacles, reaching up through his entire body. The world darkening around him, he slumped to the ground, motionless.

CHAPTER TWO

"Hurry up, Rory. We're going to be late."

Jade Tanner looked at her watch for what felt like the hundredth time in the last five minutes. She was on edge, she knew, and she shouldn't be taking it out on her son. But today was the first day in her new job. And quite possibly her last posting with Police Scotland if she didn't get it right.

Rory stood in the front doorway to the house.

"I can't find my dinosaur picture, Mummy."

Jade felt her shoulders slump. "It's still at school, sweetie. Remember? Miss Brown wanted to post it on the wall."

His forehead crinkled. "No, Mummy, I brought it home."

Jade approached her son. She scooped her hand around his face and stroked his cheek, crouching down to get closer to his level.

"I promise you, hen, it will be on the wall at school when you get there."

He looked into her eyes, as if sizing up whether she was telling him the truth or not.

"It's in my bedroom, Mummy."

"It's not, sweetie. I promise you. Now, come on, we need to get to school. You don't want to be late, do you?"

"OK." He didn't look convinced.

She grabbed Rory's hand and edged him towards the car, strapping him into the back seat. She checked the boot for her own briefcase and smoothed down her hair in the rear-view mirror as she got into the driver's seat and started the car.

Five minutes later, they still hadn't moved off the short slip road they lived on.

"What's up, Mummy? Have you forgotten *your* picture?"

She chewed her bottom lip. Her knuckles were white on the steering wheel.

They were at the end of their driveway which emerged straight onto the A82, Jade waiting for the traffic to lighten.

"There's a gap, Mummy."

She nodded.

There'd been plenty of gaps.

"Mummy?"

"Yes, sweetie?" She smiled into the rear-view mirror.

"There's a new girl in my class. Anita. She asked about my mum and dad."

Jade swallowed. "And what did you say?"

"I told her my mum's a police officer and my dad works with birds."

Jade dug her front teeth into her lip. "Is that all?"

"Did I do wrong?"

She turned to him. "Of course not, Rory. You did fine." She lied about Dan herself from time to time, so it was hardly surprising her six-year-old son would.

"Mummy?"

She rubbed the skin under her eye. "Yes?"

"We're going to be late."

The matter-of-factness made her want to cry. They were always late. She would have to apologise to his teacher again. Take him in through the main entrance.

They'd understand. Every time she went into the school she got those same looks from the staff. Pity and concern.

She swallowed and took a deep breath, then leaned forward over the steering wheel, peering out along the road. A car was coming, far enough away for her to get out in front of it. But still she couldn't move.

"Mummy, why aren't we moving?"

Jade felt her muscles clench. *Because this road bloody terrifies me. After...*

She turned towards the back seat. "There's just a lot of traffic this morning, that's all."

He sniffed and nodded, then went back to playing with the action figure he'd brought with him.

Come on, she told herself, *you can do this*. If she didn't learn to deal with her feelings about this road, she was going to have to move house. But this was Rory's home, it was the only place he'd ever known. And she loved their wee house. There were so many happy memories here. She needed to get a grip.

Come on, eejit, she told herself. *It's clear*.

She looked up and down the road, satisfied that the gap was big enough. She pulled out. Immediately, she pushed down on the accelerator, making the car rev and sending smoke billowing from the exhaust pipe.

"Mummy, I don't like that."

"Sorry, sweetheart."

She slowed the car. She needed to drive like a normal

person. She needed to do *everything* like a normal person, for the sake of her son.

But it was four months since it had happened, and still nothing felt normal.

Her phone rang and she hit the hands-free button.

"Hi, boss."

"Hi, Patty."

DC Patty Henderson had been part of her previous team, and Jade had managed to wangle getting her onto her new team as well. It was good to have at least one familiar face to work with.

"I'm going to be late, I'm sorry," she said.

"It's OK, boss. We need you to hang by Glasgow Queen Street on your way."

"Really? That will make me hopelessly late."

"The new guy's train gets in in half an hour, he needs somebody to pick him up. And you're kind of on the way."

Jade *was* 'kind of' on the way. The new office was in the outskirts of Glasgow, some nasty business park far away from any other Police Scotland premises. She preferred not to think about why they'd banished her to that godforsaken place, but instead focused on the fact that it gave them easy access to the motorway network which meant they could run investigations all over the country.

"Which train's he on?" she asked.

"It gets in at 9:13."

"OK. And what does he look like?"

"He's a Muslim, a Brummie and a copper. And he'll have suitcases, I imagine. I don't think you'll have any problem spotting him."

Jade nodded.

"Hi, Patty!" Rory called out from the backseat.

"Hey, Rory. How ya doing? Going to school?"

"I'm gonna be late again."

Jade frowned. "I've got to go, Patty."

"No problem, boss. See you in a wee while."

Jade hung up and peered over the steering wheel. At least she'd left the A82 now.

At last they reached the school. She parked as close as she could – double yellows again – and hurried Rory inside, making her usual apologies as they reached the reception desk. As ever, there were no reprimands. Rory wouldn't be getting a late card, unlike the other kids. She wondered whether they resented him for that. How they felt about having a child who'd suffered trauma in their midst.

"Thanks," she breathed as she left the building, running towards her car.

Now, she thought, *Queen Street*. At least the rush hour was over and she wouldn't have to fight the traffic getting into Glasgow. This Mo Uddin guy, she hoped she could find him.

CHAPTER THREE

Dr Petra McBride handed over her passport and tapped her glossy red fingernails against the desk as she waited for the check-in attendant to skim through it. She smiled sweetly as the woman looked up at her, comparing her face to the photo. As far as Petra was concerned it didn't look anything like her; the camera had caught her on a good day. Clear skin, minimal makeup, not like she felt today. But it seemed it had passed muster.

"Thank you, Dr McBride," the woman said, offering that broad smile that only Americans could manage.

Petra smiled back. It was nice to be called 'Doctor' for a change. Officials like this had a habit of calling her Ms – even Mrs, which had replaced Miss over the last few years.

She pocketed her passport and turned to Ursula, the smile still on her lips.

"This is it, hen," she said. "I'll be back in three weeks."

Ursula raised an eyebrow. "I could come over to visit you."

Petra shook her head. "I'll be busy with work."

"Your new job."

"Uh-huh. Come on."

Petra grabbed Ursula's hand and walked towards the departure gate. She was wearing her highest heels; she didn't want to reach up too far to kiss her girlfriend goodbye.

She cocked her head and eyed Ursula as they reached the gate.

"You've seen *When Harry Met Sally*, haven't you?" she asked.

Ursula shrugged. "No, why?"

Petra laughed. "Billy Crystal's got a theory. People only take you to the airport when the relationship's new. Next time I come, you'll be busy. You won't have time to drive me all the way to JFK."

Ursula brushed a stray hair away from Petra's face. "I'll always have time to drive you to the airport, honey."

Petra felt her limbs melt. She knew it wasn't true, but it was good to hear. She leaned in and gave Ursula a kiss, glad of the heels. Petra was four foot eleven and these four-inch stilettos were mandatory if she wasn't to go through life looking up everyone else's nostrils.

"Right," she said, pulling her bag higher up her shoulder. "Time to go."

"Your flight isn't for three hours. Let's grab a coffee."

"I like to get myself settled," Petra said. "Besides, I need to do some shopping."

"What kind of shopping are you going to do in the airport?"

"Duty Free, hen. Get myself some nice American bourbon."

Ursula laughed. "Now I know you're pulling my leg."

Petra gave her a smile, feeling Ursula's hand tighten on hers.

"I just like to get myself settled. I booked myself into a lounge, maybe I'll have a snooze."

"You could have had a snooze with me back at my apartment." Ursula raised an eyebrow.

Petra shook her head. "It's best this way, hen. And I'm not sure we'd have got that much snoozing done. Just give me a kiss and wave me off. I'll see you in three weeks. Hopefully..."

Ursula's face fell. "Hopefully?"

"It depends on this new unit I'll be working in. No idea what Fraser Murdo's going to be like as a boss."

"Fraser Murdo," Ursula repeated, a faraway look in her eyes. "It doesn't get more Scottish than that."

"What about me?" Petra asked, staring back at her. "Dr McBride. Short, fat, Scottish lassie."

"You're not fat."

"I am," Petra said. "Don't try and butter me up."

"OK, honey."

Petra couldn't be anything other than fat, at her height. If she was going to achieve a body mass index that made her GP happy, she'd have to be thin as one of those supermodels. A thought that made her shudder. Ursula was slender; not skinny, not fat. Just right. Lumps and bumps in all the right places.

Ursula leaned in and gave Petra another kiss. "You have a good flight. Call me when you get to Edinburgh, yeah?"

"I will," Petra replied.

She squeezed Ursula's shoulder and turned away, forcing herself not to look back. She'd only known Ursula for two months, and they were definitely still at the stage of taking each other to the airport. But Petra had seen *When Harry Met Sally* too many times, and that airport theory had stuck with her. Personally, she'd never taken a girlfriend to the airport. And she'd had plenty of opportunities, with her erratic dating history.

If she'd been in Ursula's shoes, she'd have stayed back in the apartment, dozing under the covers. But it was nice to be driven here, and if Ursula did prove to be true to her word and drive her every time: well, that would be a bonus.

Two and a half hours later, her plane was boarding. She hurried towards the gate, a bag of duty free in one hand and her shoulder bag bumping against her back with every step, her heels clipping on the smooth floor. In front of her, a wee old lady struggled with a bag that looked too big to be properly classed as carry-on luggage.

"You alright there, hen?" Petra asked, catching up with her.

The old lady smiled up at her. She was one of those rare people who was shorter than Petra. Well, shorter than Petra in her heels, at least.

"I'm fine, lassie. You go on ahead."

"You on the flight to Edinburgh?" Petra asked.

"I am. I've been visiting my son, he lives in Queens." The woman wrinkled her nose. "Too busy, too smelly. Looking forward to getting back to the Highlands."

Petra nodded. "Let me help you with that bag."

It was a rare bag without wheels, a relic of the twentieth century. The woman probably hadn't travelled with it in years.

Where was this woman's son? Why hadn't he brought her to the airport? But then, Petra remembered, they were past the departure gate. Even if the woman's son had accompanied her, he wouldn't have been allowed this far.

"Let me help you with your bag." She grabbed at it, not taking no for an answer.

"You're a sweet wee lassie, aren't you?" the woman said.

Petra shook her head. "You should see me on my off days."

She hoisted up the woman's bag, struggling to carry it along with her own duty free bag and keep her shoulder bag in place.

"OK," she said. "Gate five. Let's go."

CHAPTER FOUR

JADE COULDN'T QUITE BELIEVE it. As soon as she'd picked up her new colleague from Glasgow station, she'd had to turn the car around and head straight back north again. She sat on the M8, her hands gripping the steering wheel as she waited for the traffic to move.

"So," she said, glancing at the DS, "where will you be staying?"

He screwed up his nose. "They found me a room in a Premier Inn in Glasgow, just until I get myself sorted."

"That's not what I meant," she told him. "I mean, where will you stay, where will you bide?"

He looked at her. "A hotel in Glasgow, Premier Inn. It's just around the corner from Queen Street."

Jade smiled at him. "You're gonna have to get used to the lingo, pal. Where will you be *living*?"

"Ah!" he replied. "Not quite sure yet. Depends on my wife."

Jade raised an eyebrow. "She lives up here already?"

"No, we've got a house in Northfield, south of Birmingham. She's applied for a transfer to a GP practice in Stirling. If she gets it, we'll probably live there."

"Stirling's not too bad from the office," Jade said. "Good roads, as long as the Forth Bridge doesn't give you any trouble."

He looked at her, his face blank.

"Have you been to Scotland before?" Jade asked.

"Just to visit family," he said. "Catriona's family live just south of Aberdeen."

"So nowhere near Stirling?"

"No," he replied. "But we figured Stirling was sort of central for her family and my work."

"Makes sense," she told him.

The traffic was moving now. She shifted her focus from her new colleague to the road, pulling into gaps when she spotted them, using the training she'd received in Uniform to glide through the traffic. Away from her home, and the dreaded A82, she was a good driver.

And she had to be. These days she was permanently running late, always delayed by the school run or by her paralysis on leaving the house. It meant that she generally needed to make her journeys faster than the satnav told her was possible. Nine times out of ten she made it; the other time, she relied on abject apologies and the fact that people felt sorry for her.

She didn't like people feeling sorry for her.

"So, where do *you* stay?" he asked.

"Loch Lomond," she replied, her voice flat.

"Nice," he said, then hesitated. "*Is* it nice?"

She smiled. "It's beautiful. I don't want to talk about it, though."

"OK."

He placed his hands between his thighs, squeezing them together, almost as if in prayer. She wondered whether he was religious. She hoped his hotel would be able to cater for him if he was.

"So, this case," he asked her. "When did it come in?"

"Hang on a minute." A gap had appeared in the traffic to their right. She pulled out into it, gunned the engine, passed a few cars, and then slid back in again. Jade might have liked beating the traffic, but she was a stickler for driving in the correct lane.

"It was called in this morning," she said. She'd taken the call just as she'd arrived at Queen Street, from Patty again. "Local Uniform are already there. The deceased is an American millionaire. Billionaire, maybe."

"Oh." Mo's voice betrayed a mix of sympathy and anticipation. Just the right combination for a Detective Sergeant. "*Which* American billionaire?"

She looked at him. "Phineas Montague. Heard of him?"

Mo frowned. "Never."

"That makes two of us."

"So, does he live in Scotland?"

She raised a finger to correct him. "You mean, does he *stay* in Scotland?"

Mo adopted a puzzled expression. "I suppose so. So, what do you say when somebody is on holiday here, or just here for business?"

"I can see how it gets a bit confusing," she said. "For that, we'd say *where are you staying*?"

"OK. I'm staying in a Premier Inn. Phineas Montague might have stayed at Loch Lomond. Have I got it right?"

"You're a quick study, I can see." Jade took the slip road

to leave the motorway. "He's got a house overlooking the loch."

"Near you," Mo suggested.

She laughed. "A little more grand than my wee place. It's over on the other side of the water, one of those places that you can't see from anywhere public."

"So where was he found?"

"On his own land, out walking. Gunshot wound."

Mo winced. "And why have we been called in?"

She raised a finger, once again bringing his train of thought to a halt. She turned left at the roundabout and onto the A82. She'd be taking it as far as Balloch and then turning off to travel up the eastern side of the loch. She could deal with that.

"Sorry," she said. "What was your question again?"

"Why is it being given to the Complex Crimes Unit? Surely it's a straightforward murder?"

She glanced at him. "Straightforward? American billionaire found with a gunshot wound on his own land near Loch Lomond? I don't think that's all that straightforward."

"Oh." His face fell. "Sorry."

"Or is that straightforward where you come from?" Jade asked. "You brummies getting yourselves murdered all the time, are you? Gunshot wounds ten a penny?"

"No," he replied. "It's not like the Americans think it is. We don't have 'no go areas'."

"Good," she said. "I think Fraser has passed it to me because of another case I was working in my last team."

"Which case is that?"

She shook her head. "I'll give you the details when we get there. I want you to make your own judgments first."

CHAPTER FIVE

As PETRA CROSSED the sky bridge towards the plane, her phone rang. She fumbled in her bag and pulled it out, only to be accosted by a steward.

"I'm sorry, Ma'am," he said. "You can't use your phone on the plane."

She pulled herself up to her full height, still five inches shorter than he was. "We're not on the plane yet, laddie."

He smirked. The lad had a cute dimple in his cheek and short hair that was slicked up in a quiff. His cheeks were pierced by high points of colour.

"I know that, Ma'am. But still, you can't answer your phone."

She put a hand on his shoulder. "Just give me a wee moment. I'll be done by the time you've got everyone on board."

He eyed her.

"And besides." She paused for effect. "It's about a murder." She went for the full roll on the first 'r'. *Murrrrder.* It never failed to impress Americans.

His eyes widened. He glanced over her shoulder – which wasn't difficult – at the other passengers, then gave her a wink.

"So long as you're quick."

She grinned.

The lad was cute, and camp as a troop of boy scouts. Her favourite kind of young man.

She answered the phone. "Dr McBride, make it snappy."

"Petra," came the voice at the other end.

Petra rolled her eyes. She looked at the steward, who grinned at her. She wished she'd listened to him now.

"Fraser," she said. "What can I do for you?"

"Where are you?" he asked.

"Legally, nowhere I think."

"You know that's not what I mean. Have you landed in Edinburgh yet?"

"Not yet." She checked her watch. "Should be there in about seven and a half hours."

The steward threw her a nod and a smile in confirmation.

She sighed. "What can I do for you, Fraser?"

"That case I emailed you about. I just wanted to fill you in on the details."

"OK." She tapped her fingernails on her bag as a solidly built American couple pushed past her, turning to give her unfriendly looks. "Can't you do that by email?"

"It's... sensitive. And your email isn't secure."

"Fair enough. Is it the one I saw on CNN this morning? Montague?"

"Yes." He hesitated. "I believe you'll find it interesting."

"My idea of interesting and yours can be quite different, Fraser."

He sighed. "We're under pressure. I've put my newest team on it."

"You forget that I don't know any of your teams. Just you." Petra had met Detective Superintendent Fraser Murdo at an event bringing law enforcement and academia together a year or so earlier. He'd been surprisingly lively, for a copper.

"No. Anyway. DI Jade Tanner, she's heading up the new Complex Crimes Unit. She's good."

"Glad to hear it."

The steward leaned towards her. The other passengers had passed and the two of them were alone.

"I'm sorry, Ma'am. But I must insist..."

"It's fine. I'll talk to you when I land, Fraser." She hung up.

The steward smiled and Petra gave his arm a squeeze. "Gi' us an extra dram of whisky on the flight, eh sweetheart?"

"Er... of course." He frowned, clearly worried she might be a drunk. But if she was going to be dealing with the murder of a world-famous billionaire, she'd need a lot more than a bag of peanuts.

CHAPTER SIX

PHINEAS MONTAGUE HAD INHABITED a broad modern house on the eastern shores of Loch Lomond. To reach it, Jade and Mo had to drive ten miles along a single-track road, pausing occasionally for other vehicles to pass. Jade wondered who they belonged to.

At last they arrived at the house. A tall slim man whose features were hidden by a forensic suit gestured to one side, showing them where to park. Jade did as she was told and got out of the car.

She approached the man, her hand outstretched. "DI Jade Tanner," she said. "Are you the Crime Scene Manager?"

"That's me," he replied. "Jamie Douglas." His handshake was firm.

"Pleased to meet you, Jamie," she said. "So what are we looking at?"

"We're working our way over his house, seeing if we can find anything pertinent."

"He's in there?" she asked.

He shook his head. "Uh-huh." He pointed towards the loch. "Just over a mile that-away, down near the water. The bastard got him from a distance."

Jade narrowed her eyes. "How so?"

"Gunshot wound. The shot might have come from across the water."

"Really?" Loch Lomond was half a mile wide up here.

"I can't see any obvious lines of sight from inland." He shrugged. "What d'you want to see first? The body, or the house and paperwork? Heather's inside, boxing stuff up."

Jade had no idea who Heather was but could guess she was one of the CSIs. "The body," she said. Mo was now standing beside her, watching the two of them in silence.

"Very well," Jamie said. "Follow me."

Jade followed him past the house and along a broad path. It looked like it had been recently renovated: widened out and tarmacked. Possibly by the latest owner of the property.

"How long has he owned the place?" she asked.

"There's documentation from the sale. Just six months ago."

"And what else have you been able to find out about him?"

Jamie raised an eyebrow. "You're the detective inspector, Detective Inspector."

She sighed. "Your team have been going over his house, Jamie. I'd hope that you'd have discovered a few things about him by now."

"That we have," he replied. "He's an American billionaire, and I imagine this is one of dozens of houses he owned around the world. This one's got a vast, light-filled study, the lucky bastard."

Jade sniffed. She wasn't sure lucky was quite the word,

given what had just happened to the man. "How far away from the house was his body found?"

"Just over a mile."

Jade exchanged glances with Mo. "I wish someone had told me," she said. "I'd have changed into boots."

"It's fine," Jamie replied. "It's still frosted over up here, the ground's hard. You won't get muddy."

"Good."

They walked on in silence, Jade mulling over her thoughts. She could sense Mo was itching to ask questions, but at the same time, wanted to listen and get the lie of the land.

At last, she spotted two more CSIs up ahead, and a forensic tent.

"That's where you found him?" she asked.

Jamie pointed. "He was spotted by a dog walker this morning, the usual cliché."

She smiled. It may be a private estate, but Right to Roam still applied. And without dog walkers, half of Police Scotland's CID officers would probably have to be laid off.

"OK," she said. "Let's take a look at him."

Jamie led her to the tent and lifted the flaps. Jade shuffled inside. A photographer was already there. He looked up at Jamie and then at her, cocking his head.

"I'm DI Tanner, Complex Crimes Unit." Jade showed her ID.

The photographer grunted and got back to work. *Friendly*, she thought.

Jade didn't know any of these people. She was used to Strathclyde Police, as it had been before Police Scotland had amalgamated. Her former colleagues were in Glasgow and despite living just over the other side of the loch, she'd never met a soul from up here.

She felt a shiver run across her skin. She might have met some of them, actually. But not in a professional capacity. When...

She shook her head out. *Focus.*

Now she was in the Complex Crimes Unit, these people were her colleagues. The whole of Police Scotland was, potentially. Would they put two and two together and work out who she was, what had happened to her family?

She looked at the photographer. "I'm the senior investigating officer. I'll need copies of those."

"Yes, ma'am." He glanced at Jamie and shuffled out of the tent.

Jade rounded the inside of the tent, surveying the body. Phineas Montague was dressed in expensive-looking walking gear. Apart from a hole in the knee of the trousers and the blood that had dried around it, there was no sign of wear or tear. No mud, no scuffs. Either Montague wasn't a regular walker, or his clothes were new.

She crouched down to get a better view. The body hadn't been here long and the cold was preserving it. No smell.

"How did he die?" she asked.

Jamie pointed. "There's a bullet wound in the back of his leg, under that hole. Bullet passed straight through, we're still looking for it. Looks like he's wearing thermals underneath, they'll have soaked up a lot of the blood. Pathologist'll need to determine the actual cause of death though."

"You know when we're expecting them?"

"Him. Soon."

Jade nodded.

Mo had moved around the tent and was standing on the

other side of the body. He surveyed it in silence. A man of few words, her new DS.

She wondered if he was picking up anything that she wasn't. She'd read the man's personnel file, but preferred to reserve judgement until she'd worked with him.

"That's all there is?" she asked the crime scene manager. "A bullet wound in the back of the leg?"

He nodded. "'Fraid so."

"He was left out here overnight. Exposure might be what did for him." Jade shivered, thinking of another case she'd worked.

Jamie shrugged. "We'll have to wait for the pathologist."

"Nobody missed him for all that time? No staff? No security guards?"

"It's all high-tech. No human guards."

"It didn't do him any good though, did it? I still want to know why none of his staff noticed him gone." She looked towards the entrance to the tent. "Any forensics in the vicinity? Footprints, fibres?"

"The ground was too hard for footprints. There are faint marks between here and the house. Nothing left by the shooter, if that's what you mean."

"You still think they were across the loch."

A shrug. "We'll search the area thoroughly, of course. But I haven't found any trace nearby."

Jade stood up. "Who's in the house? Employees? Family members?"

"Employees. No family. There's a PA who seems to be in charge: Taylor something. Domestic staff, a groundsman. They've been rounded up by Uniform."

"I can go back there," said Mo. "Start collecting statements."

Jade nodded. "I'll come with you. Find out why the hell they didn't notice he was gone. Let me know when the pathologist gets here," she told Jamie.

"Of course."

She stretched her arms, her muscles stiff. She'd slept badly last night. As always.

"Come on," she told Mo. "Let's start on those statements. We can come back here once the pathologist's arrived."

CHAPTER SEVEN

TAYLOR GANNON CHEWED HER FINGERNAILS, staring out of the upstairs window and watching the detectives as they worked.

The officers had arrived and put on their white suits about an hour ago, and now there were more of them. Some in uniform, some in plain clothes. Taylor had no clue how British police operated and didn't know how long it would be before they wanted to speak to her. Would they talk to her here? Perhaps they'd take her into custody for a statement.

She also didn't know the circumstances of her boss's death. All she knew was that some dog walker had found him out there early this morning.

Would she be blamed? When Phineas was on his deep thought weeks, she was his only connection to the outside world. She managed his Instagram account, sharing photos of him with his followers, making sure his blog posts were published.

Phineas liked to maintain the fiction that these weeks involved him switching off from the world, entering a bubble of calm where he could do nothing but think. But the reality was that Phineas went nowhere without Taylor, and Taylor went nowhere without her phone.

Only last night, she'd uploaded a photo of him enjoying haggis, neeps and tatties. Grinning at the camera with his perfect and expensive teeth, knife and fork held aloft.

Phineas also liked pretending to be a Scot, but the truth was, he was as American as they came. He'd made his billions developing a novel approach to cryptocurrency. Well, he'd made his billions being the face of a novel approach to cryptocurrency.

The reality was that Henry Jones, Phineas's former business partner, was the brains behind the operation. It was Henry who'd come up with the idea, Henry who'd explained it to Phineas over late-night drinking sessions. It had taken Phineas months just to understand it, but he had the kind of charisma that allowed a man to convince the world the emperor was wearing new clothes. And as a result, both Phineas and Henry had become fabulously wealthy – Phineas in particular, as a result of his offshoot businesses.

Henry, of course, hadn't done so well. He'd died of leukaemia a year ago, leaving his two sons very wealthy indeed.

One of the detectives turned and looked up towards the building. Taylor swallowed, pulling away from the window.

Her nails were almost down to the quick. She knew they'd want to talk to her.

Taylor was an anonymous figure. As far as Phineas's followers were concerned, she didn't even exist. They didn't know there was a woman who acted as the filter between him and the world, who tended to his every need – from booking travel and managing his diary, to organising hookers when he travelled. Taylor did everything. There were things only she knew about Phineas. Things the police would surely ask her about.

There would also be questions about her, things she wasn't so sure she wanted to tell them. The detective had been looking up at her, had made eye contact before Taylor had pulled away. She was in her early forties, by Taylor's reckoning. Mid-length blonde hair, and a suit from a mid-range chain store by the looks of it.

Taylor inched forward. The detective was still looking up at the window. She raised her hand over her eyes to get a better look.

Taylor shivered. The woman was looking right at her.

If she moved away again, that might make her look guilty. She stood very still, her heart racing. She didn't want them knowing how she'd truly felt about Phineas Montague.

CHAPTER EIGHT

JADE PAUSED on the threshold to Phineas Montague's house.

She never liked entering the homes of the dead. It made her feel like a trespasser. Even more so when, like this one, the house was still occupied.

Montague had staff, and plenty of them. Domestic staff, professional staff. He was the kind of man who had different individuals to tend to his every need, and she and Mo would need to speak to every last one of them.

"Right," she said to him. "You take the domestic staff, I'll take the business."

"Yes, boss."

"It's alright," she told him. "You don't have to be so formal."

He frowned. "Sorry?"

"You can call me Jade," she said. "I'm only one rank above you, and I've only been a DI for a couple of years. How long have you been a sergeant?"

"Time enough," he replied.

She grunted, wondering if he was hiding something.

"Who was your last DI?"

He blanched. "DI Finch," he said. "Zoe. She was my best friend."

"Was?"

He smiled. "Still is. Don't worry, nothing's happened to her."

"Good," Jade told him. "I wouldn't like to think you were bad luck."

He looked at her for just a moment too long. She wondered whether he'd researched her before arriving. Whether he knew about her own personal tragedy.

"OK," she said, injecting a note of brusqueness into her voice. That moment of familiarity had probably been too much. Time to put things back on a professional footing. "Let's find some rooms we can use for these interviews." She looked along the hallway. It was wood-lined, dark. "Where's the PA?"

A young woman descended the stairs, her footsteps light. She was unnaturally thin, with caramel skin, blonde hair pulled back in a ponytail, and lipstick that was almost luminous. Jade raised an eyebrow.

This woman certainly didn't look like the Scotswomen Jade associated with.

"You must be Taylor," she said.

"Taylor Gannon," she replied in a drawl that came somewhere from the southern states. "Mr Montague's PA. Can I help you?" The young woman gave her a bright smile but the skin around her eyes was creased.

Jade held up her ID. "I'm Detective Inspector Jade Tanner, Police Scotland. I'd be grateful if you could help us organise interviews with the staff here."

"Of course." The woman's smile didn't drop.

"My colleague here, DS Uddin, is going to be speaking to the domestic staff. I'd like to speak to professional colleagues. That'll include you, I guess?"

Taylor nodded, her face pale. Scared? Jade wondered what she had to hide.

Something flickered across Taylor's face and she lifted herself up, pulling her shoulders back and straightening. Suddenly, her cheeks were flushed again, and the air of confident professionalism returned.

"No problem, Ma'am," she said. "I'll round everybody up and we'll work our way up from the most junior upwards."

"No," replied Jade, "we'll start with the most senior. I'm assuming you're the most senior business colleague here?"

The woman swallowed. "Give me a moment to check on everybody else's whereabouts and yes, sure, I'll be with you first. It's no problem."

"Good," said Jade. "And the domestic staff?"

"That's no problem either, Ma'am. Mrs Carrick the housekeeper, she can come first."

Jade glanced at Mo, who nodded.

"I'm on it," he said. "Leave it with me."

"Good," she replied. She turned to the young woman. "Now, Ms Gannon," she said. "I'd be grateful if you could give me a list of all of Mr Montague's colleagues who are either in the building or the vicinity. Make sure they're all ready for us and then I'll be speaking to you. Got that?"

"Got that," the woman said, her gaze level.

CHAPTER NINE

Mo HAD BEEN ALLOCATED A SITTING room at the back of the house, with views over the loch. From his perch on an armchair, he could see birds swooping over the water, making for a small island in the distance. He wondered whether the island had a name. He knew this was Loch Lomond, but that was only because he'd heard the DI say so, and other than that he was feeling a little lost. His luggage was still in the back of his new boss's car, and his feet had barely touched the ground since leaving the train at Glasgow. He was hoping he'd get a chance to catch his breath at some point.

A young man entered. He had weathered skin and a deep tan. He wore a Barbour jacket and had no shoes on.

The man noticed Mo's glance at his feet. "Dropped my wellies off at the door."

Mo nodded. "You're the groundsman, then?"

"That's me. Angus Robertson."

The man had a broad Scottish accent. Mo, despite being married to a Scotswoman, had no idea which part of Scotland it was from.

"I was expecting the housekeeper."

A tight smile. "She'll be along in a mo."

Mo wrinkled his nose. No point kicking the man out just because it didn't fit with the boss's plan. He gestured for Robertson to take a seat. The man remained standing.

"We're just asking preliminary questions for now," Mo told him. "Finding out what people in the house know about Mr Montague's movements in the last day or so. And where each of you were when he died."

The groundsman grunted.

"Why don't you sit down?" Mo said.

The man looked around the room, then perched on the edge of a seat opposite Mo, his hands gripping the arms. Mo wondered how often he actually ventured inside the house, and whether he'd ever been permitted to take a seat in here.

Mo had been given a list, printed off by Montague's PA. It named all of the staff working in the house, six in total. Some were employed by Montague personally, others by the business. Jade was dealing with the business associates. Mo, he felt, had been landed with the less interesting job.

He checked the list. Just names, nothing that could give him any insight into the man sitting opposite him.

"How long have you worked for Mr Montague?"

Robertson scratched his nose. "Since he bought this house."

"And how long is that?"

"Six months, six and a half maybe?"

"Did you work at this house before Mr Montague bought it?"

"No."

"So you came here when he bought the house?"

"That I did."

"Where did you work before?"

"Forestry Commission, Cowal Peninsula."

Mo had no idea where that was. He looked up from his pad. "Did you have much interaction with Mr Montague?"

A shrug. "Little as I could manage."

Mo raised an eyebrow. "You didn't enjoy interacting with your employer?"

Robertson sniffed and dragged the back of his hand across his nose.

"Sorry, pal. Got a bit of a cold, comes with the job." He checked his watch. "I need to get out soon, dogs need walking."

"Mr Montague's dogs?" Mo asked.

"They belong to the house more than him. Dogs live here, he doesn't very often. He likes – liked – walking them when he's over here, country gentleman and all that."

"Mr Montague liked to pretend to be a country gentleman?"

Angus gave a curt laugh. "He was as American as they came, but when he was over here, he liked to dress up in tartan and pretend he was a Scotsman."

Mo remembered the outfit Montague had been wearing when they found him. Walking trousers with a tartan waist-coat over expensive-looking leather shoes. Mo wondered what the man had worn when he was at home in the States. Not tartan, he imagined.

"I'm getting the feeling you didn't like Mr Montague," he said.

Angus sniffed. "He was my boss, that's all."

"That doesn't answer my question."

"I did my job, looked after the grounds." Robertson swept a hand out in front of them, gesturing towards the window. "I love working in this place. Who wouldn't? But, let's just say it's easier when the boss isn't here."

"Why so?" Mo asked.

"He's... particular, shall we say. Or he was."

"In what way was he particular?"

"Liked to change his mind. He'd go to bed, tell you he wanted to do X, Y, Z the next day. You'd get up at the crack of dawn and make sure everything was ready for him. Say he told you he wants to go hunting; guns ready, Land Rover, all set. Then he'd wake up and declare he wanted to go fishing instead. So we'd have to change our plans, get set up for fishing. And he always denied he changed his mind, insisted that that's what he'd said in the first place. I knew better."

Mo knew what it was like to have a difficult boss. Until a year earlier, he'd worked for David Randle, the mere mention of whom made Mo's skin crawl. But for the last year, he'd worked for Zoe. Best boss he'd ever had. He hoped Jade would be half as easy.

Still, Montague being a difficult boss wasn't a motive to kill him.

"What did the rest of the staff here think of him?" Mo asked.

"You'd have to ask them."

"I'm asking you."

"Look, I'm not speaking out of turn. I don't want to get anybody else into trouble. I'm sure you'll be talking to them all individually. I'm not getting involved."

Mo looked at him. "Fair enough. As I imagine you know, Mr Montague was out walking when he was shot. Did you see him before he went out walking? Were you involved in any preparations for his walk?"

Robertson shook his head. "Walking was easy. All he

needed was his coat and shoes. Mind you, he had a habit of forgetting where he left them."

"Isn't there a designated place in the house?"

"Boot room." Angus gestured behind him. "But the boss didn't like leaving his boots there, he used to just dump them wherever he fancied. It was Mrs Carrick's job to clean them up."

Mo nodded. He hoped to interview the housekeeper next.

"So did you have any contact with Mr Montague in the twenty-four hours before he was found?"

"No. I was over on the other side of the estate doing some work on the High Copse."

"What does that entail?" Mo asked.

"Clearing ground, pollarding trees, that kind of thing. Satisfying work. Not the kind of thing the boss had the slightest interest in."

"And where is the High Copse?"

"Along the loch, opposite direction from where... from where you found him. Inland a bit. Quite a bit."

"I'd be grateful if you could show me on a map."

"You want to know if I had time to head over to the shore and bump him off."

Mo winced at the turn of phrase. "Please, show me on a map."

Robertson brought his phone out. He had the Ordnance Survey app open. He pinched to zoom in and showed Mo a spot on the map. It meant nothing to Mo; they'd need to print out a map of the estate and mark up everyone's position. Sometimes old-school was best.

"So Mr Montague didn't get involved in that kind of work?"

A laugh. "You're kidding, pal. The man didn't like to get his hands dirty. He didn't even like to tell us how to get our hands dirty. Outdoors was just about being a country chap. Hunting, shooting, fishing, and he was crap at all of them. So no, he never got involved in any proper work on the estate."

Robertson clearly hadn't liked his employer. But that wasn't exactly uncommon, especially when the employer was a billionaire.

Mo frowned. "You said you came here when Mr Montague bought the house. So how did he hire you?"

"He put out an ad, I answered it, got the job. Simple."

"OK." Mo stifled a yawn.

He was tired, still recovering from his journey, the packed train, the swiftness with which he'd been thrown into a murder investigation. These were just preliminary interviews. If the DI wanted to speak to Angus Robertson in detail, he'd be brought into the station.

Mo still didn't know exactly where the station was. He hoped he'd find out today; he needed to feel settled.

"Very well," he said. "Thanks, Mr Robertson. If we need anything else, we'll contact you."

The man grunted, stood up from his chair, brushed himself down, and left the room in silence.

CHAPTER TEN

"Follow me, Ma'am, we can talk in my office."

Jade followed the PA down a warren of corridors leading to a small office looking out over some bins. Despite being tiny, it was almost unnaturally neat. The only thing on the desk was a laptop. It was closed and arranged at exact right angles to the corners of the desk.

Shelves lined one wall, a few business books and neatly stacked reams of paper along with a couple of snapshots. A family: two women, one man and two children. Jade wondered if these might be a niece and nephew.

She looked around for the printer that the paper might be used for, but there was no sign of it.

"Is this your office?" she asked.

Taylor nodded. "Sorry. It's not all that roomy, is it?"

Jade shrugged. "Is there anywhere more suitable we can talk?"

Taylor frowned. "Phineas doesn't like me..." She pulled herself up short, her face crumpling. "I guess so. We can sit in... we can sit in his study?"

There was a question mark at the end of the sentence, as if she was asking Jade's permission.

"Did you go into Mr Montague's study often?" Jade asked.

"When he needed me to. *Never* alone."

"OK," Jade replied. "Why don't we talk in there?"

Taylor looked at her for a moment and then nodded. "Follow me."

She led Jade back along the warren of corridors and through a set of double doors into a wide room overlooking the loch. At its centre was a large desk made of what looked like cherrywood and a modern chair that Jade imagined would have cost at least a thousand pounds. To one side were two easy chairs, positioned to get the best view of the loch.

"Let's sit there," Jade suggested.

Taylor looked at the chairs, her mouth twitching. "If you're sure."

"It's fine," Jade told her. "Nobody's going to stop you."

Taylor frowned and nodded. "If you say so." She stood, staring at the chairs.

Jade shook her head then picked one of the two chairs. It was soft and comfortable, the view of the loch even more impressive from this angle.

It seemed that every chair in this house, or at least every chair that Montague had used, faced a window overlooking the loch. The building had been explicitly designed to afford the best possible views. Jade's own compact house also faced the loch, but was about a tenth of the size of this one. One downstairs room, and two pokey eaves bedrooms. It was the views they'd bought it for, and the birds.

Dan's passion, the birds.

Jade shook herself out. She'd trained herself not to think about Dan while she was working. She couldn't break now.

She looked up at the PA, waiting for her to take a seat.

Taylor frowned and Jade put out a hand.

"Please. Sit down."

At last, the woman sat down. Jade gave her her most reassuring smile.

"So, I'm assuming that as his PA, you're the person who kept track of Mr Montague's movements?"

Taylor's expression was intense. "I was, but not so much when we were at this house."

"No? Why's that?"

"He was here for his deep thought week." Taylor gazed towards the window. "A week where he switches off from the mainstream. No WiFi, no phone, no shop talk."

Jade had heard of this kind of thing. A fancy of tech millionaires. People who had a PA to keep an eye on the outside world could safely switch off for a week, knowing that if there was an emergency, they would be alerted.

"So, this house isn't connected to the outside world at all?" she asked.

"There's 4G in places," Taylor replied. "I use it on my phone. Instagram updates, emails, that kind of thing. Phineas needed to know if there was an emergency."

I bet he did, thought Jade.

"But he didn't use a phone?" she asked.

"He would hand his devices over to me when we arrived. Even his personal phone. There's a safe in a room off the kitchen. I was under strict instructions not to let anybody access it."

"And are the phones still in there?"

"I should think so." Taylor looked at Jade, her eyes wide. "I haven't touched it."

"Does anybody else have access to that safe?"

Taylor frowned. "No. Why?"

"No reason, but I'd be grateful if you could let us have the access code."

"I can open it for you—"

"No, thank you. My colleagues in the forensics team will want to examine the safe, and the phones. Was anything else kept in it? Valuables, paperwork?"

"No. Nothing."

Taylor's gaze flickered. Jade wondered what might be on those phones.

"So you say you didn't track his movements while he was here," she asked. "Does that mean you didn't know he'd gone out?"

"He always went out in the evenings at around sunset. He liked to go for a walk around the perimeter of his land."

"How much land was that?" Jade asked.

"There's a three-mile route. It takes him along the loch and then inland across heathland and through woods. He walked it in the same direction every evening."

"And that's what you believe he was doing last night?" Jade asked.

Taylor nodded.

"Didn't you notice when he didn't come home?"

Taylor pursed her lips. "He used to go out for his walk when we'd all been dismissed for the day. He didn't like to be disturbed after that. He had a strict rule. I was only to enter his office when explicitly summoned."

"Summoned?" Jade asked. That was a very specific word.

Taylor nodded.

"So at what point did you notice that he was missing?"

"Mrs Carrick the housekeeper, she told me he hadn't asked for his breakfast this morning."

"And what time was that?"

"Around half past six."

"Around?" Jade suspected Taylor wasn't the kind of PA who described anything as *around*.

Taylor looked away from the window and at Jade. "Six thirty-four."

The discovery of the body had already been called into local police by then. The dog walker had found him just before six.

"And that was the first you knew of Mr Montague being missing?"

"It was." Taylor's voice was thin.

"And what kind of boss was he? You said he had rules and he liked to summon you."

"He was fine. He was a good boss."

Taylor had drawn in on herself, bringing her feet beneath her chair and her hands into her lap. Jade was no psychologist, but she knew the woman was hiding something.

"It's OK," she said. "This is confidential. If you didn't get along with Mr Montague, you can tell me."

"It was fine," Taylor said, looking at Jade. "He was a good boss. He paid well, he treated his staff with respect. We're going to miss him."

Jade looked at the young woman. Her voice was flat, her expression dull. Jade had the feeling that nobody in this house was going to miss Phineas Montague.

CHAPTER ELEVEN

Fraser had given Petra an address on a business estate on the edge of Glasgow. She paid the taxi driver, leaving a generous tip, and watched as he pulled her bags out of the boot. Petra was a firm believer in the idea that if you were paying somebody and they were prepared to do a task for you, you should let them do it. She had friends who liked to jump in and stop taxi drivers helping with bags. She knew people who'd probably stop them driving the bloody taxi if they could, and grab the wheel themselves. But as far as Petra was concerned, this man was doing a job, and he was doing it better than she could. She'd hauled those bags all the way to New York and back, and she was damned if she was going to stop anybody from helping her at the end of the journey.

She smiled her thanks to the man as he got back into the car and grabbed the handle of her largest suitcase, dragging it along behind her, and shouldered her holdall. The tarmac of the car park was uneven, rutted in places. She pulled the case up onto the curb of the pavement and headed towards a doorway marked with the name of the business park. There was no sign for Police Scotland.

She checked her phone again, and the address Fraser had given her. She double checked Google Maps. He'd told her this was a new location for his team, but it wasn't like the police not to mark their territory.

She pressed a random buzzer.

"Hello, Higgins and Clark."

"I think I've got the wrong buzzer. I'm looking for Police Scotland."

"Police Scotland? I think you're in the wrong place, hen."

"Sorry."

Petra frowned and eyed the buzzers again. One of them was unmarked. She pressed it.

"Can I help you?"

"My name is Dr McBride, I'm here to see DI Jade Tanner."

"Oh OK. Hang on a wee minute."

Petra waited as the buzzer sounded and the door opened. She wedged it open with her suitcase then picked up her holdall, slung it over her shoulder, and made her way inside the building.

She peered through a door into an empty ground floor office. Where the hell was everyone?

There were only two floors; they must be upstairs. And there was a lift, thank God. She waited for it to arrive then shoved her bags inside, panting as she did so. She hadn't slept on the plane and she was knackered.

The lift heaved its way up and the door opened. Standing in front of her was a middle-aged woman with greying blond hair scraped back in a bun. She wore an austere blue suit that didn't quite fit. Just that bit too loose around the bust.

Petra gave the woman a smile. "DI Tanner?"

The woman laughed. She had a low, guttural laugh, the laugh of a woman who'd smoked for many years.

"Fat chance," she said. "No, I'm DC Patty Henderson. I work for DI Tanner. You must be the forensic psychologist?"

Petra smiled at the correct use of her title. Too many people referred to her as a profiler. Or worse, 'the female *Cracker*'. "So you were warned that I was coming?"

"We certainly were. The Super told us."

"Is Jade expecting me?"

Patty shook her head. "Jade's not here yet, she's out at the crime scene with the new guy."

"So I'm not the only one new to the team?"

"You're certainly not. We've got some lad up from Birmingham, DS Mo Uddin."

Petra knew that name. Could it be the same DS Uddin that she'd worked with on the gay village killings in Birmingham, the so-called Digbeth Ripper? She guessed she'd find out soon enough.

"OK," she said. "So where do you need me?"

"Follow me."

Patty turned on her heel, not offering to help with Petra's bags, and walked through a door, holding it open behind her. Petra dragged her suitcase and holdall along behind her. She'd had enough of carrying the holdall, and preferred to scrape it along the floor. And if she made a meal of it, she might get some help.

Inside was a large open plan space, with only one desk occupied. Patty sat down at the desk next to it. At the other desk was a young man. He wore a sharp suit that looked like it had cost a bit of money and had neatly trimmed black hair. He gave Petra a knowing smile.

"You're the profiler."

"Psychologist," she replied.

A smile flickered on his lips. He had a mole on his right cheek. It lent his face just the right air of imperfection. This man was good-looking, and Petra had the feeling that he knew it.

"So who are you?" she asked him.

"DC Stuart Burns." He held out a hand, not standing up. "Pleased to meet you."

His handshake was brisk and efficient. Petra knew he was trying to convey the impression that he was the more senior member of the team. She caught Patty's eye-roll and smiled.

"So, which of these desks is to be mine?" Petra asked, scanning the room. It was full of empty desks, dotted around the broad space. None of them even had a computer.

"Take your pick," said Patty. "No skin off my nose."

Petra grunted. She picked up her holdall and placed it on a desk two rows away from the two DCs. She didn't want to come across as unfriendly, but at the same time, she didn't want to be in their laps.

"So when will DI Tanner be here?" she asked.

Fraser had assured her that DI Tanner was efficient. But he'd also told her that she'd been posted to this godforsaken place in the middle of nowhere, made to head up a new team that nobody really knew much about. Maybe she was a disaster on two legs?

"She's at the crime scene, like I said," Patty replied. "She'll be back soon."

Petra dumped herself into the chair and yawned. If she'd known that DI Tanner wasn't going to turn up, she'd have gone home. Maybe there wasn't time for a nap, but she could have had a quick shower. The fog of an international flight coated her clothes and skin. Her face felt tight and crusty, in need of a gallon of moisturiser.

"Have you got her mobile number?" she asked. "I'll give her a call."

Patty shrugged. "You can try, not sure how much signal there is up there, though."

"Where is she?"

"Loch Lomond, eastern shores. The uninhabited part."

"At the crime scene?" Petra asked.

"Uh huh. Complex one," said Stuart.

Petra looked at him. "Well, this is the Complex Crimes Unit after all."

He grinned. "Good name, huh?"

Patty rolled her eyes. Stuart grunted and went back to his computer.

"That phone number, please?" Petra said, holding out a hand.

"Ah, yes. They had cards printed for us all, here you are."

Patty went into her desk and brought out a box full of business cards. *DI Jade Tanner, Complex Crimes Unit.*

Petra took one and placed it on her desk. She wondered if she'd be provided with a computer, or if she'd need to bring her own laptop. For now, she could work from her mobile phone. And besides, this wasn't going to be a full-time job. She picked up her phone and dialled the number on the card.

CHAPTER TWELVE

Jade looked up as a slim, middle-aged woman entered the room. Taylor didn't look up from her mobile phone.

The woman frowned. "Sorry to bother you," she said to Jade in a broad Highland accent, "but the pathologist's arrived. Crime scene people told me to tell you."

"Thanks," said Jade. "And you are?"

"Mrs Carrick. Mr Montague's housekeeper."

"I'm glad you're here, Mrs Carrick. My colleague DS Uddin wants to speak with you."

"No problem." The woman smiled, remarkably breezy for somebody whose boss had just died. She closed the door behind her and Jade stood up.

"Thank you for your time," she said to Taylor. "If you think of anything that might be useful, please call me. And I'll need to speak to any other business staff."

"There's Kyle, the intern. And Rhianna, my assistant."

"You have an assistant?"

Taylor shrugged. "I need her."

Wow, Jade thought. An assistant with an assistant. This was another world.

She fished in the pocket of her jacket and brought out her business card. It was an old one, tatty from being carried in her pocket, and with the wrong address. But her email and phone number hadn't changed, and that was all people cared about. Hopefully there would soon be a supply of new ones with all four corners intact.

Taylor pocketed the business card and shrugged. "I'll be heading back to the States soon."

"Still," Jade said. "You have my number."

Taylor pursed her lips and tightened her grip on the card. Jade had a feeling its next destination would be a rubbish bin.

She looked towards the door. "How do I get out of the house from here?" she asked. She remembered the warren of corridors.

Taylor smiled and folded the business card in her palm. "I'll show you."

She followed Taylor out of the double doors and into a narrow hallway at the back of the house. Taylor led her round corners and through a side door to the pathway running alongside the house towards the water.

Jade shook the PA's hand. "Tell me before you leave for the US, please."

"Oh? OK." Taylor turned into the house and closed the door, bringing her phone to her ear.

Jade looked at the closed door. Was the PA normally this rude, or was it the shock?

She turned to get her bearings. The body was a mile away along a path that ran along the front of the house. Jade sighed and trudged towards it, hoping the pathologist and CSIs were still waiting.

As she walked, her phone rang.

"DI Tanner," she said.

"Jade, this is Petra McBride. I've been assigned to work with your team."

Jade slowed her pace.

"Dr McBride, good to hear from you."

"I'm afraid things seem to have got off to a bit of a slow start. I'm in your office," the doctor replied. "I thought you'd be here?"

Jade swallowed. "I'm at the crime scene. Is Patty there? Has she briefed you?"

"I wouldn't exactly say that."

Jade wrinkled her nose. She knew that Patty was wary of outsiders and would probably see a psychologist as some kind of quack. She hoped her DC hadn't put the woman off.

"OK," she said. "Why don't you head up here?"

"I don't have a car." The doctor's voice was stern. "I arrived in on a plane from New York this morning, and I got a cab straight to your office."

"You don't have a car at all?" Jade asked her. "Or you just don't have it with you?"

"I don't own one. I've not had need for one."

"OK." Jade scratched her cheek.

Did this mean she was going to be ferrying this woman around every time she needed to visit a crime scene or speak to a witness?

"In that case, why don't you stay in the office and I'll speak to you when I get back?"

"How long will that be?"

Jade was walking faster now, aware that the pathologist would have started.

"I'm sorry," she said. "But the pathologist has just arrived and I don't know how long his examination is going to take. I can't tell you exactly how long I'll be."

There was a grunt at the end of the line.

"Well, in that case, I'll go home. Call me when you're ready for me."

Jade opened her mouth to object, but then realised she had no right to insist that this woman stay in the office with nothing to do.

"That's fine," she said. "Can you let me have your address though? I might be able to hang by on my way home from the office."

"Very well."

The woman read out an address in Glasgow's West End. That was good, Jade thought. Not too far out of her way.

"I'll call you when I'm leaving," she said. "And I'm sorry that we've messed you around."

"I've worked plenty of police investigations before. I know how it can be."

The line went dead.

Jade felt her body slump. Fraser had said he wanted her working with Dr McBride on multiple investigations. The woman seemed snippy and irritable. Jade hoped it was down to jet lag.

Up ahead of her was the crime scene. A forensic tent had been erected, but there was no one in sight. The crime scene manager and pathologist would be inside. But still, there should always be a police guard. Even here, in the middle of nowhere.

Jade cleared her throat, took a deep breath and tried to push her worry about the new psychologist out of her mind. She needed to focus on the body.

Forget the shrink. This was physical evidence, and hopefully it would help her solve the case.

CHAPTER THIRTEEN

JADE PUSHED OPEN the flaps of the forensic tent. Sure enough, Jamie Douglas, the crime scene manager, and Dr Pradesh, the pathologist, were inside.

She cleared her throat to get their attention, and the two men turned. Both of them were stooped over the body, peering at it. She got the impression they'd only just started.

"Morning," Jade said, trying to sound brisk and professional. "Sorry it took me a while to get up here, I was interviewing a witness."

The pathologist sniffed and turned back towards the body. Jamie gave Jade a smile.

"No problem. Dr Pradesh has only just started."

Jade stepped forward.

Jamie put out a hand, gesturing at the protective plates that he'd placed on the floor. She wasn't entirely sure how important they were. After all, the victim had been shot, and probably not from close range. But they couldn't be too careful.

She stood on one of the plates, glad that she was short

and slim so she could balance, and watched as the pathologist twisted his head this way and that, trying to get a better angle on the body. Jay Pradesh was a large man, his jacket stretching across his shoulders as he bent over. Jade was impressed that he could balance on the plates.

"What's your first thought?" she asked.

He pointed at the man's leg. "He was shot just above the knee," he said. "It would have been debilitating. Certainly not fatal, though."

"So what killed him?"

He turned, an eyebrow raised. "I've been here five minutes, DI Tanner, and you're after a cause of death already?"

She held his gaze. She'd attended plenty of crime scenes with Jay and she knew his irritation rarely ran deep. "Cause of death helps us start an investigation."

"Hmm." He wrinkled his nose and squatted, getting closer to the body. "I'll need to confirm this in a post-mortem, but my first impression is that he bled out."

Jade tried to peer over his head. "What makes you think that?"

"The colour of the skin. Look at his face."

Montague's skin was pale. Almost blue. But that wasn't exactly uncommon.

"Couldn't that be down to blood pooling lower down?"

Jay shook his head, his back still to her. "There is none." He reached out and lifted one of the victim's shoulders. The man's jacket and shirt had fallen down, exploding bare flesh.

"See," the pathologist said. "No pooling."

"But you'd expect blood everywhere. There's hardly any."

"Maybe he moved," Jamie said. "After he was shot."

'Dr Pradesh?" Jade asked. "Does it look like he moved?"

"I can't tell from the body." He looked at the CSM. "But surely you guys would know from the forensics."

"The stones have been moved too much," Jamie said. They were on a shingle and pebble beach, footprints hard to capture. "But Heather's searching for a blood trail. If he bled out, he didn't do it here."

"He can't have bled out and then walked here," Jade pointed out.

Jamie lifted a flap of the tent. "We're not far from the water's edge. Maybe some of the blood was washed away."

"This is an inland loch," Jade reminded him. "No tides."

Jamie screwed up his face. Jade could tell he was as puzzled as she.

Jade looked at the pathologist. "You don't think anybody could have come and finished him off after the first shot?"

"There's no sign of a struggle," the pathologist said. "Look at his hands, they're clean. Very clean. No defensive wounds, no blood, or skin, or hair under his fingernails. There's no scarring or bruising to his body. All there is, is that wound to his leg."

"He's still fully clothed, though," she said.

"That's true," the pathologist admitted. "And it may be that we discover injuries to areas of his body that we can't make out just yet. But his neck is clean, his wrists, his face, and his head."

He looked at the crime scene manager.

"Is there any evidence of anybody else having been in the vicinity?"

"Not that we've found yet," Jamie replied. "There are faint footprints leading in this direction, consistent with Montague walking here. A few blood stains, leading from a spot by the trees over there. And then nothing, just the victim."

"OK," Jade said. "Are we thinking he was over by the trees when he was shot?"

Jamie stood up, grimacing. He stretched his back out, leaning back. "Not jumping to any conclusions yet, but it's likely. We'll work it out, don't worry."

The pathologist stood and made for the tent's exit. "One moment."

Jade exchanged glances with Jamie then followed him out. Jay had rounded the tent and was facing the loch, scanning the horizon.

"You're trying to work out where the shot came from, aren't you?" Jamie asked.

"It's impossible to say, from the wound. He moved too much, afterwards."

"We've taken plenty of photos," Jamie said. "We'll be aiming to work out exactly where he was standing when he went down. If we can do that, and get the trajectory of the bullet from the post-mortem, we might be able to work out where the shooter was."

"Tying up pieces of string and working out trajectories?" the pathologist asked.

Jade looked past the two men, across the loch. Surely the shooter hadn't been over there? It had to be a mile. Maybe more.

Jamie shook his head, a wry smile on his face. "Far more sophisticated than that. Digital 3D mapping, it'll visualise where that bullet came from. And hopefully, it'll lead us to the gunman's exact location when he fired the shot."

CHAPTER FOURTEEN

TAYLOR STOOD in the window of the side scullery and watched the detective walk away from the house towards the spot where Phineas had been found. She was still expecting him to appear at any moment. Even while she'd been talking to the detective, she'd found herself glancing at the door time and time again, expecting him to throw it open and berate her for invading his personal space.

She shuddered.

Personal space was a big deal for Phineas. Especially when he was here, on his deep thought weeks. She wondered if anyone had made physical contact with the man for years. Certainly not his parents, and there was no partner. Just the dogs.

The dogs. Who did the dogs belong to now? Was that even her concern?

She pushed out a breath and rubbed her eyes. There was a lot to do. Lawyers in California were already leaving voice-mail messages every five minutes. Hell, the estate. She had no idea who Phineas had left his wealth to, but there was one thing she was sure of: the sharks would be circling already.

She rubbed her nose. She had a cold coming, and it would only get worse with an eight-hour flight back home. Still, she wasn't about to hang around here any longer than she needed to. Those cops made her uneasy.

She pushed her shoulders back, rubbed under her eyes – her mascara would be a mess but who cared now? – and opened the door into the corridor. It was quiet. She made her way back to her cramped office. Could she move into Phineas's study, just for the final few days?

No. Even if he never knew, *she* would.

As she was about to put her key in the lock, Angus Robertson appeared from round a corner. He had his head down and was walking fast. She put out a hand to stop him barrelling into her.

"Angus? Everything OK?"

He skidded to a halt and looked up. His eyes were dark.

She cocked her head. She'd never seen the groundsman inside the house. "You're in one hell of a hurry there."

He shrugged. "Got to get back to the High Copse. Work to do."

"I think you can get away with—"

"No, Taylor. The estate continues, with or without your sainted Phineas Montague. It still needs me."

She drew back. "OK." Taylor knew that some people found solace in work after an event like this. Maybe Angus was one of those people. "Look, I'm kinda in charge around here now, and if you need to take some time off..."

He stared at her. "You aren't my manager."

"No, but—"

"Just mind your own business, Taylor. You can bugger off to America now, can't you?"

He pushed past her. Soon he was gone, his hurried footsteps fading to nothing.

Taylor watched, her hand on the key in her door. She wasn't going to miss these people.

CHAPTER FIFTEEN

JADE WALKED AWAY from the crime scene towards the main path leading alongside the loch. Her phone was buzzing in her pocket. Fraser, her boss. She needed to take this.

She gave Jamie and Jay an apologetic wave. "Sorry."

"Sir," she said. "I'm at the crime scene. Phineas Montague."

"I know," he said. "I just called into your office and they told me you'd gone haring off up there."

"Not exactly haring off, Sir. I can practically see my own house from here."

There was a pause at the other end of the line.

"Sir?" she asked. "Is everything alright?"

"I'm not sure you should be working this case."

She clutched the phone tighter. "I'll be fine. It's not a problem."

"You've just told me you're practically in view of your own house. That means you're also practically in view of where it happened."

"Of where my husband died, you mean?"

She hated the way people pussyfooted around her. That nobody ever said what had happened on that awful night.

"You're still seeing the psychologist," he said. "You're still processing it. I know you're having nightmares."

"I told you that in confidence."

"And this conversation is in confidence too. I can put another DI on the case."

"With all due respect, Sir," she said, "I'm back at work, and I should take any case that's assigned to me. If it happens to be the death of a multimillionaire on the opposite side of the loch from where I live, then so be it."

Another pause.

"Sir?" she asked, her senses prickling.

Behind her, she could hear birdsong. The distant sound of a 4x4 engine. Access to this crime scene was tricky. Ideally they'd be able to use a chopper, but the only place to land it was too close to the body.

The sound of birds made her think of Dan. That was the reason they'd moved here: proximity to the water and to nature. Not to mention his job with Forestry and Land Scotland.

Stop it, she told herself.

"Sir?" she repeated. "I promise you, I'm fine. When I said I was in view of my own house, I was being flippant."

"I know you were," he replied. "But I also know that people can use humour to mask despair."

She gritted her teeth. "I'm not in despair, Sir. Not while I'm at work."

"You know as well as I do that it's not easy to compartmentalise these things. If you feel it getting to you, I expect you to tell me straight away. I won't be responsible for you having another mental breakdown."

"It wasn't a breakdown, Sir."

A grunt. "Potato, potahto. Just look after yourself. You've got a new team member to manage, and a new team to head up."

"Patty will keep an eye on me," she said. "We go back a long way."

"She's a DC. She can't order you to stop when it gets too much for you."

"And you can?"

"I can, Jade, and I will. Just look after yourself and tell me before it gets too much."

Jade sighed.

She still needed to speak to Kyle and Rhiannon. The assistant's assistant. She shook her head, bemused.

"Yes, Sir," she said, injecting professionalism into her voice. "I'll be sure to tell you if there's anything you need to know."

She hung up, not waiting for a reply.

CHAPTER SIXTEEN

Mo watched his new boss as she navigated the single-track lane back towards the main road. He could sense the tension in her. She'd been taciturn when he'd asked if there was anything he needed to know about the call from the superintendent. She'd closed him down, her face hard.

They'd been sitting in silence for the last fifteen minutes. She hadn't been like this on the drive up. She'd been chatty, filling him in on what she knew about the case, pointing out local landmarks. But now her gaze kept flicking towards the loch.

"So," he said, blinking at the road ahead of them. It was starting to get dark. "Will we need to be back up here tomorrow?"

"How did you get on with your interviews?"

"Covered all the domestic staff. Nothing untoward from any of them really."

"Really?"

"No one liked him. But that isn't enough."

"No."

"What about the business staff?" Mo asked.

"I had a chat with Taylor Gannon. She didn't like him much either. And the other two worked for her, never even spoke to Montague."

"He was like that?"

"Seems so."

She tapped the steering wheel. Her fingers were long and slim. She wore a wedding ring, Mo noticed. "The techs can give us everything they need to back in the office."

"You sure? Surely tramping the crime scene, getting to know what happened here, is the best way of working out what happened?"

She frowned. "Phineas Montague died on that beach, but that wasn't where his killer was located. We need to see what Jamie gets from his 3D modelling. Once we've got that, we can find out where his killer was, and then we'll go there."

"You got any theories?" Mo asked.

A nerve under her right eye twitched. "Could have been on the other side of the loch."

"Really? It's a long way."

"It depends on the weapon he was using. You'd be surprised."

Mo nodded.

He hadn't worked many cases involving long range firearms in West Midlands Police, but he knew the theory. In a place like this, with open spaces and fewer people around to hear the crack of the gunshot, he could imagine they'd be more likely to come into play in an investigation.

"So am I right in thinking we're getting Petra McBride in?" he asked.

She looked at him. "You're talking like you know her."

He shrugged. "She worked with our team on a case in

Birmingham, homophobic hate crimes. She helped us get to grips with the type of person who would have done it."

The boss nodded. "She's not a permanent member of the team," she said. "But Fraser wants her in on the complex investigations."

"And seeing as we're the Complex Crimes Unit, that would probably be most of them."

The DI smiled, her mouth twitching but her eyes not moving.

"She's good," Mo said. "Rubs people up the wrong way sometimes, but she seems to know her stuff."

"Let's hope so," the DI replied. "I imagine forensics will turn out to be important to this case. We need to know where that bullet was fired from and what kind of gun it came from. There aren't many people with access to long range weapons like that. Once we know that, we'll be able to narrow it down."

"You think whoever did it would have walked into a gun shop and openly bought the weapon?"

"Weapons are easier to come by up here than they probably are where you come from. Hunting is a big deal, especially up in the Highlands."

"The glorious twelfth and all that?"

She threw him a smile, and he shuddered. "I thought that had all been banned?" he said.

The boss shook her head. "That's fox hunting, doesn't affect us much. Grouse, deer, other stuff. All fair game." That nerve twitched again.

"You don't approve?" Mo asked.

"My husband was a conservationist," she told him. "The idea of killing animals for sport..." her voice trailed off.

Mo noted the 'was'. But he'd only met the woman this morning. He wasn't about to pry.

He stared ahead at the road. They were past Balloch now, sailing down the A82 towards Glasgow.

"Are we heading for the office?" he asked.

She nodded. "I want to introduce you to the team. Where are you staying?"

He smiled. "My hotel?"

Her face flickered into a smile, but it was genuine this time.

"That's exactly what I mean. You're learning."

"I'm in a Premier Inn."

"Oh, yes," she said, remembering. "Just round the corner from Queen Street. We'll pop back to the office, you can meet the rest of the team, and then I'll give you a lift back to your hotel."

"Are you sure it's not out of your way?"

"I've got to drive all the way back up here when we're done." She pointed out of the car back behind them. "I live on the other side of the loch."

"Nice," he said.

Her jaw tightened.

Mo wondered what had happened to make his new boss so ambivalent about the beautiful place she lived in. Surely the kind of person who was prepared to hold down a police job while commuting from up here would do it because they genuinely loved the place. But then, she'd said her husband was a conservationist. Had they lived up here because of his job?

Mo shifted his feet in the footwell. He'd find out soon enough, and in the meantime, he needed to focus on the case.

CHAPTER SEVENTEEN

PETRA HAD NEVER OWNED her own home. At Dundee University, she'd had a small but adequate studio flat as part of her contract, and before that she'd been too nomadic to put down roots. Still was, at heart.

She'd never been interested in the idea of buying her own place. She didn't like to be tied down. The thought of picking not only an individual city or town, but a street and a house and a number. How could people know they'd be happy within one set of four walls for the rest of their lives? Petra had never held down a relationship for more than a year. She wanted the flexibility to move around, follow jobs where they took her, and girlfriends too.

She conveniently ignored the fact that she'd actually lived in her pokey little flat at Dundee University for the last six years. She hadn't spent all that much time in it. It was small and dingy, the decoration old-fashioned with a damp patch in the kitchen where the ceiling met the wall. It had been nothing more than a base. Somewhere she used when she was working, and where she stashed her stuff when she wasn't. Somewhere adequate, but no more than that.

But now, suddenly, she was the owner of a flat. This flat was in the west end of Glasgow. From the photos she'd seen, it was an impressive residence, halfway along a U-shaped block of Georgian terraces, the sort of place that made Petra shudder. But an aunt she hadn't had contact with since she was sixteen years old had died, and in the absence of any other relatives, Petra was now the proud owner of the place.

She emerged from the Clockwork Orange, the fond term for Glasgow's limited underground railway system, and checked the location on her phone. Around her, the city buzzed. The road was thronged with traffic and people hurried past her. The street had trendy cafes and a whole-foods shop. It would do.

Petra followed the map, exchanging nods with one or two people as she walked. Despite the bustle, the area seemed friendly. Maybe she could settle down here? She shuddered again.

She took a left and then a right, and found herself in her new street. She squinted. All the houses looked the same. How was she going to find it? She checked the photos again, sent by the solicitor who'd contacted her about the will. No, that didn't help. She'd have to find the number.

She trundled up the hill, pulling her wheeled suitcase and holdall behind her, picking out house numbers as she went. Not every house had one and they weren't odd and even on either side of the road, but consecutive.

At last, she found the correct number. She pulled the keys out of her bag and sifted through them. Three of them. She tried one, and it worked. She smiled.

The front door was heavy and stuck a little as she pushed

it. She heaved her shoulder against it and dragged her bags inside. The hallway was high ceilinged, chilly. The kind of communal space that people didn't take much care of.

She pushed down the handle of her suitcase and picked it up, preparing to climb the stairs. She hauled the holdall over the other shoulder. It wouldn't be easy in her heels, but she wasn't about to make the trip twice.

At last, after plenty of pauses and much heavy breathing, she reached the top floor. She tried the next key on the ring and got lucky again. Perhaps this was some kind of sign.

She pushed open the door to the flat and steeled herself. This had been the flat of an elderly woman. Aunt Morag had been in her nineties. Eccentric and bohemian, according to family rumour. Should Petra feel guilty that someone she hadn't seen for forty years had left her all her worldly belongings?

Petra left the bags in the hallway and wandered through to the living room. It was an open space, a kitchenette at one end and a broad window overlooking the square at the other. She went to the window and pulled the net curtains to one side. The view was impressive. Directly below was the garden square, locked and to be used by residents only. Maybe that was the third key. Paths ran across it and a pond sat at the centre. Beyond that, Glasgow stretched out before her like a map. She had to admit it, Aunt Morag had chosen wisely.

Her phone rang in her pocket. She dropped the net curtain and pulled it out.

"Dr McBride."

No response.

"Hello?"

Nothing.

She pushed the phone closer to her ear, listening.

"Who's that?" she said.

Silence.

Could she hear breathing? A distant click of machinery? She wasn't sure. She wasn't familiar with the sounds of this building and whatever she could hear could be coming via her other ear.

"Hello?"

No answer. The line went dead.

Petra shoved her phone back in her pocket.

Shit. It was happening again.

CHAPTER EIGHTEEN

Patty looked up as Jade entered the office, Mo trailing behind her.

"Boss," Patty said, her forehead creased. "Are you OK?"

Jade yawned. "As OK as you can be when you've just spent two hours sitting in Glasgow traffic."

Patty nodded, unsmiling. "That's not what I meant."

Jade walked over to Patty and put a hand on her shoulder.

"I know what you meant, Pat. It's fine. You don't have to worry about me."

Patty shrugged the hand away. "I do, boss."

"And I appreciate it."

Jade turned back to Mo, rolling her shoulders to relieve the tension.

"Everybody, this is our new DS, Mo Uddin. He's moved up from the West Midlands force, so let's all give him a warm welcome, yeah?"

Patty stood up, smoothing her hands on her trousers. She put her hand out and Mo took it. His handshake was firm,

Jade noticed. Stuart, the other member of the team, stayed in his chair. Jade gave him a frown and jerked her head, indicating that he should stand up. Mo was his supervising officer, after all. He should at least treat the man with some respect.

"Sorry," Stuart said. "Welcome to Glasgow."

Mo smiled back at the two DCs.

"Thanks," he said. "I'm looking forward to getting stuck in, hit the ground running as they say."

"On that note," Jade said. "We need to bring Patty and Stuart up to speed with the case."

Patty looked at her. She tilted her head. "Loch Lomond."

Jade sighed. Yes, the crime had taken place almost within view of where it had happened. But there would be plenty of reminders to come. If she was to lead any sort of life at all, she'd just have to cope with them. Patty had to stop handling her with kid gloves.

"That's the one," she said, leaning against an empty desk.

There were twelve desks in here, and another in the office at the far end of the room. The space was empty and blank, a unit in a soulless business estate at the arse-end of Glasgow. Not what she was used to.

Patty and Stuart had helped themselves to two of the desks, and Jade guessed Mo would pick another close by. He was looking between them now, clearly trying to make a decision.

"Help yourself," Patty said. "Take whichever one you fancy."

Mo raised an eyebrow. "Any recommendations?" he said. "You tried any out?"

She laughed. "What? Like Goldilocks?"

"Something like that."

"I'd go for the one by the window," Stuart piped up. "Gives you a view over the car park."

Mo walked to it and placed his bag on the desk. He stood by the window, peering out.

"Nice view," he said.

"That's one way of putting it," Stuart replied.

"OK," Jade said. "Now that's settled, let's get up to speed with this case. Phineas Montague, an American billionaire, found dead on his estate early this morning."

"Gunshot wound, yes?" Stuart said.

"Yes," Jade replied. "But he didn't die quickly. The pathologist thinks he bled out. Could have taken hours."

Patty winced. "Poor soul."

"Poor soul, my arse," said Stuart. "D'you want to know how the people who worked for him were treated?"

"Stuart—" Jade began.

"The contracts they were on in America. Still are," he continued.

Jade waved a hand in dismissal. "That's not relevant. The man's dead. Let's show some respect, eh?"

Stuart's stare dropped.

"Actually," Mo interrupted, "it might be relevant. How much fuss was there in the media about working conditions at his offices?"

Stuart looked up. "Not so much in the mainstream media, more the bloggers and YouTubers."

"OK," Jade said. "Well, let's find out what we can about that."

"It might be that somebody wanted to punish him," Mo suggested.

"That's pretty drastic, isn't it?" said Patty.

"We have to keep all options open," said Jade. "Stuart,

you look into that. Find out if there are any individuals or organisations who might hold a grudge against him because of his working practices."

"No problem, boss."

"What about the staff?" Mo asked. "There was plenty of tension there."

Jade nodded. "He didn't come across as the best of bosses," she said. "So, yes, we do need to consider the fact that one of his team might have decided to kill him. It's a fairly drastic way to get out of an employment contract, though. So my hunch is that that isn't what this is going to turn out to be."

"And then there's the fact that whoever killed him was a fair way away," Mo said.

"Exactly," Jade replied.

"What, a sniper?" Stuart asked, his eyes wide.

Patty rolled her eyes. Jade flashed him a look. This wasn't something to get excited about.

"Forensics are doing a detailed analysis of the trajectory of the bullet using computer software. Hopefully we'll be able to calculate approximately where the gunman was when he fired the bullet."

Stuart winced. "Blimey, Loch Lomond, too." He caught Jade's expression and paled. "Sorry, boss."

"It's fine," Jade replied, her voice terse. She couldn't help glancing towards Mo, who was looking between them, frowning, clearly aware that there was something going on here.

"So if there was a sniper," Patty asked quickly, "Could this be some kind of governmental thing? Security forces? MI5? CIA?"

Jade scoffed. "Now you're getting excited. Let's not jump to conclusions until we've got more evidence, yes? We need to look into a number of things. Firstly, there's Montague's relationships with the people who work for him in Scotland. Secondly, there are the forensics. We need to know exactly where the gunman was, and we need to know more about the scene of crime. Once we can pin down a location for the gunman, we'll examine that crime scene and hopefully pick up some traces."

Stuart shook his head. "Somebody like that isn't gonna leave anything behind. You're talking about a professional."

"Either way," Jade said, "we collate what evidence we can. Jamie Douglas is on it. He'll liaise with Mo and let you know what's happening."

"You want me on forensics?" Mo asked.

"Please."

"No problem. Can you let me have Jamie's mobile number?"

"I'll get that for you," said Patty.

"And after we're done here," Jade added, "I can fill you in on who some of the key people are that we work with."

"That would be great, thanks," Mo said.

"Right," Jade continued. "Then there's this psychologist the DCI has brought in."

"She came here," said Patty. "She was looking for you."

"I know," Jade replied. "She called me."

She looked at the clock. It was gone six. She'd suggested hanging by the psychologist's flat on her way home, but her mum had Rory and she didn't want to keep her waiting any longer. "Is she coming back in the morning?"

"Think so," Patty replied.

"You think so, or you know so?"

"Sorry, boss. She said she'd be back at half nine."

Jade frowned. She'd been planning on heading back up

to the crime scene in the morning. It would be easier to go there straight from home, rather than coming to the office first. But Fraser wanted her to use the expertise of the psychologist and she shouldn't leave the woman hanging.

"Boss," Patty said. "What about the Severini case? Do you think there's any connection?"

Jade raised a hand. She'd been thinking the same thing, but she didn't want to make that leap just yet. "Let's focus on this case first," she said. "I'll tell Dr McBride about Severini in the morning, see what she thinks. But I don't want to put two and two together until we know that we've got at least three."

"Fair enough, boss," Patty replied.

Jade nodded. She was tired, couldn't remember the last time she'd slept well. It wasn't just her own nightmares: Rory's, too. "There's not much else we can do until we get the forensics in. We need to go through these witness statements, but I'm still not sure we're looking at someone in that house. They were all present on the property at the time. Our shooter was possibly on the other side of the loch."

Patty tilted her head again. Jade felt the muscles in her neck tense.

"I'm fine, Patty."

"Just concerned about you."

"I know."

Jade smiled at the DC. Patty meant well. The two of them had worked together for over fifteen years, and Patty had Jade's best interests at heart. But sometimes, it could be a little cloying.

CHAPTER NINETEEN

JADE HADN'T REALISED JUST how dog-tired she was until she walked through her front door. She paused for a moment, closing it behind her, and took a few breaths. She dumped her bag on the floor and yawned.

"Mummy!"

She braced herself. The kitchen door flew open and Rory sped out, hurling himself at her. She ran her hands through his hair.

"Hello, sweetie," she said. "How are you?"

"I'm good," he said. "Dougie Murphy's cat had kittens!"

She laughed. "Kittens? Lucky him."

She knew what was coming next. Rory had been needling her for years for a pet. He didn't care what kind of pet it was, as long as it had fur and adoring eyes.

She crouched down and looked into his eyes. "How many kittens?"

Was she ready for this? Responsibility for another life?

His eyes gleamed. "Six." The excitement was palpable in his voice.

"Six!" she said. "Wow! That's some busy cat."

He giggled. "They're tiny, like little sausages."

She pulled him in for a hug.

"Mummy," he said, his voice muffled through her shirt.

"Yes, Rory?"

"Can I have one?"

His voice was tentative, expecting a no.

She gritted her teeth and closed her eyes. He needed this. Maybe they both did.

She took his head between her hands and angled it towards her own. "Yes, sweetheart. If there's one still available, you can have it."

He pulled away from her and stared into her face, looking for the trick, for the moment she changed her mind. "Really?"

She nodded, smiling. "Really."

"Yes!"

He pumped the air with his fist, running back into the kitchen.

"Nana, Nana! Mummy says I can have a kitten!"

Jade stood up, her gaze going to the ceiling. There was no getting out of this now.

She followed her son through to the kitchen, where her mum was wiping down the worktops. She gave her daughter a look. "A kitten? You agreed at last?"

"Yes."

Jade knew her mum would be wary about this, worried that she was making a snap decision in her fragile mental state. But it was too late now.

"I figured it'd be good for both of us," she added.

Rory was at the kitchen table, drawing with crayons. A kitten.

"Not one kitten. Two, three. I'm going to draw them all, Mummy," he said. "I'm going to show them to Dougie."

"I'll call his mum, see if there's a kitten still available." Jade put a hand on the kitchen table. "But don't forget, kittens are popular. They might already have been allocated."

"What's allocated, Mummy?"

"Sorry, sweetie. There might already be people who said they want them."

"But we can get a rescue cat!"

"We'll see, Rory. I'll call Mrs Murphy and we'll see what happens."

Over by the sink, her mum gave a snort. Jade ignored it.

"Right," she said. "No time like the present."

She pulled her phone out of her pocket and dialled Rory's friend's mum, hoping she wouldn't have to disappoint him.

CHAPTER TWENTY

JADE WAS IN HER BEDROOM, tidying away the clothes that her mum had washed for her today. Rory was asleep, or at least, there was no sound from his bedroom.

It hadn't been easy getting him to go to bed: the prospect of a kitten had him bouncing between the walls, running around the house, shrieking, laughing, asking her questions about how you looked after a kitten. What toys would they buy for it? What food would it eat? Could they buy it one of those scratching climbing frame things? She'd laughed and said yes to all the questions. The big question had been answered. Adding some paraphernalia to the mix felt like nothing.

She put the last of her clothes into the chest of drawers and sat on the bed, smoothing the duvet beside her. The tiredness washed over her again. She flopped backwards to lie staring up at the ceiling.

Even now, after three months, this bed made her think of him.

Maybe she should move rooms, swap with Rory, shift

into the spare room. Maybe she should move house. Then at least she wouldn't have to navigate that junction in the morning.

She shook her head and sat up. Rory needed stability. He didn't know about the junction, and she hoped to keep it that way. For a good while, at least.

She needed to make a phone call. It was late, but it had been niggling at her all day. She dialled the number she had already saved into her phone.

"Dr Petra McBride, can I help you?"

"Dr McBride, this is DI Jade Tanner."

"Ah, the elusive DI Tanner."

Jade tensed. "Look, I'm really sorry I didn't get a chance to come by your flat. I'm hoping we can get off to a better start in the morning?"

There was a chuckle at the other end of the line. "I'm sure we will, DI Tanner."

"Call me Jade. You're a civilian."

"OK. It'll be nice to meet you in person, Jade."

Jade felt her muscles unclench. So the doctor was being pleasant after all. But there was no *call-me-Petra* in return.

"So, what can you tell me?" the doctor asked.

"We've got an American billionaire found dead on his estate on the shores of Loch Lomond. He was shot from a distance."

"A sniper?"

"We're still trying to work that out."

"What kind of a distance?" the psychologist asked.

"We think it was off the victim's land. There are cameras."

"Which means the killer didn't trespass?"

"No."

"Could he have been on the opposite side of the loch?"

Jade shook her head. These questions were for forensics, not for a profiler.

"Why do you need to know all this?" she asked.

"It's important to know how close the shooter had to be in order to kill his victim. It makes a difference to the psychology of the crime. And if he went onto your victim's land, then there's more likely to be a connection between the two of them."

"You think it's a member of his staff?"

"I'm going to need a lot more information before I can draw up a profile for you."

"Is that what you'll do?" Jade asked. "Give us a description of the perpetrator?"

A pause.

"Something like that," the doctor replied. "It won't be a narrow description though. I'll give you some probabilities, options. This is the kind of person who might do this sort of thing, these are the most likely scenarios, and the most likely personality traits you're looking for. I try and focus on the history of a potential criminal, imagine what they might have gone through in their lives to lead them up to this point."

"Don't you think that if the bullet was fired from a distance, we're looking at a professional?" Jade asked. "Not at some disturbed individual, killing for emotional reasons?"

"Either way, the psychology of a person who can shoot somebody in cold blood from a distance could be important to your case. And I'd like to get to know the psychology of the victim. What kind of man was he? Who did he associate with? How much time did he spend in Scotland? And did he identify as Scottish or American?"

"I'm pretty sure it was American," Jade said. "He just came over here for his 'deep thought' weeks."

"Deep thought, what's that?"

"A week where he shut himself off from the internet and his work, and focused on strategic thinking."

A laugh. "Lucky bastard, wish I got a chance to do that."

Jade smiled. "Anyway, I'm planning to go to the crime scene tomorrow morning. I was wondering if you might want to come along?"

"Of course. Seeing where it happened will help me get into the head of the victim, and the perpetrator."

"Good," Jade said. "And I am sorry about today."

"It's fine," came the reply. "You're a busy woman. I envy you."

CHAPTER TWENTY-ONE

Mo SHIFTED his fingers on the sticky steering wheel of the pool car he'd been given for the drive up to Loch Lomond. There was no sense in waiting for the boss to pick him up, seeing as she lived just around the corner from the crime scene, and Dr McBride, the profiler, needed a lift.

They were on the M8, stationary. In front of them, another stationary car. Beside them, more stationary cars, and behind them, a whole row of the things. It reminded him of Spaghetti Junction at rush hour. He wondered if more of Glasgow would remind him of Birmingham.

But there was no point in getting settled here. The plan was to live in Stirling closer to Catriona's parents. She was coming up at the weekend so they could look at houses. He was looking forward to seeing her and the girls.

"So," he said, releasing the steering wheel and stretching his fingers out in front of him, "are you still working at Dundee University?"

The doctor grunted. "I'd rather not talk about that, if you don't mind."

"Sorry." He wondered what had happened.

He lived – had lived – in a part of Birmingham a few miles away from an area inhabited by academics, and his old boss Zoe lived in Selly Oak, where all the students were based. He knew that academic careers could be insecure. Certainly more so than police careers.

"How much has the DI told you about this case?" he asked.

"American billionaire over in Scotland for a deep thought week, shot from long range on his land on the banks of Loch Lomond."

Mo wrinkled his nose. That was about the size of it, but it sounded brusque, put like that. Phineas Montague might have been a billionaire but he was a human being, and there were people who would be grieving his loss.

When Mo had worked with Petra on the Digbeth Ripper case, she'd shown more interest in delving into the details. He wondered if whatever had happened at Dundee University would affect her ability to do her job.

"Thanks for the lift," she said, changing the subject.

"That's fine," he replied. "Didn't make sense to take two cars up."

She cleared her throat. "And I don't have one anyway."

"You're between cars too?"

"That's one way of putting it. Never had a car in my life. Never needed one, never getting one."

Mo looked at her. The car in front had moved by about half a metre but then stopped again. No one bothered to follow it.

"You've never had a car?" he asked.

"Dundee's got good public transport and I tend to rely on friends when I need a lift places."

"OK." Mo couldn't imagine what it would be like to not have access to a car. But then, Petra didn't have children, and as far as he could tell, she lived alone. It was probably easier using public transport when you didn't have kids moaning at you, asking how long it would be before you got wherever you were going.

"So," she said, "now that you've established I'm a Luddite, tell me more about the case. You went up there yesterday, yeah?"

"I did," he said. "It's a remote spot, alright. He was found on the edge of his land on a kind of beach."

"And how far away is the neighbouring house?"

"Well I couldn't see it, that's for sure."

She nodded. "Tell me about his staff, did you interview them?"

"I talked to the groundskeeper, housekeeper and a cook," Mo replied. "The DI talked to his PA and her team. There are others, Uniform have been taking statements from them, but we'll try and get more from them today."

Petra shifted in her seat. She was wearing tall stiletto heels and had her hair piled immaculately on top of her head. Her fingernails were pink, and equally neat. Mo wondered how long that outfit would last at the crime scene.

"I want to watch them," she said. "Don't tell them who I am, don't mention profiling or psychologists. I don't want everybody going all *Silence of the Lambs* on me."

Mo laughed. "You get that a lot?"

"I do. Bloody FBI."

"So what do you want me to tell them about you?"

"Just tell them I'm helping you with the case."

"You don't want me to introduce you by name?" Mo asked.

"Your DI will be there, won't she? She'll know what to do."

Mo didn't like the insinuation that he didn't know what he was doing.

The car in front moved again, not stopping this time. Mo sighed, relieved, and followed it. He checked his rear-view mirror for an opportunity to overtake and then shifted into the flow of the outside lane.

"That's better." The doctor stretched her feet out in the footwell, slipping off those stiletto heels. She wore tan tights underneath them, again, hardly the most practical of outfits for police work. But then, she wasn't here for police work, was she? Not really.

At last they reached a sign for Loch Lomond and Mo turned off.

More motorway. He blew out a breath. But it didn't last long, and twenty minutes later he was on the A82 heading along a river. He had no idea which one.

"It's nice down here, isn't it?" Petra said.

Down? Mo had been thinking of this as very much *up*. He shrugged.

Countryside wasn't his thing. He was used to the city, being surrounded by people who looked like him. He hadn't spotted many people with brown skin so far, and he doubted there'd be any near Loch Lomond.

"It's OK," he said. "If you like that sort of thing."

She laughed. A deep, gutsy laugh that came out as a single *ha*. "So you're a city lad?"

"Are you analysing me?" he asked.

Mo hadn't worked directly with Dr McBride before. He'd been in a couple of briefings where she'd been present, advising Zoe. She hadn't got close enough to analyse him. Now he imagined he'd have to get used to the idea.

"Go on then," he said, "tell me about myself."

She turned to him and wagged her finger.

"Oh, no, laddie. It doesn't work like that. I don't do readings to order."

"Readings?" he said. "You're a psychic?"

She leaned towards him, her eyes wide. "Don't you blaspheme in front of me."

Mo laughed. "Sorry."

She reached out and squeezed his shoulder.

"It's OK, DS Uddin. I'll tell you if I spot anything interesting about your psyche. But in the meantime, you can rest easy. I'll be focusing on the case."

CHAPTER TWENTY-TWO

JAMIE HAD REQUISITIONED a study at the back of the house for his forensics team. It wasn't a room that Phineas Montague had used, but a more humble one for the staff. He'd examined it for any forensics, declared it clear, then obtained permission to take the place over. Now computers sat on both the desks and photos and notes had been pinned to the walls.

In a corner were boxes containing evidence bags. Materials from the area where Montague's body had been found. Soil, blood samples, twigs and branches. Although they believed that the killer had been a way off, they wanted to check that nothing had been brought into the scene from outside, that the killer hadn't perhaps come to examine Montague's body after making the shot. It was unlikely, but the unlikely sometimes blew a case open.

Jade sifted through the bags in the topmost box.

"Anything useful yet?" she asked.

"Sorry," Jamie replied. "It's all fairly random so far. No sign of anybody else having been there. The blood we found inland from the body was all his and the only sign of disturbance was from the dog-walker discovering him the next day."

She nodded. "How are you doing with the bullet trajectory?"

"Making progress."

He bent over a computer and fired it up. Jade stood behind him, squinting at the screen. She needed to get glasses, but had resisted so far.

Jamie brought up a plan of the immediate area: aerial photographs showing the roof of the house and the land around it. They were recent, taken by a police drone the previous day. They showed the vegetation in the state that it would have been at the time Montague died.

Jamie clicked a button and blue circles appeared on the image. At their centre was the crime scene.

"So those show the range within which we think the bullet was fired."

"The range?" Jade asked.

"Based on the wind conditions and the type of bullet. I've spoken to a ballistics expert and to a mate in the Firearms Unit. These two circles show the inner and outer perimeter of the potential range.

The range began within the boundaries of Montague's land, skimming out over the loch. The outermost circle reached to the other side of the loch, and was elongated.

"Why isn't it circular?"

"The vegetation. The shooter would have needed a clear line of sight, and there just isn't the visibility inland."

"Makes sense. So you think it came from across the loch?"

"Difficult to tell. Montague could have moved in any

direction as he fell. And he was out there a while. But my best guess would be that the shot came from the north."

"The north?" Jade asked. "So not the west, across the loch?"

"The west would have given the shooter the clearest line of sight. But it's too far. There aren't many guns that would have that degree of accuracy at that distance."

"So, where do you think the shot was taken from?" she asked.

Jamie ran his finger across the screen, tracing a line towards the water south west of where Montague had fallen.

"I think if you follow this line here," he said, "you've got a line of sight. We still need to do more analysis, run the 3D modelling, but while we wait for that I'd like for you and me to go there, check it out."

"Good idea." Jade pulled on her coat.

She was wearing walking gear, clothes that she'd bought for hiking with Dan. She'd forced herself not to think about the last time she'd worn these clothes. Today, they were what she needed. Practical, that was all.

"Can you bring the laptop with us?" she asked Jamie.

"I'll send it to my phone."

Jade nodded.

The door opened and the new DS walked in.

"Mo," she said, giving him a smile. "How are you today? Decent night's sleep in your hotel?"

He wrinkled his nose. "Not too bad. Looking forward to getting a place of my own."

"I can imagine."

Another figure appeared behind him, a short woman whose height was partially offset by her ridiculously tall heels and the fact that her hair was piled on top of her head. The woman had to be less than five foot tall, but today she was almost eye to eye with Jade.

"DI Tanner, I presume?" she said in a Dundonain accent.

Jade stepped towards her. "You must be Dr McBride." She held out her hand. "Good to meet you, finally."

"You too." Dr McBride's voice was terse. "What have you got for me then? Interviews with the staff?"

Jade shook her head. "We're heading up to the crime scene, we wanted to have a look at where the fatal bullet came from. Care to join us?"

"Absolutely," the doctor replied. "Walking the scene helps me get a feel for how it happened. Which in turn, gives me a feel for the mind of the shooter."

"Good." Jade flicked her gaze down at McBride's shoes. "You might want to change your footwear."

The doctor sniffed. "I'll be fine."

Jade could make out red on the soles, were they Louboutins? And the woman was about to ruin them by tramping through a crime scene.

"Are you sure?" she asked.

"Positive, DI Tanner."

"Jade."

"Positive, Jade."

Still no *call-me-Petra*.

Dr McBride gestured towards the door. "Let's go and check out this crime scene then, yes?"

CHAPTER TWENTY-THREE

PETRA MADE sure to keep up with Jade's pace as they strode towards the crime scene. She'd seen the look on the woman's face when she'd noticed her shoes and was determined to confound her expectations.

Petra was used to people assuming she wouldn't be able to get around in her heels. But the truth was, flats slowed her down. She was used to the way heels projected her hips forward and gave her body a kind of momentum. It was helpful when your legs were as short as hers.

She strode alongside the DI, with DS Uddin and the crime scene manager following behind. Petra surveyed the surroundings as they walked, making mental notes. They were on a wide path, about twenty yards inland from the loch. It was clear here, but to their right the area became dense with shrubs and trees. This didn't look like a managed piece of woodland.

To the left was the loch, broad and grey under a flat, cloudy sky. An island about a mile out behind them seemed to be attracting flocks of birds that skimmed across the water and disappeared into its vegetation. Beyond that was the hum of the A82 from the other side of the loch.

The smells were the ones you'd expect in a landscape like this. Water, mud, nature. Petra had a keen nose, it wouldn't be long before she detected the tang of blood, even if Montague's body had been removed.

A flash of white appeared up ahead, a forensic tent. They slowed their pace, the crime scene manager hanging back and looking at his phone.

She turned to him. "Are you checking something specific?"

"We're calculating the trajectory of the bullet, software's running through the options. If we get that, we can work out where the killer was, and then treat that as a secondary crime scene."

"You'll take me up there with you?"

"If we can find it yes. And after we've made sure it's protected."

She sniffed. "I have done this before you know, laddie."

"I'm sure you have," he replied, an eyebrow raised. "But I still need to protect the scene."

"That you do," she said. "I'll be careful, I promise."

She raised her fingers to the side of her head in a mock salute.

He grunted and looked back at his phone.

They'd reached the forensic tent. A white-suited tech emerged.

"Jamie," she said, "I've found evidence of stones that might have been brought in after Montague died."

The CSM looked up from his phone. "What kind of stones?"

"Here." She turned away.

Petra glanced at Jade who nodded at her and Mo. They followed the two CSIs around the tent and further along the shore of the loch. After a minute or so they came to a small pile of stones, nothing Petra would have considered out of the ordinary.

"Do you think this came from elsewhere?" she asked.

The CSI pointed at the ground. "The gravel around them has been disturbed. And they've been arranged."

"They could have been arranged at any time," Jade said. "Why do we think they were brought here after he died?"

"The disturbance to the gravel is recent," she said. "It rained here three days ago and the ground is dry."

Jade shook her head. "Still. It doesn't make sense. Surely it's more likely it happened in the two days before Montague died? Why would someone take the trouble to shoot him from all that way off and then approach the body?"

"Murders don't always make sense, DI Tanner," Petra said, her voice low.

Jade's cheek twitched. "I know that." She walked around the stones, surveying them.

Stones and physical forensics weren't Petra's thing. She was more interested in walking through the crime scene, sniffing the air, scenting out the emotions of the killer as he'd spotted his prey and gone in for the kill. She wanted to find where he'd been when he'd fired the fatal shot. To put herself in his head, imagine what he'd been thinking as he'd done it. Had this been a cold ruthless killer, somebody hired to take out a business rival, perhaps? Or had it been somebody wanting revenge? A former employee, angry at the way he'd been treated by Montague's company? She hoped that staking out the scene would help her get closer to the answer.

"Jamie," she said, "does this get you any closer to working out where the gunman was?"

He shook his head. "Not just yet."

Jade raised a hand. "Let's give Jamie time to do this properly."

Petra eyed her. So DI Tanner liked procedure. "OK, what should I do then? Sit down here and have a picnic?"

Jade frowned. "Let's get back to the house while we wait."

Petra sighed. "OK."

CHAPTER TWENTY-FOUR

PATTY YAWNED.

"Late night last night?" asked Stuart.

"Don't you start," she grunted.

Stuart was fifteen years younger than she was. He knew nothing about late nights and how they made you feel the next morning.

She rubbed her cheeks with her fingertips, kneading the balls of her fingers into the skin to try and wake herself up. She knew that her face was grey. One too many whiskies round at her friend Shona's house last night. Shona was going through a messy divorce and Patty was the rock that Shona was leaning on. Patty worried that Shona was drinking too much, and that she was drinking too much with her. But when you had a pal in trouble, what were you supposed to do?

She put her hand in front of her mouth, suppressing another yawn. Stuart smirked and she ignored him.

"Right," she said, "what are we doing again?"

Stuart chuckled. "Digging into Montague's staff."

"Yeah," she said. "That."

She shuffled in her chair. "Tell you what, I'll grab us a coffee."

Stuart stood up. "I'll go. Need to get my steps in."

She looked him up and down. He was thin as Glasgow Tower. "You, exercising?"

He frowned. "What's wrong with that?"

She shook her head.

Stuart was mid-height and lean with prominent muscles on his arms. He didn't need exercise.

"Do you really need to get steps in as well as whatever it is you do that gives you those muscles?"

He raised an eyebrow. "Rowing."

"Rowing, in Glasgow?"

"You'd be surprised." He turned to the door.

Patty yawned, glad he wasn't watching, and returned to her computer screen.

She was looking into Taylor Gannon, Montague's PA. Jade had described the woman to her. Short, perky, blonde hair, flawless skin. Teeth like, well, teeth like an American. Patty knew the type. Well, maybe she didn't. But she watched enough Netflix to think she did. She yawned again as she scrolled through the documents, not bothering to put her hand in front of her mouth this time. She wondered how long it would be before the DI and the DS got back.

There was a folder full of files, all taken from the Montague server. The PA had been helpful, provided passwords. They didn't even need to bring computers down from the house; everything was in the cloud.

Patty wondered what the house was like, and if the views were what she imagined. In her spot at the bottom of the CID ladder, all she got to do was sit in front of a computer screen in this godforsaken office at the arse-end of nowhere. It wasn't good for her figure, or her skin.

Stuart returned and placed a coffee on her desk, spilling some of it over the book she had waiting for her lunch break.

"Hey," she said. "Watch out."

"Sorry." He pulled his sleeve over the heel of his hand and wiped her book.

She tutted and batted him away. "I've got tissues in my desk."

"Sorry," he repeated, and retreated to his own desk with his mug. He slurped noisily and Patty resisted telling him to mind his manners. She wasn't his mum.

She opened up another file, then frowned. "Hang on a minute."

Stuart looked up from his screen. "Found something?"

"Might have done."

Patty leaned in and magnified the document in front of her. "I have."

"What?" Stuart leaned back in his chair and stared across the desks. Despite the need to get his steps in, it seemed he wasn't going to bother getting up and having a look for himself.

"NDA." She gave him a look. "Nondisclosure agreement."

"I know what an NDA is."

"It's between Taylor Gannon and Montague's company."

"Why did she need an NDA?"

Patty frowned. "Probably standard procedure in these big American companies. Make sure your employees don't tell people how crap you treat them right from the start."

She scrolled up the list of documents and checked the date. Six months ago.

"When did Taylor start working for Montague?" she asked, as much to herself as to Stuart.

Stuart shrugged. "Buggered if I know."

She sighed and went back through Taylor Gannon's paperwork files. Taylor had worked for Montague for more than seven years.

In which case, why had she been required to sign an NDA six months ago?

The list Patty was scanning through included a brief summary of each document. She tried to make sense of the description of the NDA, but it was vague, couched in legalese, nothing saying exactly what it was the woman wasn't supposed to disclose. NDAs, by definition, meant that you weren't supposed to find out what they were about. But this was a murder case, and Patty was police.

She looked at Stuart. "Phineas Montague's PA signed an NDA six months ago, years after she started working for him. We need to know why."

CHAPTER TWENTY-FIVE

"OK," said Jade as they approached the house. "Strictly speaking, you're only supposed to advise me on the approach to these interviews. You're not supposed to sit in."

Petra shrugged, keeping pace with Jade as they walked along the driveway leading to the low building. Jade was glad that, despite the heels and diminutive stature, she hadn't once had to slow down for Petra.

"That's fine," Petra said. "I can do whatever you need."

Jade stopped walking and turned to her. "Really? You don't want to look them in the eye, see if they're lying?"

Petra gave her a condescending smile. "It's not so easy to tell if somebody's lying as people like to think. I know you coppers have your tells. Scratching the chin, looking away, shifting in the chair. The reality is, being interviewed by the police makes people do that stuff anyway."

Jade nodded.

"Fact is," Petra continued, "there's no sure sign that somebody's lying. Your lot are more likely to know if somebody's not telling the truth because of other evidence that contradicts what they're telling you."

Jade felt her cheek twitch at that *your lot.* "So what are you hoping to get here, in that case?"

Petra laughed. She turned away and carried on walking, tapping the side of her nose with a forefinger.

"The psychology, Detective. Even if their body language doesn't tell me how truthful they're being, I can give you a fair few clues as to what's really going on in the relationships between these people."

"Like what?" Jade hurried to catch up.

"You'll be asking the victim's staff about their relationships with him, yes?" Petra asked.

"Of course."

"You'll be asking where they were on the night that he died?"

"We've already done that."

"But what you also need to consider are the relationships between all of the people in that building. There are webs there, connections, simmering resentments, unrequited love affairs. I can spot that kind of thing. I can read between the lines and tell you what Montague himself might have been thinking, or how he might have been feeling before he died."

Jade slowed her pace. "You can't think it was suicide?"

Petra laughed. Her laugh was shrill, high pitched in contrast to her voice.

"What? Pick up a sniper rifle, ricochet the bullet off a nearby tree, shoot yourself and then hide the evidence? No, Detective. I certainly don't think it was suicide."

"Good," Jade replied.

"But there is an outside possibility," Petra added, "that he hired somebody to do it." She pursed her lips. "It's a pretty daft possibility, but it's there."

"Pretty daft," Jade agreed. She'd never known a victim to stage such an elaborate suicide. "Phineas Montague was the type of man to have enemies," she said. "If one of his staff didn't do it, it could have been a business rival."

"Or maybe an old friend, jealous of his success," Petra said. "I've heard about these men. They come up with their ideas in conjunction with somebody else and then make off with the intellectual property, turning themselves into billionaires and leaving their old mate behind in the dust."

"That's what Montague did," Jade told her. "He had a business partner, Henry Jones."

"See. Told you so. He a suspect?"

"He died a year ago."

"Ah. Still, I was right about Montague's type."

"You know a lot about billionaires?"

"You'd be surprised the type of people I come across in my line of work."

They were at the door to the house. Jade looked at it for a moment before pulling on the bell.

"Right," she said, "you can sit in, see if there's anything about these people you can tell me. Let's see who we can speak to first."

CHAPTER TWENTY-SIX

TAYLOR GANNON WAS young and pretty, blonde hair in perfect waves. It seemed natural, like she was lucky enough to look that way when she climbed out of bed in the morning. But Petra knew it was the kind of thing that necessitated getting up early and spending time in front of a mirror. Something the woman had clearly done this morning, with her boss lying in the morgue.

The PA was slim and athletic, with the caramel tan that only Americans seemed to have. Petra eyed her as they took three comfy chairs in the living room overlooking the loch. Jade would ask the questions. Petra could watch and listen.

"So," Jade said, "we've already spoken once."

Taylor nodded. "Yes. And this is...?" She smiled at Petra.

Petra put out a hand and adopted a neutral smile. "Petra McBride. Helping out with the case."

She spotted Jade's raised eyebrow.

Taylor took her hand and shook it. Her handshake was as limp as Petra had expected. Petra let go and sat back in her chair.

Jade leaned forward. "We're still trying to find out what we can about Mr Montague's relationships with his staff and business associates. We need to understand who might have wanted to hurt him."

Taylor blinked back at her, her eyelashes heavy with mascara. "Well, clearly someone wanted to kill him," she replied. "Or he wouldn't be dead."

Petra allowed herself a smile. Oh, she did enjoy the directness of Americans. Like Ursula, who'd walked up to Petra in a bar, placed a hand over hers, bought her a drink, and then after two more martinis, leaned in for a kiss. None of the games that the British habitually adopted.

Petra needed to call Ursula, they hadn't spoken since JFK. But then, they were still at the stage where Ursula took her to the airport.

"So," said Jade, "I'd be grateful if you could give me some background on Mr Montague and the people that he most frequently came into contact with. I assume you managed his diary."

"I did," said Taylor. "Do you want to know about people he would have been in contact with here, or back home?"

"Both. Let's start with here in Scotland."

A nod. "So there's me, to start with. He probably spent more time with me than anyone else."

Jade nodded.

Petra wanted to ask if the woman had been more than his PA, but she knew better than to interrupt. And besides, she'd soon work that out from watching the way the woman spoke about him.

"Not that we had a personal relationship, you understand," Taylor said. "But Phineas was a private kind of man. He didn't make friends easily. He spent more time with business associates than anyone else. And as his personal assistant, I was the one who helped steer him through life. I was... I guess you could say I was a gatekeeper between him and the world."

She paused, looking down at her hands, clasped neatly in her lap. She sat very still, her legs crossed at the ankles.

"Phineas struggled with people. He was..." She looked into Jade's face. "A classic geek, I suppose." She smiled. "He needed somebody like me to act as that conduit."

"Conduit?" Jade repeated. "That's how you saw yourself?"

Taylor nodded.

"Interesting," Jade said. "A lot of PAs just see themselves as a gatekeeper, as somebody keeping the world away from their employer. Not as somebody facilitating their employer going out into the world."

Taylor shrugged. "He needed both of those things. Conduit and gatekeeper. Whatever he needed, that's what I became."

Jade's phone buzzed in her pocket. Petra watched for a reaction but Jade ignored it.

"So who else did Mr Montague have frequent contact with?" Jade asked.

"Here, it was household staff. There are only the three of us from the business who travel with him. Well, I travel with him. The other two go back in coach. The staff here stay in Scotland, they don't move around with him." A pause. "Didn't."

"So who among the household staff did he have the most interaction with?"

Petra sniffed. The fresh air was bringing out her hay fever.

"Not anyone, really. Mrs Carrick, the housekeeper, I suppose. She sometimes served his meals. But he preferred me to bring things to him. He locked himself away on his deep thought weeks, didn't like distractions."

"He often went out walking, would he have had company?"

Taylor smiled. "Hell, no. It was all about the solitude for Phineas." She wrinkled her nose.

"And he wouldn't have come into contact with anyone while he was out walking? Neighbours?"

"He chose this place for the solitude."

"What about in the US? Who did he have the most contact with there?"

Taylor looked at Jade. "His immediate inferiors in his company."

"That's how he saw them?" Jade asked. "As inferiors?"

"Well, they were, weren't they? Phineas was the man who built up the company, they would have been nothing without him."

"Surely he built the company up with Henry Jones?"

Taylor shook her head. "Phineas's work was mainly focussed on his offshoot companies. Henry wasn't a part of that."

Petra noticed that the PA was consistently referring to her boss by his first name. Her body language was showing no evidence of the woman having been in love with him, but she wondered just how close they'd been.

"You've provided a list of all those employees to my colleagues?" Jade asked.

"I have," Taylor replied.

"And was there anybody in particular that Mr Montague

was having difficulties with? Any arguments, fallings out, people who'd left the company under a cloud?"

"There were plenty of those." Taylor's voice was hard. "But nobody in Phineas's inner circle."

"And what about in the UK?" Jade asked. "At the Scottish house. Any problems with any of the staff here? Any associates who spent time here while he was on his retreats?"

"Nobody. No one came here. He liked to cut himself off."

Jade looked up. "But he had you, his conduit."

Taylor blushed. "I only told him about anything happening outside this building if it was absolutely urgent."

"And what sort of thing would be considered absolutely urgent?"

"Major stock market changes, shifts in the board. That kind of thing."

"Business stuff?" Jade said.

Taylor sighed. "Everything was business stuff with Phineas."

Jade's phone buzzed in her pocket again. This time she pulled it out and looked at it, and there was a sudden shift in her body, in the way she was sitting. Something personal, Petra wondered, or to do with the case?

Jade put her phone in her lap. She bit down on her bottom lip.

"Ms Gannon," she said, "Can you tell me why you signed a nondisclosure agreement with your employer six months ago?"

Petra resisted the urge to let her jaw drop. She watched the PA, whose chest rose. Her eyes widened just for a moment and then normalised again.

This woman was good at hiding her emotions.

Taylor blinked a few times, then raised her chin.

"You know I can't discuss the contents of a nondisclosure agreement." She leaned forward. "That's the whole point. Nondisclosure."

Jade looked back at her. "I understand you can't discuss the content, but can you tell me a little about the circumstances?"

"Of course not. If I told you the circumstances, you'd be able to figure out the content."

"This was six months ago. When you'd been working for Mr Montague for six and a half years, is that correct?"

"It is." Taylor uncrossed her legs and placed her feet on the floor. Her knees were squeezed together, her hand sandwiched between them. Petra knew anxiety when she saw it.

"Did you sign a nondisclosure agreement when you started working with Mr Montague?" Jade asked.

"Of course I did. It's standard procedure in a large company."

Jade nodded. "But then you signed another one after you'd been working for him for quite some time. Did something happen that led to that being required of you?"

Taylor drew her hand out from between her knees and balled it on top of her thighs.

"I've already told you, I can't discuss the contents of a nondisclosure agreement."

Jade glanced at Petra who shrugged in response. She was no lawyer.

"Very well," Jade said. "But if this nondisclosure agreement turns out to be pertinent to Mr Montague's death, then I will obtain a warrant."

Taylor stared back at her, silent.

"And that warrant will enable me to look at the contents

of the agreement. You might want to consider talking to me about it instead."

Taylor stood up. "I have work to do. If that's all?"

Jade looked up at her, puzzled.

"Like I say," Taylor said, "I have work to do. There is much to be done in terms of the arrangement of Mr Montague's estate and his funeral."

"I'm afraid we won't be releasing the body until we've concluded the investigation."

"I understand that," the PA replied. Her cheeks were pale now, her breathing fast. "But there will be a memorial service nonetheless."

"Of course," Jade said. "I'd be grateful if you could give me the details when you've set a date."

Taylor's jaw clenched. "Of course." She turned away from Jade, slid her gaze over Petra then left the room.

CHAPTER TWENTY-SEVEN

JADE WALKED out of the living room then stopped, realising she had no idea how to get out. This house had been designed in such a way that the layout made no sense whatsoever. She turned around, peering along the corridor.

Petra was behind her. "Everything OK?"

Jade nodded. "Can you remember how we get out of here?"

"Of course." Petra tapped Jade's arm. "Follow me."

Jade allowed herself a sigh of relief as she followed Petra along a maze of corridors. How had she become so absent-minded? Jade was known for her photographic memory, her ability to retain facts and information.

When they reached the external door, she paused to take a few breaths, running her fingers through her hair.

"You sure you're alright?" Petra asked her.

"Don't I look alright?"

"I haven't known you very long but you seem a bit pale."

"Paler than I was earlier?"

A shrug. "A wee bit. You seem distracted."

"I wasn't distracted in that interview."

"No. Clearly you have an on switch."

Jade looked at her. "I wasn't expecting you to analyse me as well as the suspects."

Petra laughed. "Sorry, habit. What I mean to say is that you're very professional."

Jade gave her a smile. "Flattery will get you nowhere."

Petra pushed open the door and they emerged onto the gravel driveway. It was starting to rain. Petra drew back under the cover of the wide porch. Jade was about to pull up the hood of her raincoat but stopped, aware that the psychologist wasn't dressed for the weather.

"So," Petra asked, "what was all that about the nondisclosure agreement?"

"How did you think she reacted to it?"

"Nice one. Deflecting a question."

Jade clenched her teeth. "You're here to help me, not the other way around."

"We need to help each other if we're going to get the job done."

Jade clenched her fists. The psychologist was right. She couldn't treat the woman like a subordinate.

"Sorry," she said. "I'm used to, I don't know... So, yes, the nondisclosure agreement. Patty found it, DC Henderson."

"I met her yesterday."

"Of course, yes. She was doing a trawl of paperwork that we picked up in the house and she found a reference to the NDA. Still hoping to get sight of the document itself."

"What do you think it was about?"

"No idea," Jade replied. "That's the whole point of a nondisclosure agreement, as Taylor said."

"Can you get access to it?"

"If I can obtain a warrant," Jade replied. "But I'm not sure if I have grounds. If Taylor was a suspect..."

"Which she's not right now, is she?" asked Petra.

"No," Jade said. "You saw her. Cool as a cucumber."

"Not entirely. Although I can tell you she wasn't in a romantic relationship with her boss. The mention of the NDA made her antsy, though."

Jamie Douglas was approaching, a plastic box full of evidence bags in his arms.

"You think that was her genuine response?" Jade asked Petra, ignoring the CSM for now.

"Very few people are genuine when they're questioned by a police detective about the death of somebody close to them. She says she was the person he spent the most time with, almost a wife to him, but without the sex. But her reaction when you mentioned the NDA was quick. She didn't have time to dissimulate, didn't see it coming."

"Wife. You think that's the kind of relationship they had?" Jade asked.

Petra shrugged. "Not romantically. But practically, probably. Maybe the NDA will help us find out, if you can get it."

Jade grunted. The psychologist was right, they couldn't put the cart before the horse. The nondisclosure agreement would only become available to them if they had other grounds to suspect the PA.

"Jamie," she said as the CSM stopped to place his box on the floor next to one of the CSI vans. How's it going up at the scene?"

"We have a new piece of evidence," he said.

"What kind of evidence?"

Jamie dropped the plastic box to the ground, breathing heavily.

"Bloody hell, that thing's heavy," he said. "Well, it is when you have to lug it a mile and a half along a narrow track."

Jade didn't want to know about the challenges of carrying evidence from the crime scene. "What have you found?"

He bent over and lifted the lid off the box, rifling inside it. He pulled out an evidence bag and held it up with a satisfied smile on his face.

"Found this," he said. "In amongst some fallen leaves."

Jade grabbed the bag off him and held it up to the light.

"It's a bullet."

"Indeed it is," he said. "And it might be a match for a previous case you worked."

Shit. She'd been meaning to talk to Petra about that.

She turned the bag in her hands and squinted at Jamie. "Really?"

"We'd have to check it on the system to be sure," he replied. "But you don't see these very often in Scotland. It's not the kind of thing they use for hunting."

Petra had drawn closer, looking at the bag. She'd be wondering what was going on.

"Okay," Jade said. She turned to Petra. "I want to talk to you about another case that might be related."

CHAPTER TWENTY-EIGHT

"What case?" asked Petra. She felt like she was being excluded from something. Police did this from time to time, unsure whether to trust her.

Jade scanned the space around them, her movements jerky. Apart from Jamie, no one was around.

Jade put a hand on Petra's arm and drew her away from the porch. Petra forced herself to ignore the rain that would no doubt be ruining her hair, and followed.

"I want to take you to another crime scene," Jade said as they moved away from the building.

Petra frowned. "We found where the sniper was?"

"No, it's the bullet. There was another shooting using the same kind."

Petra shrugged. "Where?"

"Glasgow."

"Surely you get shootings in Glasgow all the time? Is it that unusual to have the same bullet type?"

Jade looked at her. "How long have you lived in Dundee?"

"Twelve years."

"And do you visit Glasgow often?"

Petra shrugged. Truth be told, she'd kept promising to visit her aunt, but hadn't actually done so for five years. And now the woman was dead. Petra tried not to dwell on how she felt about that.

"Last time I came was probably five years ago," she said. "Five and a half."

"You seem to have some sort of idea that Glasgow is the Bronx."

"Well, it is one of Scotland's crime hotspots."

"We don't get shootings every day down here." Jade gave her an irritated look. "Two shootings with the same kind of bullet isn't run of the mill. Not by a long stretch."

"OK, sorry." Petra raised her hands in apology. "So you're taking me to the Glasgow crime scene?"

"I'd like to."

Jade looked around again. "Damn. We still haven't spoken to Angus Robertson."

"Who's he?"

"The groundsman."

Petra turned at the sound of a car. A blue Fiesta pulled up next to them and DS Uddin got out.

"Mo," Jade said. "Perfect timing."

"Boss," he replied. "Sorry I took a while. Further than I thought."

Mo had been over the other side of the loch, getting an angle on Montague's property in case the shooter had been across the water. They knew it was a long shot, in every sense, but even long shots had to be looked into.

"Any joy?"

"No. The only spots where you have a line of sight over to this side are much too close to the road."

Jade sniffed. "Well, Jamie's found a bullet now."

Mo looked surprised. "What kind?"

"6mm Creedmoor," Jamie said. He was still with them.

Mo shrugged. "Means nothing to me."

"We found the same type at another crime scene, seven months ago," Jade told him. "In Glasgow."

"You think they're related?"

"It's an unusual bullet type," Jamie said.

"So are you going to take me to this crime scene, or what?" Petra asked. She could feel her hair sticking to her face.

"Sorry." Jade turned to Mo. "I need you to speak to Angus Robertson."

"I already did."

"Tell him about the bullets. Watch his reaction."

"Shouldn't Dr McBride be here for that?"

"It's fine," Petra told him. "You can debrief me afterwards."

"You're sure?" Jade asked. "That's enough."

"The alternative is for you to leave me here with DS Uddin and forget about this other crime scene."

Jade pursed her lips. "I want to take you there.'

"OK. Surely it can wait?"

Jade frowned. She looked confused. "Yes. Yes, you're right. OK, you and I will speak to Robertson."

"What about me?" Mo asked.

"Can you go up to the scene, see if Jamie's got any further?"

A frown flickered across his face, but he said nothing

before turning away. Jade scratched her chin and nodded at Petra, who hoped she'd be able to find a bathroom before the interview.

"OK," Jade said. "Robertson, then we go to Glasgow."

CHAPTER TWENTY-NINE

"I DON'T SEE why you have to interview me again," the groundskeeper said. "I already spoke to your colleague yesterday."

"We won't keep you long," Jade told him as they walked through the house towards the living room that was now being used for interviews. "Just clearing a few things up."

Petra trailed behind, not speaking. She was here to watch and listen, no more.

As they reached the door to the living room, Robertson hung back, waiting for the two women to go ahead. Old-school, Petra thought. Despite his youth. He couldn't be much more than thirty. She gave him a quizzical look as she passed him to enter the room.

Jade was already in a chair facing the window. Petra wondered if she'd chosen it strategically, to ensure that Robertson wouldn't be distracted by the view. Robertson took a seat at an angle from her and Petra sat slightly back, on a sofa that was too soft and all but swallowed her up as she sank into it.

Jade gave the man a smile. "Thanks for giving up your time again."

'I've got work to do."

"We won't keep you."

"I already answered questions about how long I've worked here and what I do. How I got along with the boss. I hardly ever saw him, so there wasn't much opportunity to be pals."

"And that's all good," Jade said. "Very helpful. We just want to piece together some specifics."

Robertson rubbed his hands together then placed them on his lap. "Go on then."

"Very well. You're the person who looks after guns and ammunition for Mr Montague, who I gather liked to go hunting."

"He did."

"And you looked after the equipment?"

"I did."

"Can you tell me what kind of guns Mr Montague used?"

"They were all kept under lock and key, if that's what you're getting at."

"I just want to know the type."

"He had a 12-gauge shotgun, two .22 centrefire rifles and a .243 Winchester."

"That's all?"

"He hunted alone. That was plenty."

"He never invited friends or business associates to hunt with him?"

"No." Robertson pursed his lips.

"Did he own a Creedmoor?"

"No."

Petra watched the groundskeeper. His body language was open, his skin even in tone. He seemed relaxed with the subject at hand.

"OK," said Jade. "So did you have to sign an NDA before working for Mr Montague?"

"I did."

"I know you can't tell me the detail of it, but did it seem pretty standard to you?"

"No idea."

"No?"

"I've never signed one of those things in my life. I've got no clue how standard it was. It's an American thing, isn't it? Not the kind of thing we need here in Scotland. We trust each other, instead."

"Did it annoy you, the feeling that you weren't trusted?"

Robertson's gaze flicked from Jade to Petra and back again. "You're trying to get me to say it annoyed me so much I topped the fella?"

Jade smiled. "I'm just asking how it made you feel."

"It was a piece of paper. Couldn't have got the job without it, so I signed it."

"OK. What's your relationship like with the other staff here?"

"Mrs Carrick keeps me fed, along with everyone else. There's Jim who maintains the building and Heather who oversees any disputes with neighbours—"

"Were there a lot of those? Disputes?"

He shook his head. "You're doing it again, putting words into my mouth. There was a ruckus over a path leading across this estate. About four months ago. Apart from that, virtually nothing."

"Virtually nothing?"

"Nothing. That was what I meant to say."

But you didn't, Petra thought. She knew the police would be looking into Montague's neighbours, getting background on them. Even if none of them was the killer, they might have allowed access via their land.

"How do you get along with Taylor?" Jade asked.

"Taylor?"

"Taylor Gannon. Mr Montague's PA."

"I know who Taylor is. That's about all, though. She comes here a couple of times a year, with the boss. Runs around after him, fetching and carrying, like some sort of puppy. Pathetic."

"So you don't have much direct contact with her?"

"Nope. Sorry."

"What will happen to your employment, now Mr Montague has died."

A shrug. "No idea. All I know is I've got a job right now. Which is why I want to do it well."

"You hope to be kept on?"

"Someone will buy this place. In the meantime, it'll need to be tended. Else no one'll buy it. So yes, I'm hoping that whoever's responsible for the estate now will keep me on."

"You enjoy your job."

"I do."

"But you didn't work in this line before starting here."

Another shrug. "No law against changing professions, is there?"

"There isn't, Mr Robertson." Jade stood up, glancing at Petra as she did so. Petra wasn't sure if there was something specific she'd been expected to keep an eye out for.

If there was, she'd missed the instruction. The jet lag was

catching up with her, she'd slept little more than nine hours in the last three days.

Petra yawned. Right on cue, she thought. Not a coincidence at all.

Jade was looking at her.

"Sorry," Petra said. She wiped her hand on the pocket of her trousers; some saliva had transferred to it as she'd raised it to stifle her yawn.

"We don't have any more questions, do we?"

Petra looked at Jade. She wasn't supposed to be asking questions. Jade knew that, as well as she did.

What was she trying to achieve?

She looked at Robertson again. He was watching the two women, his expression alert.

"No, DI Tanner," Petra said. "I think we've got everything we need."

CHAPTER THIRTY

"What did you think?" Jade asked as they headed out of the building once again.

Petra scratched her head, carefully so as not to disturb her hair. It was damp, but quickly drying.

"He's trying too hard."

Jade's steps slowed. "How so?"

"Well, it's clear that Phineas Montague was far from loved by his employees."

"That's more than a fair assessment."

"But when someone's died, it's normal to pretend you held them in higher regard than you really did."

Jade nodded. "Like Taylor did."

"Exactly. She'd have had more reason than most to hate the man, she was practically his slave."

"She might have had some respect for him."

Petra turned to Jade. "It isn't about respect, though. It's about regard."

"You think the fact that she didn't hold him in high regard means she wanted him dead?"

Petra shook her head. The DI had it all wrong. "No. Besides, it's not Taylor I'm talking about. She's an open book."

"You think so?"

"Yes. Her face, it's very expressive. I know she's American and all that, but it's how she is. She couldn't hide committing murder from us any more than she could act like a snooty Edinburghian."

Jade smiled. They were nearing her car. Petra guessed she was about to be taken on a trip to Glasgow. She hoped she wouldn't be brought back here again, those single-lane roads had made her nauseous.

"So Angus Robertson, then?" Jade asked, stopping at the car. "He was lying?"

"He's been putting on a show."

Jade's gaze was steady on Petra's face, clearly waiting for more.

"I talked to your man Mo," Petra said, "on the way up. DS Uddin. He described the conversation he had with Robertson yesterday. The man's clearly decided he's not going to pretend to like his late employer. So he's feeding us a few morsels of disdain, just enough to make us think he was being genuine."

Jade leaned on the car. Her coat was going to get wet, but it was a practical navy waterproof and Petra imagined she didn't care. Again, she didn't speak. Petra imagined what this woman would be like in a proper interview situation, with the tape and a caution and everything. Effective, she suspected.

"Do you think it's significant?" Jade asked at last.

"No idea. But it's interesting."

"Interesting isn't enough."

"Sorry. I'll never promise to give you more than I can."

Jade put a hand on the door handle. "If you spot anything else interesting, let me know."

Petra nodded.

"And I'd be grateful if you could give me more than interesting. Else I'm not sure what Fraser's spending his budget on."

Petra raised her eyebrows. Direct. She liked this woman.

"I'll be sure to tell you anything I come up with."

"Good." Jade opened the door. "And you'll be doing a profile."

"After I've seen the Glasgow crime scene."

"You think that'll make a difference?"

"I've no idea. But I want to see it. You'll probably be getting two reports from me. And please don't call them profiles."

Jade smiled to herself. Her eyes were hooded, dark circles beneath them. And the smile made it nowhere near far enough up her face to lift them.

"DI Tanner?" Petra asked.

Jade looked up, alert to the change in Petra's voice. "Yes?"

"If you don't mind me asking, are you OK?"

A frown. "Of course I'm OK." She turned and opened the car door.

"Only, you seem preoccupied."

Petra had noticed Jade's gaze travel towards the loch on multiple occasions. She hadn't been looking towards the crime scene but back over the water to the south. Every time she did it, something came over her face. Fear?

"I'm fine. You stick to your job, and I'll stick to mine."

"Fair enough."

"OK, let's get on the road." Jade brought up her watch,

her expression blank. "I'll drop Mo a text, make sure he's OK for getting back, and—"

"He's got a pool car."

Jade looked up from her watch. "Of course. Well, I'll check he's happy with being left in charge."

"I imagine he'll be fine."

"I'm sure he will. I'm jus—"

"Don't call him," Petra said.

"I'm not, I'm texting him."

"Still. Don't."

Jade closed the car door again. "Since when were you in charge of this investigation?"

Petra hesitated. She had a habit of putting her foot in it like this. She saw things about people, it was her training. More than one girlfriend had accused her of being psychic, something Petra had responded to with an ill-concealed roll of the eyes. It was no wonder those relationships hadn't lasted. But then, nor had any others. Perhaps she needed to rein in her professional instincts.

"Sorry," she said. "You carry on."

Petra rounded the car and opened the passenger door, ignoring the sensation of Jade's eyes on her back. If she was going to develop a working relationship with this woman, she had to do better.

CHAPTER THIRTY-ONE

Mo was slowly getting used to being up here. It was chilly, at least a couple of degrees colder than at home, but the air was fresh and if he ignored the distant hum of the A82 he could hear distinct bird calls from the trees around the loch. It was beautiful.

Or at least it had been, before Police Scotland had filled the beach on which Phineas Montague had died with equipment and forensic tents.

They were on a small pebble beach, half a mile from Montague's house. Uniform had told him that this was the spot Montague habitually used to access the house, as it was the best place to land a helicopter. Police Scotland had plenty of those, but weren't about to sully the crime scene by bringing one anywhere near. So instead, they were using SUVs, slowly making their way up the rutted but broad West Highland Way. Mo had bounced up here from the house in one of them and had decided about thirty seconds in that he'd walk back.

Jamie was inside the forensic tent, his colleague Heather

just outside it. She stooped low, examining the ground around it for evidence. Two more CSIs who Mo hadn't been introduced to were not far away. Mo watched them for a moment, establishing that they were using a spiral pattern for their search. Further out, uniformed officers were doing the same, closer to the trees where most of the blood had been found.

Mo knocked on the fabric of the tent, realised how stupid that was, and pushed through to the inside.

Jamie stood up. "DS Uddin, how's it going?"

"Fine. You can call me Mo, though."

"Mo. How's it going?"

"The DI and Dr McBride have gone back to Glasgow."

"Checking out the Severini crime scene." Jamie nodded, his expression grim.

"Did you work that scene too?"

"I did. Nasty."

"Can you tell me about it?"

"Come outside."

Mo followed Jamie out of the tent and away from the activity of the CSIs and uniformed officers. Jamie exchanged nods with people as he passed, seeming to know everyone. With the DI in Glasgow, Jamie was in charge of the site as the CSM. But Mo needed to get to know some of these people and to assert some authority. He was second in command in the Complex Crimes Unit, after all.

Jamie found a log at the edge of the beach, where the stones met the trees. He lowered himself down to perch on it and gestured for Mo to do the same. As Mo sat, Jamie pulled a pack of chewing gum from his pocket and offered a stick to Mo. Mo took it, unsure what he would do with it when he'd finished but not wanting to appear rude.

"Steve Severini," Jamie said. "Has Jade told you much?"

"Practically nothing."

"That makes it easier, then." Jamie leaned back, chewing on his gum. Mo shifted his around his mouth. It had been years since he'd chewed gum. How did you not choke on it?

"Glasgow-based millionaire, made his money from property development. Buying up empty land. Sometimes not empty land at all but areas full of homes. Run-down, but homes nonetheless. Unpleasant bloke, but never did anything actually illegal. Well, not so far as anyone was able to pin on him, anyhow. I know it's a cliché, millionaires and money laundering—"

"When things become clichés, it's usually because they're true," Mo interrupted.

"You've got experience?"

Mo nodded. "The Canary case. Big one. Big business, local politics, money laundering and," he shivered, "child exploitation."

Jamie sucked his teeth. "Bastards. Well, Severini was nothing like that, not so far as CID were able to find out. And they moved fast after his death, his offices were cleared of computer equipment within hours."

"How did he die?"

"Long-range shooting, like this one."

"He bled out too?"

"Died of exposure. Poor bugger. Found near the river."

"He was dumped in the Clyde?" Mo didn't know much Scottish geography but he'd seen a sign as they'd crossed the river yesterday.

Jamie shook his head. "He was found on the top of one of his own buildings. Over by the squinty bridge, an office development. They've since been finished and sold, unbelievably."

"The squinty bridge?"

"Sorry. Clyde... Clyde Arc, I think is the official name. It's by the Armadillo." Jamie smiled. "The SECC."

"I've heard of that." Catriona had taken the girls to a concert there one time they'd been up visiting his in-laws. Miley Cyrus? Mo couldn't remember. He wished he'd gone now. He missed them. "He was shot by a similar bullet?"

"That's another reason why Jade thinks there's a link. Glasgow's got plenty of crime, not so much as the press would have you think, but enough. But two sniper killings in one year, well that's too much of a coincidence."

"Do you think the cases are linked?"

"Not my place to draw that kind of conclusion, pal. That's for you lot. But I think the bullets make it a definite possibility."

Mo leaned back. He needed to stand; his legs were cramping and if he stayed down here on this log any longer, he might never get up again.

"So Severini was another millionaire?" He stood up, stretching out his legs.

"You'll be wondering if the two of them were connected. No idea. But if there's any connection to be found in the forensics, we'll uncover them for you."

"I know." Jamie was good at his job, Mo could tell. He thought of Adi, Zoe's favourite CSM from the West Midlands Force. Poor Adi and his unrequited crush on Zoe.

"OK," Mo said. "Well, in the meantime we'll go through the financial forensics, business records, that kind of thing. Find out if the two men had any dealings."

Jamie shrugged. "Not my area. But yeah, makes sense."

Jamie joined Mo standing. "I'd best get back. That Taylor woman wants the site cleared ASAP."

"She can't stop you doing your job."

"She's managing the estate of one of the wealthiest men on the planet. I'm pretty sure she can do whatever she wants."

Mo thought back to the glimpses he'd had of Montague's PA. She didn't seem the type to go throwing her weight around.

"Great. Thanks, Jamie. Let me know if you find anything else, yeah?"

Jamie put a hand on Mo's arm. "Sure thing."

CHAPTER THIRTY-TWO

Jade's car was a nondescript affair, a mid-range saloon in an instantly forgettable shade of beige. In the back was a child's car seat, but despite this clearly being a family car, there was no litter on the floor. No balled-up sweet wrappers, empty packets of crisps, or half-drunk cartons of orange juice.

Petra was impressed. If Jade had a child young enough to inhabit that car seat, then she was a tidy woman indeed to keep her car like this.

She settled into the passenger seat, shuffling her backside to get comfortable as they took the narrow lane away from Phineas Montague's house.

"So," she said, after they passed the second car coming in the opposite direction. Jade had waved at both of them, clearly police. "Tell me about this second crime scene?"

"Of course." Jade drummed her fingernails on the steering wheel as they sped up. Petra put a hand on her seatbelt. "It's from seven months ago, a case I worked when I was in Glasgow."

"How long have you been with the Complex Crimes Team?"

Jade glanced at her. "Fraser didn't tell you?"

"Fraser didn't tell me what?"

"This is our first case, we're a brand new team. I only started yesterday."

"You and me both, then," Petra said. "We can be newbies together."

Jade smiled.

There were creases deep in her forehead and bags under her eyes, Petra wondered if that kid ever let its mum get some sleep.

"So it was a case that you investigated when you were working in Glasgow?" Petra asked.

"Yes," Jade said. "Steve Severini. Glasgow-based property developer. Found dead of exposure after being shot on the top floor of one of his own buildings."

"Exposure, in a building?"

"The building wasn't completed yet."

"Ah."

"At first we thought it had to be someone in the building with him, but the bullet was just like this one. From a long range weapon."

"Let me guess. No one except the victim on the CCTV."

"Correct. He went up in the construction elevator, walked around the top floor for a bit, then suddenly collapsed. It was all captured on film."

"So you know which way the bullet came from?"

"We do. We searched neighbouring buildings but came up blank. Whoever shot him wasn't new to it."

"And you think it might be the same shooter."

"Similar MO. I'm not assuming anything about the identity of the gunman yet."

Petra clutched her seatbelt tighter as they took a bend. "Yet you're using the word gunman."

Jade turned to glance at her. "I am, aren't I? Is gunperson a word?"

"Shooter will do."

"Yeah." The car came to an abrupt halt at a junction. Jade edged it over the line and Petra held her breath. At last Jade decided the road was clear and pulled out.

Petra sucked in air between her teeth. Jade was muttering under her breath.

"So you think there's a connection because of the bullets?" Petra asked.

"Not just that," Jade replied. "Both unfeasibly wealthy, billionaire in the case of Montague, multimillionaire in the case of Severini. Both of them unpopular."

Petra nodded. "The Montague house was full of unspoken tensions. I had the feeling that everybody was hiding. Sometimes people hide when there's been a death in a house. Like if they remove themselves from it, they can almost pretend it didn't happen. But that house felt like somewhere people always hide."

"You reckon they hid from Montague?" Jade asked.

Petra shrugged. "He was the dominant individual in the house. The atmosphere in any building always comes from the alpha."

"The alpha male?" Jade said.

"Not always a man. Sometimes it's a woman. Sometimes it's not even the most powerful person there, not in the formal sense. It can be a child, or even a member of domestic staff if they're obnoxious enough."

Jade chuckled. "Mrs Danvers."

"Exactly." Petra liked that Jade could make literary references. It surprised her.

Petra leaned back in her seat.

"How many police investigations have you done?" Jade asked her. "How many murder cases?"

"Enough." Petra went over them in her head. "Seven murders, eight abductions. How about you?"

"I stopped counting years ago," Jade said. "That's the kind of thing that leads to madness."

"You're not wrong there."

"And have you done a lot of work in Scotland?"

Petra shook her head. "Despite being based at Dundee University, most of my work took me away from Scotland. There's been a couple of cases in Birmingham, a few in the States, some in Spain. One in Dorset not that long ago."

"But now you're going to be working with us more closely?"

"Seems I am."

"Good," Jade said. "If these are the kinds of crimes we're investigating, getting the psychological angle could be just as helpful as the forensics and the pathology."

"I'm glad you think so," Petra told her. "Not everybody would agree."

"Well." Jade turned to her and gave her a grin. "We'll ignore them, won't we?"

"Right."

They were coming off the A82 now, making for the motorway. Petra was glad she didn't have to drive this. Not having a license could be a blessing.

"It's near the BBC offices," Jade said. "Shouldn't take too long. We'll go into the building and I'll show you where it happened.

CHAPTER THIRTY-THREE

JADE WRAPPED her arms around her chest, wishing she'd brought more layers. Petra wore a long purple wool coat that coordinated with her shoes. It might have been utterly wrong at Loch Lomond, but it was just right here.

They wandered the empty space on the eighteenth floor of the tower block. The block had been completed but this floor was yet to be let. It had floor to ceiling windows and she suspected the heating had never been activated. It was bloody freezing.

Petra sniffed and made guttural sounds under her breath as she peered around the space.

"Is there anything particular you're looking for?" Jade asked.

Petra turned and shook her head. "Nothing specific. I just want to get a feel for the place. This was where Severini worked, yes?"

"He would have spent most of his time in his office in central Glasgow," Jade told her. "But yes, we think he was fairly regular here. Had his own hard hat."

"And would he have been giving instructions to the workers here? Or would he have just been coming here to inspect?"

"Inspecting, I think," Jade said. "His company worked through a variety of subcontractors. He kept as far away from the nitty gritty as he could."

"But still," Petra said, "he liked to visit his buildings while they were being erected."

"Doesn't everybody?" Jade asked her. "You're creating something, you want to see what it's going to look like?"

"He would have been a busy man," Petra replied. "Does a man like that normally have time to come out and inspect his building sites? Wouldn't he delegate, if there were enough of those sites to make him a multimillionaire?"

Jade frowned. "You think it's relevant?"

"I don't know," Petra said. "But you might want to look into whether he was a regular visitor to his other sites. I'm assuming he had multiple building sites?"

"He did."

Jade hadn't thought about that. It had been seven months ago and as far as she was concerned, she had exhausted all bases. And now Petra, within five minutes, had come up with a new angle that hadn't even crossed Jade's mind. It made her feel inadequate. Was she up to leading this new Complex Crimes Unit? She'd already told Fraser that it should be a DCI heading the unit, but he'd reassured her that he had complete confidence in her. And they both knew that made things cheaper.

Petra was over by the windows. There was no furniture, nothing to block the view. It made Jade uneasy. She shuffled towards the psychologist, her heart rate increasing.

"Be careful," she said.

Petra was crouching, looking at something on the ground. She turned to look up at Jade and smiled. "There's a window. Toughened glass."

"It still makes me nervous."

Jade had never liked heights. This case had given her the creeps when she'd been working on it seven months ago. At that point, the building had been little more than a shell. The wind had blown hard through here when she'd visited the crime scene, and she'd been shivering for days afterwards. Dan had wrapped his arms around her and said he'd warm her up.

She swallowed. *Dan.*

Don't think about him.

Behind her eyes was an image of Petra falling, preceded, bizarrely, by an image of her pushing Petra out of the window. Why did vertigo do that to her? Why did it give her the feeling that she might do something stupid?

She took a few steps back, anxious to ensure she wasn't within striking distance of the psychologist.

"Please," she said. "Can you come back just a bit?"

Petra stood slowly and turned to Jade. She took a few steps towards her and put a hand on her arm.

"Are you OK?" she said. "You've turned pale again."

Jade shook her head.

"I'm fine. Just a bit wary of heights."

"More than a bit, I'd say. So why did you bring me up here?"

"I wanted to show you the crime scene."

"I appreciate it," Petra replied, her hand still on Jade's arm.

Jade pulled her arm away. She was embarrassed.

"So," she said, pushing some brusqueness into her voice, "what do you think?"

"I'm intrigued by the fact that a busy man like Steve Severini took the time to come to building sites like this, particularly this one. I'd like to know the full history of the project, as well as his other work. The fact that he was shot here instead of in his office or at his home might be pertinent."

"Of course," Jade said. "We've got files in the office. I'll get Patty to pull them out for you."

Petra shrugged her shoulders and flicked something off the fabric of her coat that Jade couldn't make out.

"I'm done."

"That's it? You don't need longer?" Jade asked.

"You're clearly struggling up here, and I have what I need."

Good. Jade turned and led Petra to the lifts.

CHAPTER THIRTY-FOUR

As Petra and Jade arrived at the office, Mo was getting out of his pool car.

"Everything OK?" Jade asked him.

"Fine," he said. "I had a chat with Jamie, there wasn't much else for me to do up there."

"That's fine. Anything of interest from Jamie?"

Mo shook his head. "He told me a bit about the Severini case."

Petra watched as Jade put her keys into her bag, taking care to place them neatly in a pocket. She smiled.

Jade turned to her and frowned. "Everything OK?"

"Of course. Sorry." Petra wasn't about to tell the DI she was observing her.

"Good." Jade turned back to Mo as she made for the door to the offices. "That's where we've just been."

Mo looked at Petra. "Helpful?"

Petra grunted. She'd have preferred to see the crime scene in its original state.

"We need to check in with Patty and Stuart," Jade said.

"I want to bring some structure to this investigation, now we think we're looking at both killings."

"Still not sure about that," Petra said. They were in the dark hallway to the offices. Jade went first, taking the stairs two at a time. She slapped her knees as she went. *Yeah, I'm tired too*, Petra thought.

At the top of the stairs, Jade paused. "No. Still not sure. We'll wait till we've got the official post-mortem, and more on those bullets." She opened the door to the office and Mo stood back for Petra to follow. She went ahead, giving him a nod.

Inside, Patty and Stuart were at their desks, music playing from somewhere. Patty looked up and the music stopped.

"Boss," she said to Jade. "Productive morning?"

"Something like that. Come on, let's get all our heads together."

"There's an office in the corner we can use." Patty stood up from her desk and walked to an empty office. Stuart pushed his chair back and followed, his footsteps slower. They all filed inside, Petra at the back.

The office was large and empty, a featureless wipe-down table in the middle and six chairs. There was a blank magnetic whiteboard on the wall.

"Why hasn't anybody filled this in?" Jade turned to Stuart and Patty.

"Sorry, boss," Patty said. "I've got a load of stuff on my desk, shall I...?"

"Yes," Jade replied. "Please."

Patty left the room. Stuart was in one of the chairs and Mo stood by the door, waiting for the DI to take a seat.

He was still getting the measure of her, Petra thought,

just like she was. But the difference for Petra was that this woman wasn't her senior officer. She needed this job now that she didn't have her income from Dundee University. But she didn't need Jade Tanner's patronage in the same way that Mo would.

Patty reappeared and approached the board. She had a pile of post-it notes in a box file, scraps of paper, photographs printed out. Jade watched as she arranged them on the board. Patty stood back, tilting her head to admire her handiwork.

"You've missed some," Stuart said.

Patty turned to him. "Which ones?"

"The Severini case. We need to put that on there, too."

Patty looked at Jade. "You really think there's a connection, boss?"

"The bullets," Jade said. "Both victims ultra-wealthy, both probably shot by a sniper. We need to consider that they could have been killed by the same person."

"I don't reckon they were," said Stuart.

"No?" Jade asked.

Petra watched him. He was leaning back in his chair, his feet crossed at the ankles and his hands steepled in front of him. Projecting confidence, Petra thought. But there was a tremor in his shoulder. He was less at ease than he was pretending to be.

"No," he said. "These are professional killings. Somebody was hired to carry them out. They might be the same bullet type but that doesn't mean it was the same person pulling the trigger."

"It's possible," said Jade. "But what are the chances of two professional assassins working in this area?"

"We have to keep our options open," Stuart replied.

"Stuart's right," Petra interjected. "I know it's tempting

to look for one suspect. But the reality is we could be looking at two people. Possibly more if this is a professional operation."

Jade looked at her, her teeth gritted. "Carry on. What else have we got on the psychology side of things?"

Petra surveyed the board. "If somebody did hire a professional, their motive is one that has been brewing for a while. This isn't a crime of passion, it's going to be a business rival or somebody who was wronged by these two men some time ago. If indeed it is the same person who hired both gunmen. You have to consider the fact that there might be a professional who's been hired by two people for two separate killings."

"So any combination of killers and people hiring them," Stuart said.

"They might have been referred," Patty added.

"Referred?" Mo asked. "What d'you mean?"

Petra had almost forgotten Mo was there, he'd been so quiet by the door.

"You can sit down, you know," Jade told him.

He shrugged and took the seat closest to him, next to Jade. Stuart and Patty both gave him wary looks.

Petra noted that he hadn't attempted to take charge of the two DCs yet, he was letting Jade lead them. At some point, he would need to step in.

"Well," said Mo. "There are networks, yeah? Organised crime, that kind of thing. If we've got one person who wanted to commission a hit on Severini, then they may have somehow passed on the details of the individual or organisation that they hired to whoever wanted to commission the hit on Montague."

"People talk about that sort of stuff?" Patty asked.

He raised an eyebrow. "You'd be surprised."

"Have you got much experience of organised crime?" Jade asked him.

He nodded. "In Birmingham, I worked the Canary case. We uncovered an organised crime gang that was selling drugs, trafficking prostitutes, and grooming children for a paedophile ring."

Patty winced. "Bastards."

"They certainly were," Mo said. "They had a few coppers in their pocket, too." He sat back in his chair, his body language uneasy.

"OK," Jade said, standing up and going to the board. "So let's add the Severini case."

She grabbed a whiteboard marker from a tray beneath the board and wrote Severini's name at the top.

"We'll need mugshots. Who have we got? Who did we interview when the case was ongoing?"

Patty stood up. "I'll go on the system," she said. "Dig out the file."

"You can't remember?" Jade said.

"Did you two work the case together?" Petra asked.

Jade turned to her. "Patty was on my team in Glasgow."

Petra nodded. "OK. Let's hear what we've got on Steve Severini."

CHAPTER THIRTY-FIVE

Jade stood at the board, her back to the team as she waited for Patty to call things out from the file. She had a pretty good memory of the Severini case, but she didn't want to rely on it. She wanted the hard evidence that was in the file on Patty's laptop. At some point they would need to go down to the evidence store in Glasgow and pull out forensics. But for now, they could rely on what they'd stored during the investigation, and all the information they could get from HOLMES.

She stood poised, a marker pen hovering over the whiteboard. She'd already written Severini's name, and some lines leading away from it which would lead to the people closest to him and their potential suspects.

"So there was a prime suspect," Patty said.

Jade nodded; she remembered that much. She'd interviewed the man a few times.

"Duncan Thompson," Patty added.

Jade wrote his name on the board.

"Security guard, right?"

"Yes. He was on shift, last person to see Severini alive."

"Severini checked into the building?" Mo asked.

"He did," Patty said. "Thompson had an app on his phone to check people in and out."

Jade looked at Mo. "There was more to it than that."

"We found guns at Thompson's flat," Patty said.

Mo whistled. "Circumstantial. But a match?"

"No." Jade wrote Thompson's name up anyway. Patty could add a photo later.

Jade turned to the DC. "And they didn't match the bullets that we found, did they?"

"No, it doesn't look like it."

Jade wrote *bullets?* and *guns?* on the board.

"Still, guns in his flat..." Mo said.

"They were illegal. The case is still going through, but all we were able to get him on was possession of firearms."

"Maximum ten years," Stuart added.

Patty laughed. "Something you'll discover, Sarge, is that Stuart is our walking encyclopaedia. We don't need HOLMES with him around."

Stuart blushed. "I didn't work the Severini case though."

"It's alright, Stuart," Jade said. "Patty and I aren't going to rely on our memories, either."

Stuart fidgeted in his chair and said nothing.

"Did he have motive?" Mo asked.

Jade nodded. She jabbed the pen into the board below Thompson's name. "He'd been fired, that was his last night on shift."

Mo pursed his lips. Jade could see how it looked, from outside. He'd be wondering whether their investigation was as thorough as it might have been.

Petra cleared her throat. "So did you discover if he was expecting to see Severini that night?"

Jade sniffed. "Not that we know of," she said. "Severini hadn't been intending to visit."

"Did he do that a lot? Surprise visits to his properties?"

"That's something we'll have to check on, but we know it happened sometimes."

"At what sort of time?"

"Nine pm," said Patty.

"Nine pm," Petra echoed.

"But in any event, whoever killed him wouldn't have been expecting him to be there as a matter of routine?" Mo asked.

"Most likely not," said Jade.

"But Thompson knew he was there," Petra said.

"You think it's suspicious?" Jade asked.

Petra shrugged. "It's quite a coincidence. Get fired, pissed off with the boss, he turns up on your last shift. So what was it that led you to rule him out?"

"He had an alibi," Patty said. "A friend went to the pub with him, end of his shift. Just ten minutes after he signed Severini in."

"Still doesn't mean he didn't hire someone."

"But if the guns were a factor in him being a suspect..." Mo said.

Jade sighed. "I'd like to follow that up again."

"Does that make sense, though?" Mo asked. "Given that the link between the two cases is the bullets and they're different from the bullets that Thompson had, why do we need to follow up that alibi again? Surely that points away from it being the security guard rather than towards."

Jade looked at him. Challenging her. That's what she wanted out of a DS.

"You're right," she said.

Mo was turning out to be brighter than she'd hoped. She needed someone who could add more to the team than she, Patty and Stuart did.

She also needed somebody who could focus on the evidence, the forensics and the pathology, and not so much on the human side of things. Or maybe she should focus on the more material aspects, given her current state of mind. They had Petra for the psychology, too.

"So did you have any other suspects?" Petra asked.

Patty scrolled down through her screen.

"He had an executive assistant. An ex-wife, two kids, only young. We checked the assistant and the ex out, both had alibis."

"What about business associates?" Mo asked.

"No one in particular."

"OK." Jade wrote more names on the board. "I want to go back over all the names we looked into, check for a link with Montague. Let's get photos on the board so we've got a visual cue."

"Does that help you?" Petra asked. "You're a visual processor?"

Jade felt her shoulders twitch. Petra was here to analyse the suspects, not her colleagues. "I just like to have all the options out in the open for everyone to see."

"So we're back with the sniper bullets," Mo said. "I'd like to know more about them. And double check against Thompson's guns, just in case."

"Me too," Jade replied. The more she thought about it,

the more certain she was that Thompson's gun stash had nothing to do with either murder case, but it paid to be thorough. "Mo, can I put you in charge of that aspect of the case?"

"Of course, boss." He straightened in his chair. "Stuart, you and I can look more closely into the guns used in the murders. We'll identify what guns those bullets would have come from and who supplies them."

Stuart glanced at Jade, who gave him a nod. "No problem, Sarge."

"Good." Mo gave Stuart a long look. Stuart was gazing down the notepad that he had in front of him on the table.

"OK, everybody," she said. "So Mo and Stuart, you're on the guns. Liaise with Jamie on forensics too, please. Petra, I'd like to go over the cast of characters from both crimes with you, see if we can find some more psychological stuff we might not have thought of, and Patty, can you compare the pathology reports between the two? I want to know about the injuries they sustained. I know the actual cause of death was different, but the injuries are similar."

"You think that'll help, boss?"

"It can't do any harm."

Patty shrugged. "No problem."

CHAPTER THIRTY-SIX

"Tell me about Patty and Stuart," Mo said. "You've known them long?"

Jade and Mo were in her car, heading for central Glasgow. It was just gone three, the roads as clogged as ever. She drew to a halt behind a stationary car and took the opportunity to take her hands off the wheel and stretch them out. The knuckles clicked.

"I've known Patty for over ten years. We were in Glasgow Central CID together. She's a good copper, reliable, hard-working. She can have a bit of a temper on her from time to time, but it's usually justified."

"And Stuart?"

The traffic started up again. Jade placed her hands firmly on the wheel. She considered herself a careful driver and liked to focus on the road.

"Stuart's more of an unknown quantity," she said. "He joined CID from Uniform about eight months ago. Worked in Lothian for a while then transferred to this unit."

"Ambitious?"

"Not sure. I know it's the assumption: young guy, new to CID. But he hasn't mentioned the sergeant's exam as far as I'm aware."

"Still early days."

"He was a PC for seven years before joining CID. Fresh from his Highers."

Mo nodded. "How old's Patty?"

"Late forties. She's never taken the exam, if that's what you're wondering. Some people are suited to the rank of constable, and Patty's one of them. She's right at the top of her pay band though, she's done OK for herself."

Mo pursed his lips. They sat in silence for a few minutes, crawling along in the traffic.

"I know the team's new," Mo said, "and you're probably finding your feet, but what do you see as my role? When it comes to supporting you, and how I'm supposed to relate to the other team members?"

She turned to him, then looked back at the road. She'd thought about this, of course she had, but had decided to wait until she'd seen her new DS in action and discovered where his strengths lay.

"That depends." Jade indicated to move into the inside lane and come off the M8.

Mo said nothing.

"In a small team like this," she continued as she reached the slip road, "the dynamic depends very much on the skills and personalities of the officers involved. How did it work with your last DI?"

"She and I worked together a lot. Hangover from when we were DSs together. But I tended to direct the day-to-day activities of the two DCs on the team, while Zoe oversaw the more high-level course of investigations. She involved me a lot."

Jade could sense he was testing the waters. He wanted to know if she'd do the same.

"I can't promise you I'll work in the same way as your last DI," she told him. "But if you're as good as Fraser says you are, then I expect you to be directing the DCs in much the same way."

"Thanks. Although having Dr McBride on the team adds to the mix."

They passed the Armadillo and stopped at the traffic lights leading to the bridge.

"It does," she said. "But she won't be with us full time. I'll liaise with her mostly, bring in her input on the psychological aspects of the cases."

"You think there'll be a lot of psychology to unpick?"

"Fraser does. He's passing high-profile cases to us, the ones that have proven difficult to solve or out of the ordinary. Getting an angle on the psychology of those kinds of cases could be handy."

"It's a lot of resource, for 'handy'," he said.

Jade pulled into the car park of the BBC Scotland offices and found a spot as close to the Severini scene as she could. She parked the car and turned to the DS. "You're not convinced."

He frowned, staring ahead. "I didn't say that."

"You said it's a lot of resource. You've worked with Petra before. How helpful was she?"

Mo scratched the back of his head. "It was a hate crime case. Gay men, horrible MO." He shuddered. "She helped us identify the kind of person who might have a grudge against gay men, and who might be in the mental state necessary to commit some fairly gruesome crimes."

"And did that help you solve the case?"

"To some extent. But to be honest, it was following the evidence trail that cracked it. Connie, she's a DC on my old team, she went through digital evidence with... she went through digital evidence. Found a link to a veterinary practice, which led us to the perpetrator."

"Did he fit the profile Dr McBride drew up?"

"She didn't draw up a profile as such. She hates the word. But she did give us an idea of the kind of person who might commit that crime. And yes, she was pretty accurate."

"So she might be useful."

Mo said nothing.

Jade put a hand on the door handle. "You're thinking it was your colleague's digital work that did it, and that the profile made no difference."

"It helped. It gave us more to take to the CPS, if nothing else."

"OK. Well, the Super rates her so I'm going to give her the benefit of the doubt. Come on, let's take a look at this crime scene."

CHAPTER THIRTY-SEVEN

Patty had allocated Petra a small office in the opposite corner to the room where they'd discussed the case. The open plan office had one of these rooms at each corner. This one, the briefing room, as Stuart was referring to it, and Jade's office. Not that Jade was ever here.

The fourth room, along from where Petra sat now, was filling up with junk. Every time they took over another room or another desk, its existing contents would be moved in there. Petra hoped they'd never need to use that room. But if they did, at least it wouldn't be her job to clear it out.

She'd been given a Police Scotland laptop to watch the witness interview videos. She had her own with her, but Patty had looked horrified at the idea of transferring files or putting them on a memory stick. Petra could see her point.

The laptop was old and clunky, running a version of Windows she didn't know still existed. She stuck her tongue out, teeth gripping it, as she navigated through the menus. She'd had a machine like this six or seven years ago and was trying to remember how it had functioned.

At last she managed to hunt down the video player and open the first of the files. Patty had given her a handwritten list of the suspects who'd been recorded, thank God, and she glanced at it before hitting play.

There would be three videos. Maria Watson, Severini's executive assistant. Duncan Thompson, the security guard with the gun haul. And Anthony Price, Severini's English business partner.

She'd decided to keep Thompson until last, wanting to get the measure of the other two before watching the one-time prime suspect. She'd chosen Maria Watson's video.

Petra settled back to watch. The chairs in this room were old but surprisingly comfortable.

She yawned. What time was it in New York? Should she call Ursula?

She checked her watch and did the maths. It was coming up to four pm here, so it would be late morning in New York. Ursula would be at work.

Wait until later.

Satisfied that she didn't have to feel guilty about not calling right now, she allowed the onscreen introductions to wash over her and waited for the interview to begin.

After a couple of minutes of mundane background setting, the questions started.

"Can you tell us where you were on the night of Friday March eleventh?"

There were two interviewers present. A man Petra didn't recognise, and Patty. She wondered where Jade was, if she had been watching this live via video link or a two-way mirror.

"I already went over this with your colleague, but I'm happy to help. Of course. I was at my friend Jane's house.

She had a dinner party. Four other people were there, they can all vouch for me."

Petra cocked her head. So far, so good. But if these killings had been hired out, alibis were irrelevant.

"Can you tell us the nature of your job at Mr Severini's company?"

The executive assistant's body language stiffened. Her facial expressions weren't as clear on the video as Petra would have liked, but she could sense tension.

"I was his dogsbody."

"Dogsbody?" the interviewer asked.

Petra rewound a few minutes to listen to the introductions again. The male interviewer was DS Richard Donaldson. Petra made a note of his name on her pad, wondering if she might speak to him. But if Jade had been SIO, she'd be able to get everything she needed from the DI.

She sped up the recording and found her place again.

"Dogsbody?" Donaldson asked.

Watson cocked her head. "Chief cook and bottle washer. A highly paid slave, if you will."

"I'm sorry. You're going to have to be more specific."

A sigh. "OK. My title was Executive Assistant."

Petra noted the easy use of the past tense. She checked the date stamp on the video: three days after Severini's death. But then, if Watson had hated her job so much, it wasn't all that surprising.

"In theory, my role was to ensure Mr Severini had everything he needed to be effective as the director of multiple property companies. I fielded his calls, managed his diary, occasionally smoothed the waters when a subordinate was pissed off with him. That's what I did, for the first year. But then his wife left him."

She slumped in her chair and her eyes glazed over. Onscreen, the two detectives exchanged looks. Petra knew where their thoughts were going, but she'd watched Maria Watson's body language and listened to her tone of voice when talking about her dead boss. She hadn't been having an affair with him.

"What changed when his wife left him?" Patty asked.

"He needed someone to look after his personal life too. She'd done it all, I wouldn't be surprised if that's why she left him."

"When you say personal life, do you mean you entered into a relationship with Mr Severini?"

Petra rolled her eyes. Police interviewers. So coy.

Watson shook her head and suppressed a chuckle. "Dear God, no." She curled her top lip, making Petra smile. "What I mean is that I became his personal assistant, as well as his executive assistant. I had to make sure his cleaners turned up on time, his dry cleaning was done, he was kept supplied with clean shirts. And negotiate custody details with his wife. Poor woman, I'm surprised she engaged with that at all."

"Did you have much contact with his ex-wife?" DS Donaldson asked.

"Wife, still. Legally, anyway. No, not much. Mainly by phone, some emails. Mr Severini was supposed to have his daughter every other weekend, but he rarely did. Always business getting in the way. She was angry about it, don't blame her."

"How angry?"

Another one of those smiles. "I don't think she killed him, if that's what you're getting at."

"Do you think she might have wanted him dead, though?"

Watson leaned back in her chair. She sniffed. "Well, it would have made the divorce settlement easier. It still hasn't gone through. She stands to be a very wealthy woman."

Petra noticed Patty and her colleague shuffling papers. She wondered why there wasn't an interview with the wife. She'd ask Jade about that.

She watched for fifteen more minutes. They were going over the details of Severini's financial affairs, checking that paperwork had been kept at either his office or his penthouse flat across the river from the spot where he'd died. Until his separation, Severini had lived in a house overlooking Newlands Park in the south of the city. One of Glasgow's most expensive streets, unsurprisingly. The ex-wife and child were there now.

"Some of it might be at his wife's house," Watson said.

"We've been there," DS Robertson replied. "He had a study, I assume you were required to work there occasionally."

"Not really. Carla didn't like me being in the house, I think she was suspicious of me. Until she left him, then she acted like she was my best mate. But there was a safe, too. In the cellar."

Onscreen, Robertson jotted something down on a pad and passed it to Patty, who nodded. Petra wasn't interested in the contents of any safe; Jade would have looked at all that when she'd originally worked the case. Petra was more interested in the web of relationships between Severini, his wife, and his assistant.

She was confident that Watson was telling the truth. There'd been no romantic or sexual relationship between her and Severini. But it was interesting that she'd chosen not to hide her resentment of her boss. There was none of the normal pretence of respect, or of missing him. Watson might have been hoping for generosity from Carla Severini or from the shareholders of Severini's companies. She might have chosen to play nice, in the hope of getting a generous severance package or a bequest in his will. But no, she was giving the unvarnished truth, or at least some of it.

Petra's phone rang. She reached into her handbag and fished it out. Caller ID withheld.

She frowned. On the ancient laptop, the recording had come to an end, and she closed the window as she answered the call.

"Hello?"

It would be Jade, with information on the case. Or maybe Fraser, wanting an update.

Silence.

Petra felt a shiver run across her skin. "I know who you are," she said. "I'll call the police."

But she never did. Not until she'd received at least ten of these calls. She had too much sympathy for the caller.

"Look," she said. "I'm sorry about what happened to you. I really am. But you can't keep doing this. If I call the police, they'll arrest you."

No reply. She could hear breathing.

Petra gritted her teeth and hung up. The temptation to stay on the line was hard to resist. It always was. But she wasn't going to fix this situation.

She stood up. She needed air.

CHAPTER THIRTY-EIGHT

"Stuart, long time no speak! How's it going in your fancypants complex murders unit, or whatever you call it?"

"Complex Crimes Unit. And if you saw this office you'd take back that 'fancypants' on the spot."

"Yeah, whatever. What can I do for you?"

"Who says I need something?"

"Stu. I've known you since you and me were at training college. You don't call me at quarter to five on a Wednesday afternoon unless you need something for a case."

Stuart smiled. Kate Williams was a pal from way back when he'd started on the force. The two of them had briefly dated, but not for long enough that it had ruined their friendship. Now she was a DS in the Organised Crime division. Kate was hard-working and intelligent and had thoroughly deserved her promotion, but that didn't mean it didn't rankle from time to time.

"OK, you're right. Have you heard of the Steve Severini case?"

"Stu, what do you take me for? Some kind of troglodyte

who's been stuck under the proverbial rock for the last year? Of course I've heard of the bloody Severini case. Your new boss was SIO, yeah?"

"She was." Kate knew more about his new posting than he'd realised. "So it's come up in conjunction with another investigation we're working on."

"Phineas Montague."

"Kate, how is it that you know everything about my new job?"

"I'm tracking you, Stu. Didn't you know? That's what us OC types do these days."

He laughed.

"Nah, you numbskull," she continued. "Your new posting has got tongues wagging here. We all want to know where your fancy new office is."

Stuart looked up. Across the desks, Patty was peering into her screen. Further away were empty desks with junk piled up on them, the three offices that were in use, and the fourth one that was looking increasingly like the back room of an understaffed charity shop. "It's a long way off being fancy, Kate."

"Yeah, yeah. I believe you. So DI Tanner thinks the two cases are linked? Multi-millionaires and that?"

Stuart pursed his lips. He wasn't sure how much he was supposed to be telling colleagues outside the unit.

"Something like that," he said. "But what I'm more interested to know is whether either Severini or Montague's names have ever come up in an OC investigation."

"You want to know if Organised Crime are tracking them too, just like I'm tracking you?"

"If you are, I hope you're doing a better job of it than you are with me. Given that you don't know the first thing about the office I'm working out of."

A laugh. "Your boss checked Severini out for OC links when she was heading up that case first time round."

"The case was never formally closed, so I wouldn't exactly use the phrase 'first time round'."

"You know what I mean. Anyway, we checked him out on the system. Even... well, you don't need to know what else we did. But he was clean. No organised crime connections at all. Some kind of miracle, for a guy like him."

"What about Phineas Montague?"

"Well, that's new, so I can't say for sure. But I think Superintendent Murdo has requested background checks."

Stuart frowned. Did the DI know about that? And how closely did Superintendents normally get involved in murder investigations?

"Ah. OK." He tried to sound as if he already knew what she was talking about.

"Above my pay grade, though," Kate added. "In fact, I'm puzzled that you called me."

He swallowed. "You know what it's like. Sometimes the informal stuff at lower ranks can be more useful."

"I know that. But..."

He detected hesitancy in her voice. "But what, Kate?"

"I don't mean to be funny, Stu. But this is OC we're talking about. And..."

"And what?"

"*Shit.* And... and I'm a DS now. I can't just go chatting to anyone about what I do."

"I'm not anyone, surely."

Silence.

"Kate?"

"Sorry, pal. Look, when it comes to this kind of thing, you are anyone. Our relationship isn't official, is it? You haven't gone through the correct procedure to enquire about this."

Stuart held his phone out in front of him and stared at it. Correct procedure? This wasn't like Kate.

Fuck. Now she was a DS, things were going to be different.

"OK, Kate. I'm sorry if I put you in a difficult position."

"Stu, I'm sorry. That came out wrong. I didn't mean to—"

"It's OK. I understand. I really do."

And he did. Even if it hurt. Fact was, Kate wasn't the only one of his mates who was a DS in a proper unit now. And here he was, a DC in a unit that was so crap it had been shoved in an empty industrial estate in the middle of nowhere.

"Thanks for your help, Kate." He hung up, ignoring her protests.

CHAPTER THIRTY-NINE

"It's not much help," Mo said. He stood in the window, looking out at the view of the Clyde. It reminded him of the area around the canals in Birmingham, but there was so much more space around it.

"After six months of not charging anyone, we had to let the company take charge of the site again."

"It didn't take them long."

"They'd already finished the rest of the building. Seems these modern blocks are quick to build."

"Not to fit out, though." Mo looked around the space. It was empty. There were still holes in the walls where the plasterers needed to return after the electricians had done their job. The area was neither one thing, nor the other. Not a building site, not an office.

"It seems that potential tenants are reluctant to take this place on," the DI said.

"Why? Businesses don't care about that kind of thing, surely?"

He walked to another wall, also glass-lined, and looked

out. This time, the view stretched across the city, towards hills in the distance. Loch Lomond? He had no idea.

Birmingham was like this. Constant development, new blocks popping up like moles. No views towards lochs and mountains, though. The Lickey Hills was about as good as it got.

We've got the canals though, he thought. *And it's home.*

He pushed down the tug of homesickness. It had only been two days, for God's sake. But the permanence of this move made it feel longer.

"I didn't expect it to help much," the DI said, her voice tight. Mo looked round to see that she had her fists balled at her sides. He stepped away from the window and she stretched her fingers out, her facial expression flickering.

"You OK?" he asked.

"Fine. If Petra got a chance to see it, I wanted you to, as well."

"Thanks." Mo brushed his hand against a trolley that had been left against the wall. It was thick with dust. This place made him sad. "Exactly where was he found?"

"Over here." Jade led him to a spot near the view over the Clyde. Mo followed.

Jade pointed at the floor. "He was on the ground, here. It was still bare concrete then."

"And he died of exposure?"

"There were no walls, no windows. It was March. The overnight temperature on the night he died was only one degree above freezing."

"That warm?" He gave her a smile. "In Glasgow, in March?"

She returned the smile, looking wary. So far, their interactions had been entirely factual and professional. "It's not always Baltic, you know."

Mo nodded. He shifted his foot across the spot where Severini had died, trying to imagine how it would have felt to breathe your last up here. He shivered. He closed his eyes for a moment, then straightened his back and looked at his new boss.

"Stuart is looking for links between the two cases," he said. "And the gun, he and I will work on tracking down where it might have come from."

"Good. Keep me updated, if you make any progress."

"I will. Do you want me to oversee Patty's work, too?"

Jade shook her head. "Patty's waiting for the pathologist's report. She's working on the suspect list, with me and Petra. She'll pass names onto you. You're on forensics too, remember."

"I do. I'll call Jamie as soon as we're done here."

"Good. He'll be finished up at the loch by tomorrow, then I expect you to go to the lab and go over what he has."

"Of course." *I expect you. Keep me updated.* All so formal. This was what it was like, having a boss who wasn't your best mate.

Jade checked her watch and anxiety passed across her face. "We need to get back. I'll drop you at the office."

"No problem."

"There's something you need to know about me," she said as they walked back to the lift. She was a pace or so ahead of him, not making eye contact.

He waited.

She pressed the lift button and stood watching the display. Still no eye contact. "I'm a single mum. My son is six years old. It means I have to be at home at a sensible hour. My son has been through... he needs me."

"I understand." Mo had two daughters, and his wife was a GP. If anyone knew about juggling, it was him and Cat.

"You don't," Jade muttered. Mo chose not to contradict her. She turned to him. "I pull my weight though. If I need to leave early, I take work home. I'm always available, on my mobile."

"I don't doubt it."

"Good." The lift arrived and she stepped inside.

CHAPTER FORTY

"OK," said Jade. "What have we got?"

She was back in the office, in the room they'd commandeered for meetings. The board had photos from the Severini case as well as three maps. One showed the wider area with both crime scenes marked, and the other two were closer plans of the two crime scenes and their vicinity.

"I watched all the interviews," Petra said. She was sitting closest to Jade, her sleeves rolled up and jacket over the back of the chair. She looked more business-like than she had at any point so far. Jade noticed dark rings under her eyes and remembered that until two days ago, the woman had been in New York.

"Anything of interest?"

Petra shook her head. "Duncan Thompson's body language is legit. He's telling the truth as far as I can make out. No suspicious tells, but you'd have seen that yourself. No contradictions in his statement. Did you speak to him more than once?"

"There was an informal interview," Patty said. "Before we brought him in for questioning."

"Was he arrested at any point?" Mo asked.

"No," Jade said. "We didn't have enough for a warrant."

"Not even with the guns?"

"He's been arrested for firearms possession," Patty said. "Unconnected to the murder."

Mo sniffed. He looked unconvinced.

"What about the others?" Jade looked at the photos on the board. Maria Watson was up there, Severini's assistant. Anthony Price, his business partner, and Carla, his estranged wife.

"The assistant was carefully critical," Petra replied. "Reminded me of the groundskeeper from the Montague case."

"Angus Robertson?" Mo asked.

Petra nodded. "You spoke to him first. How did he seem to you?"

Mo shrugged. "It's clear no one liked Phineas Montague much. He wasn't the only one." He looked at Jade. "Taylor Gannon was pretty unhappy with him too, wasn't she?"

Jade thought back to their interview with Taylor, the way the woman had seemed scared to occupy space in the house. "I think it's safe to say Phineas Montague was an intimidating figure."

"A bully, more like," added Petra.

"Is that a term used by psychologists?" Stuart asked.

Petra turned to him and smiled. "We speak English too, you know."

"Sorry."

"It's fine. I know what you all think of me."

"We don't," Jade said.

Petra waved a hand in dismissal. "I don't mind. Quack, charlatan, psychic. I've been called everything." She gave Mo a look and he blushed, making Jade wonder what had passed between them in Birmingham. "Doesn't matter. Your Superintendent is paying me to do a job, and that's what I intend to do."

Jade narrowed her eyes. She wanted to contradict the psychologist, to insist that they saw her as a valuable part of the team. But after her conversation with Mo in the car, she wasn't so sure that was the case.

"What about the others?" she asked.

"Anthony Price, he was Severini's business partner. English, posh as they come. I could barely understand the man, had to watch the interview three times."

Jade noticed Patty's smile. They'd had the same problem when they'd conducted the interview. She'd wondered how Price had managed to communicate with business associates in Glasgow. Or maybe Severini's role had been to translate.

"Did he come across as genuine to you?" she asked.

"Slimy as hell, but genuine. He seemed to have nothing but good things to say about Severini, and it came across as authentic. I can't cast any suspicion on him from a psychological perspective."

"So just the assistant, then?"

"To be honest, I may be grasping at straws. Compared to the other two, she was the most negative about her boss. But it seemed carefully calculated. I was wondering if you had an interview with the widow that I could watch, though."

Jade frowned and looked at the board. "Carla Severini?"

Petra nodded. "Divorce hadn't gone through yet, according to Maria Watson. As his widow, she would have inherited."

"He'd already changed his will," Patty said.

"He had?" Petra asked.

"Left it all to his daughter."

"Who's how old?"

"Er, not sure. Young."

"In which case it would be in trust, yes? With her mother as her legal guardian, you've still got a motive."

"We should go back to see her again," Jade suggested.

Petra nodded. "Can't do any harm."

Jade made a note in her pad. Having Petra here was doing her good, giving her brain the jolt it needed.

"OK," she said. "Mo, anything on the forensics yet?"

"I'm due at the lab in the morning. Jamie's been too busy clearing the site today. Sorry."

"It's fine. The job needs doing properly. What about the gun or guns?"

"Nothing on HOLMES," said Mo. "I'm hoping to get more from Jamie in the morning."

"I spoke to an old mate," added Stuart. "She said there was no link to organised crime as far as she knew."

Jade looked at Mo. "You asked Stuart to do this?"

Mo looked surprised. "Er..."

"Sorry, boss," said Stuart. "Thought you'd appreciate some initiative."

"And I do," Jade told him. "But you need to discuss this kind of thing with your sergeant. Who in this case is DS Uddin."

Stuart flushed. "Sorry."

Mo looked as uncomfortable as Stuart did.

Jade sighed. "So what did your mate have to say?"

"She said they checked Severini out for organised crime links when he was killed. Found nothing."

"It was me who asked for that check," Jade told him. She was annoyed that he'd gone behind her back. But she knew Stuart was anxious to show that he could do more.

"And apparently the Super has asked for a check to be run on Montague."

Jade felt her stomach lurch. What was Fraser doing, going to another team without informing her?

She maintained control of her facial expression, anxious not to let the team see her reaction.

"And has it come back with anything?" she asked.

"Too early to say," Stuart replied. "You want me to follow it up?"

"I'll do that. And if you think it's worth talking to anyone from outside this team about the case in future, run it past the sarge first, yes?"

The redness returned to Stuart's cheeks. "Yes, boss."

Jade took a deep breath. "OK. What else have we got?"

"The post-mortem for Phineas Montague came in," Patty said.

"Good. What's the official cause of death?"

"Exsanguination. Loss of blood, just like Dr Pradesh told you at the scene."

Jade chewed on her pen. "No surprise there. Anything else of note? Toxicology?"

"Nothing untoward in his system. Although with the blood loss, it did make it harder to do a proper analysis."

"OK. So we've got no reason to think that anyone got close to him in order to assist in his eventual death."

"No blood thinning agents if that's what you're thinking, boss," Patty replied.

Jade gave her a smile. "It was. Thanks."

Stuart was looking at Patty, his face hard. Jade rapped a knuckle on the desk.

"OK," she said. "If that's all, I need to get back to my son. Patty, can you forward the PM report to me so I can read it at home?"

"No problem."

"And Petra, we'll go and see Carla Severini in the morning."

"Sounds like a plan. Will you pick me up?"

"Where's your flat again?"

"West End."

"That's on my way. Good." She checked her watch again; she was going to be late. "Sorry, folks. See you in the morning."

CHAPTER FORTY-ONE

Mo WATCHED out of the window of the main office as Jade sped out of the car park. He hoped she'd drive safely; being late for her son was one thing, but being in an accident was something else entirely.

He turned back to the room. Stuart and Patty were pulling on their coats and Petra was in the room she'd used to view the videos, hunched over the laptop Patty had given her.

"In the morning, we'll have more on the forensics," he said. "Stuart, I'd like you to come to the lab with me."

Stuart and Patty exchanged glances.

"I normally do forensics," Patty said.

Mo swallowed. He'd seen Zoe do this; put team members on tasks which weren't their natural inclination. It could be risky, but it meant they gained a wider breadth of experience. "Patty, I'd like you to look into Carla Severini. I want to know more about her background and what she's been doing since her husband died. Is there a new man on the scene? Could there have been before Steve Severini died? That is, if you didn't look into all that during the original investigation."

"We did, Sarge, but that was months ago. Things could have moved on."

He smiled. "OK. You work on that. We've got witness statements from both cases to go through again. I want to trawl through all of them to find any potential connections."

Patti chewed her lip. "No problem, Sarge."

"Thanks."

Patty left the office, not meeting his eye. Maybe pissing her off wasn't the best thing to do on his second day, but he wasn't here to win a popularity contest.

"You want me to come here first, or meet you at the lab?" Stuart asked.

"Where's the lab?"

"Port Dundas. Just the other side of the city centre."

"In that case, I'll meet you there. 9am."

"Sarge." Stuart stood behind his desk. Shifting from foot to foot. "That all?"

"It is. Thanks, Stuart. I appreciate you showing initiative earlier. But you heard what the boss said."

A flicker passed across Stuart's face. "Loud and clear."

"Don't let it stop you coming up with ideas." Mo thought of Connie and Rhodri, the two DCs in his old team. Rhodri had gone outside the bounds of his job on a few occasions, but once he'd reined in some of his enthusiasm, it had led to some concrete breakthroughs. And when Connie had found the evidence that had identified the Digbeth Ripper and saved the life of her own brother, she hadn't been officially working on the case.

Sometimes, stretching procedure was necessary. And he

knew that one of the most important skills as a sergeant was judging when it was, and when it most definitely wasn't.

"Thanks, Stuart. I'll see you in the morning."

"Sarge." Stuart gave him a nervous smile and left the office.

Petra was still in the corner office. Mo pushed the door open.

"Everything OK?" he asked.

"Fine." She closed the lid of the laptop.

"You're going over those videos again?"

"I wasn't sure if my judgement of the Maria Watson video was accurate."

Mo raised an eyebrow. So the expert was fallible. "You've rewatched it?"

"The most important bits."

"And?"

"I still think she's calculating her answers."

"I imagine your first instincts are normally fairly reliable."

She nodded. "Sometimes. Not always. Instincts and science are not the same thing."

"No." Mo wasn't sure what to say.

"They didn't tell me you were moving up here," she said.

"Oh. Er... Yes. My wife, Catriona. Her mum's ill. She's managed to find herself a partnership in a GP practice near Stirling. And I... well, I was lucky to get a posting up here, given that there are differences between English and Scottish policing."

"Not all that many, I imagine."

"Not so much in the procedure, but aspects of the law. I'm being sent on a crash course."

She smiled. "You'll ace it."

"Thanks." He was surprised by the compliment.

"I bet Zoe misses you."

Mo swallowed. "I miss her." He was embarrassed to admit to himself that sometimes he wasn't sure who he missed more, Cat or Zoe. Although it was his girls he missed the most. Even after two days.

"You were good pals."

"We were."

"Look, Mo," she said. "I hope you don't mind me asking. But I'm buggered by jet lag and if I go back to my flat I'll just pace the floor. Fancy a drink, city centre somewhere? Where's your hotel?"

"Ummm..."

"Shit." She put a hand to her face. "You don't drink. Sorry."

He shook his head. "I'm Muslim, yes. But I do have the occasional drink. We're not all teetotal."

"Zoe was, as I remember."

"Still is."

"Sorry. But yeah, you're right. Probably not a good idea. Early start, and all." She stood up and dragged her jacket off the back of the chair. Her shoes were on the floor; she used a foot to shunt them towards her then slipped them on. "See you in the morning."

"See you." Mo followed her back into the main office. "You're getting a cab?"

"Always do, pal. Works out cheaper than a bloody car, in the long run." She pushed through the outer doors and he listened to the sound of her stilettos clipping down the stairs.

The office was quiet. His hotel room would be quieter. At least here, there was the feeling he could be useful.

He'd run through HOLMES again. But first, he'd call Cat. He grabbed his phone and dialled.

CHAPTER FORTY-TWO

THE TREES that separated the loch from the main road sped past in a blur. Jade smiled as Rory chattered in the back seat. He'd been with the childminder after school today, at her cosy house in Balloch. Rory loved it with Kelly, but Jade still felt guilty. Now she was heading up the Complex Crimes Unit, it would only get harder. But at least the Montague crime scene was local and there would be some days when she didn't have to leave the house early to get to Glasgow.

Fraser had originally intended to base the new unit in Edinburgh. There was an office there, vacated by a Road Policing team that had been downsized, which would have been perfect. But he'd known how hard that would have made things for Jade. She was still surprised he'd even offered her this job, after she'd taken so much time off over the last year.

"Mummy, is it true that a man got shot in the loch?"

Jade stiffened. She looked in the rear-view mirror.

"Who told you that, sweetheart?"

He smiled back at her. "It was on the TV at Kelly's."

Damn. Kelly had CBeebies on most of the time, which was understandable when she was minding three kids under the age of seven, but Jade couldn't ban her from watching the news.

She wished she could.

"You don't need to worry about that kind of thing. Am I right in thinking you had a visitor at school today, from the museum?"

"That was boring. Is the man still in the loch?"

Jade closed her eyes for a moment. A memory hit her, of the night she'd had to tell Rory about Dan's death. She blinked back tears.

"No, love. He was taken away. You don't need to worry."

"Poor man." Rory lifted his hand and fired a pretend shot at her in the rear-view mirror, making a 'pyoing' sound to go with it. Jade allowed herself to relax a little. For a child as young as Rory, the news of Phineas Montague's death was no more real than the cartoon violence he saw on TV. She tried to shield him, but knew she was fighting a losing battle.

The death of his father had been real, though. He'd spent six months asking when Daddy was coming home, until the questions had grown less frequent and eventually stopped altogether. She hadn't known if she was relieved he'd stopped asking, or heartbroken. Did it mean he'd accepted his father's death, or that he'd forgotten about Daddy? A year was a long time in such a young life.

She twisted her head from side to side, trying to alleviate the stiffness in her neck. "Tell me about the lady from the museum, Rory."

He sniffed loudly, then wiped the back of his hand across his nose. "She had a machine. It was boring."

Jade sighed. Maybe boring was good. Boring was better

than trauma. Both she and Rory had been receiving psychological help since Dan's death. In her case, it had been the police psychologist. For Rory, there was a nice lady who came into school and had informal chats with him. He didn't even know she was a mental health specialist, just thought she was another friendly grown-up like his teachers and childminder.

They were a mile away from the house. Rain had started to fall. Jade hated rain. She flicked the windscreen wipers on and muttered to herself. She had to get over this. If she was going to stay in this house, she needed to stop reliving it over and over. And she needed to accept that in Scotland, it rained.

The turnoff was approaching. Their house was on a slip road down to the water, running parallel to the main road. There was a right turn, not very well marked. It was dangerous, but when they'd moved in, the position and the views had been more important.

She wished she'd paid attention to her instincts.

Jade slowed the car and indicated. There was still three hundred metres to go, but she liked to give the drivers behind plenty of warning that she would be turning. There was no central reservation here, nowhere to shelter while she waited for a gap in the traffic coming the other way.

Could she do this with her son, every day, for the rest of her life? Could she put him at risk like this?

The specialists had said he needed continuity. Staying in the same house would provide that. And she couldn't afford to move right now.

She blinked, stationary in the road, waiting. The car behind her honked its horn.

"Fuck off," she muttered under her breath.

"Mummy swore!"

Shit. She hadn't expected him to hear.

"Sorry, Rory. That was a bad word Mummy used. I don't want you to repeat it."

"Why do you use it, then?"

"Because I'm very naughty, and I shouldn't have."

A gap was approaching. *Focus.* She bit down on her bottom lip and turned, foot hard on the accelerator to get through before the next car was too close. Once over, she allowed herself to breathe.

Moments later, she was in the driveway of the house. It was peaceful here, if you ignored the background hum of the road. She could hear birds, and a distant motor boat on the loch.

She loved it here. Didn't she?

She wiped her face. Tears again. She'd stopped noticing them until her face became soaked. She brought her sleeve over her hand and dried her cheeks, then turned to her son.

"OK, Rory. Tea time. How about sausages?"

CHAPTER FORTY-THREE

Aunt Lydia's flat was no less intimidating the second time Petra entered it. She kicked off her heels at the door and walked through to the kitchen, choosing to ignore the boxes of books she'd started to fill last night.

Petra liked books, she wasn't a total philistine. But Lydia had owned thousands of them. She had a feeling that the flat would feel twice as large once she'd rid the place of half of the things. And it would make the space feel more her own.

She went into the kitchen and placed the parcel she'd found in the communal hall on the worktop. There'd been a post-it note stuck to it, with a handwritten message. *Please collect parcels promptly.* Petra wondered who'd left it. The single woman in the flat immediately below, or the couple with a toddler on the ground floor?

Either way, it didn't bode well for neighbourly relations. With the amount of travelling Petra did, she envisaged parcels piling up. She'd have to get herself a PO Box, or something like that.

She tore the tape off the top of the parcel and extracted

the contents. A coffee machine. Lydia, it seemed, had been either a tea drinker or just someone who didn't care about the quality of the coffee she drank. Petra was neither of those things, so her first priority had been to buy an expensive Italian machine online. She smiled as she drew it out of the box and plugged it into the wall. She'd picked up some quality coffee after instructing the cab driver to drop her off a few blocks from the flat, where she'd seen a deli the previous day.

The smell of coffee filled the kitchen. Now it felt like home.

From the next room, she heard her phone ringing inside her bag. Closing her eyes and inhaling before she left the kitchen, she wandered through to fetch it. She just hoped it wouldn't be her anonymous caller.

She checked the display, then felt a snag of guilt.

"Ursula."

"Hey, honey. How's bonnie Scotland?"

Petra sat down on one of the two threadbare sofas. They'd both seen better days, but were supremely comfortable and she would most definitely be keeping them.

"Bonnie as always. What are you up to?"

"Up to? Who says I'm up to anything?"

"You know what I mean."

"Oh, just this and that. I had drinks with an old friend from college. It was nice, although she's a soccer mom now." Ursula made a gagging sound and Petra chuckled.

"Sounds like hell."

"No. It was fine. She's a good friend. I told her all about you."

Petra felt a pang of responsibility. Ursula liked to talk about her to her friends and family. Petra rarely discussed her girlfriends with the few friends she had. And her only family was her mother, who lived in a nursing home in Fife and had never accepted the fact that her daughter was gay.

"OK."

"She says you sound great."

Petra felt far from great. She knew she wasn't what Ursula needed, or deserved. But Ursula made her feel good about herself, and they enjoyed each other's company.

Maybe this time, Petra could make it work for longer than a few months. Other people managed that. She had to one day, surely?

"I've been brought in on a murder case."

She could sense Ursula's eyes widening at the other end of the line. "Murder?"

"American billionaire. Phineas Montague."

"Oh. I've heard of him. My cousin's son works for one of his companies. He died? In Scotland?"

"Uh-huh."

"And what's your role? No, don't tell me. You're drawing up a profile. It's like in *Mindhunter*."

"Not exactly." Petra stood up from the sofa, hearing the coffee machine click. One of these days, she might find a woman who didn't fantasise about her being Jodie Foster in *Silence of the Lambs*. Not that Jodie had even played the profiler, but that wasn't important, it seemed. "It's less dramatic than that."

"Fun, though, huh?"

Fun. A man had been shot. His staff were in danger of losing their jobs. No. It wasn't fun.

"Not really, Ursula. Look, I have paperwork to go through. I'll give you a call at the weekend, yeah?"

"That's days away."

"Sorry. I'm really busy with this case." Not so busy she couldn't make a phone call or two, but Petra was annoyed at the *Mindhunter* reference. "Speak then, OK?"

"OK. I—"

Petra hung up before Ursula had a chance to finish that sentence, mentally kicking herself. She was crap at this. Why couldn't she be better at relationships?

She sighed. No point worrying about it. She poured the coffee and pulled out her laptop. Jade had let her put a few files on a memory stick, and she had her notes from the videos. She needed to start on her report. It would keep her busy. It would distract her from her own inadequacy.

CHAPTER FORTY-FOUR

STUART WAS the first in the office. He was worried about what the DI had said to him in yesterday's briefing, and he wanted to prove that he was better than one slip-up. He knew he needed to be at the lab at nine, but there was still plenty of time.

He'd spent the night tossing and turning, the case revolving in his mind. He'd been working through all the suspects, the people associated with the two victims. Could any of them be connected? Surely two wealthy businessmen in a city like Glasgow had to have had some kind of link? Or possibly not, not if Montague's only connection with Glasgow was that he'd spent a fraction of his fortune on a pretty bit of land just outside it.

He'd thought about the killer. If it was a hired gunman, then there was a possibility they'd travelled to the area. After all, Glasgow wasn't exactly crawling with assassins for hire. He'd turned that over in his mind until 3am. And if they had come from outside Scotland, where would they have got the gun?

That wasn't an issue. Wherever the shooter came from, they had to have got the gun from somewhere. He had a sense that this wasn't someone who kept weapons in their home or office, but who was able to procure them when needed. Someone who was careful not to keep evidence where it might be found. Someone who might even lead a regular life in between contracts.

He'd smiled at his reflection as he'd shaved this morning, standing in front of his chipped bathroom mirror at 5am having given up on sleep. Listen to yourself. Gunman. Assassin. Contract. He wasn't in a Kingsman movie, for fuck's sake.

But maybe he was. Maybe this was something the like of which they'd not seen before. The thought gave him the shivers.

It was coming up to 7am and he'd been in the office for half an hour already. What with this being a remote industrial estate, each of them had been issued with a key. It wasn't like there was a desk sergeant to get past. He could work all the hours he pleased in his efforts to show how committed he was.

He'd looked at the passenger manifest for the flight Montague had taken from Los Angeles to Edinburgh. Montague, of course, had flown First Class. If you were a hired assassin trailing your victim, would you sit near them so you could watch their movements, or stay out of the way, in Economy?

It didn't really matter. The list of names told him nothing. He supposed he could widen his search, take in other flights around the same dates, and compare them to flights around the time when Severini was killed. But that would take days, and besides, there was nothing to indicate that the killer had travelled from the US. Even less so in the case of Severini.

OK. So that possibility was out, or at least, not worth exploring. But there was still a nagging suspicion that someone in Severini's circle had to be linked to Montague in some way.

How would he find a link?

He opened up HOLMES and brought up the two sets of case files. They had biographical information on all the people close to both victims. Names, jobs, home addresses, dates of birth, family.

He could input it all to a spreadsheet, see if that came up with anything. Even better, he could export a CSV file from HOLMES and dump it into Excel.

Stuart sipped at his coffee and copied the data across. In theory it wasn't possible to export blocks of data from HOLMES, but he'd worked out a way. He kept it to himself, not sure if he was breaking the rules. He'd delete the spreadsheet when he was done, not only from his computer but from the cache. And he'd make sure he was offline while he worked on it.

He leaned back in his chair and stretched his arms above his head. The fatigue was catching up with him. How much sleep had he managed? Two hours, maybe three? Not enough.

He needed another coffee.

Leaving the data dump to do its thing, Stuart left the office and went into the large but dingy kitchen to make himself a cup of instant. He gulped it down, standing beside the kettle, then made another. His fourth of the morning. He would be bouncing off the ceiling by the time the others arrived.

Stuart grabbed his mug and walked through to the office. Outside, he heard a car backfire.

The data was all downloaded and in a spreadsheet. He opened it, setting up an automated trawl for any matches. He leaned back, closed his eyes, and took a sip of coffee.

His computer beeped. Stuart put his mug down, spilling a little on his desk and ignoring it. He held his breath and blinked a few times to pull himself into alertness.

"Shit."

He stared at the screen.

That was it. There was a match.

He looked towards the window, then checked the time on his computer screen. Not even half past seven.

How long would he have to wait before he could call the sarge?

CHAPTER FORTY-FIVE

JADE NODDED as Stuart stood at the board, drawing a line between the two suspects.

"You said they were both off in the interviews, Petra," she said.

Petra had her chin resting in her hand. She was frowning. "I did. But I don't want that to sway you. All they did was complain about their bosses."

"I'd say it's fairly conclusive," Patty added.

Jade nodded. Stuart's body language was all over the place. He was jumpy and excited, but then would slump against the table from time to time. He'd drunk three cups of coffee in the short time since she'd arrived.

"Stuart, why don't you sit down?"

He nodded, his eyes bright, and did as he was told. Mo gave him a reassuring smile and he returned it with a jolt as his arm hit the table. Patty suppressed a laugh.

"It's not just the address," Stuart said. "I've found more things linking them. The rental agreement for the house, plus his Facebook. She's all over it."

"But her Facebook doesn't feature him at all," Patty said.

"That doesn't mean anything," Stuart replied. "Maybe she's locked down her privacy settings. Maybe she's just more circumspect than he is."

"If the two of them conspired to kill their respective bosses," Petra suggested, "you'd expect them to keep their relationship quiet."

Mo nodded. "You have a point there." Stuart had called him earlier, just as he'd been about to set off for the lab. What he'd found had been enough to change their morning plans.

"It's still enough to be working on," Jade said. "And enough for us to bring both of them in for a chat."

"You think we've got enough for that?" Mo asked. "A shared address?"

Jade gazed at the names on the board. Angus Robertson, Montague's groundsman. Maria Watson, Severini's assistant. Both names appeared on the rental agreement for a flat in Cumbernauld. Robertson had claimed to live on the Montague estate, but it seemed he had more than one address.

Neither of them had known that the police were connecting the two cases. When Watson had been interviewed, Montague had still been alive. So it wasn't as if there was anything suspicious about them not confessing to the connection.

But still...

"OK," she said. "We'll go see them again for an informal chat. No caution, as yet. I want the two interviews done simultaneously, with no opportunity for them to compare notes. Stuart, I don't suppose you've been able to find out where we can find Maria Watson these days?"

"She's working for Anthony Price now."

"She is, is she?"

"Based out of his office in Edinburgh."

That was no surprise. An Englishman would feel more at home in Edinburgh than Glasgow. He'd certainly find it easier to make himself understood.

"OK," she said. "Mo and Patty, I want you to go and see Maria Watson. I'll take Stuart up to Loch Lomond to interview Angus Robertson. Petra, you can take your pick."

"Maria Watson," Petra said without hesitation. "I'll go with Mo and Patty."

"I thought you'd pick her." Jade waved her pen. "Stuart and Patty, I want you to gather together any information that we can use to back up the connection between the two of them, and anything else that might be of interest, and email it to myself and the sarge. We'll leave here in an hour, by which time I want things as tight as they can possibly be."

"Boss," said Stuart.

"And good work. You've earned yourself a better night's sleep tonight."

CHAPTER FORTY-SIX

JADE YAWNED as the team filed out of the briefing room.

"Mo, can I borrow you a minute?"

He stopped walking and let Patty slip past him and out of the room.

"Yes, boss?" he asked once they were alone.

"You can call me Jade, you know. I'm pretty informal."

He smiled. "Jade it is. Thanks."

"Although not in front of Patty and Stuart."

"Of course." Another smile. She wondered what the arrangements had been between him and his last DI. Extremely informal, she imagined, what with them being pals.

"So what d'you think?"

He slid into the chair opposite her. "About what?"

"Stuart's breakthrough."

"It could be important. It could be a coincidence."

"It's not concrete evidence. But Stuart's clearly trying to compensate for yesterday's fuck-up."

Another smile. "He is. Good on him."

"Yeah." Jade scratched her arm. She was tired, and that made her skin tingle. Rory had slept badly last night, coming into her bed at 1am after a nightmare.

"I know you were supposed to be meeting him at the lab this morning, but I think this has overtaken that."

"He called me at eight, told me what was up."

"The two of you are still going to have to go to the lab at some point today. We need evidence. This connection between the cases isn't enough to build anything from without a lot more weight."

"I'll call Jamie, let him know to expect us later on."

"Thanks."

"Do you think maybe we should put surveillance on Watson and Robertson?" Mo asked.

Jade raised an eyebrow. "Already?"

"I'd like to see what they do after we speak to them. Whether they confer."

"If they live at the same address, then I think that's a given."

"But they don't. Robertson has accommodation with his job. As far as we're aware, he hasn't left Montague's estate for a few days. What if he suddenly dashes back to see her?"

"You think he'd be that impulsive?"

Mo shrugged. "Petra will probably be in a better position to predict that than me. But it's a thought."

"I don't see how surveillance can help. If he does go and see her, then we still don't know what they'll be talking about."

"I wasn't referring to physical surveillance."

"Ah." Jade tapped her phone against her teeth. "You mean online."

A nod.

"It's worth looking into, but we'd need a warrant to do it properly." She considered. "Let's see what Patty and Stuart are able to come up with before we interview the pair, then decide if we think it's worth it."

"Isn't it best to apply for the warrant as soon as possible?"

Jade pushed back a flicker of irritation. She didn't like Mo telling her how to do her job. "Let me worry about that, yeah?"

"Of course. Sorry." He stood up. "I'll get out there." He looked at his watch. "Forty minutes till we leave."

"We need to coordinate once we're on the road. I want both doors knocking on at the same time."

"Boss."

She shook her head. "Jade."

"Jade. Sorry. Thanks. Will do."

CHAPTER FORTY-SEVEN

"Shit."

Mo stopped as he passed Stuart's desk. "What?"

"Maria Watson's Facebook."

Patty looked up from her screen. "Keep it down, will you?"

Stuart shook his head, his eyes on the screen.

"What is it?" Mo asked again.

Stuart pointed. "They're married."

Mo bent to get a better look. "Robertson and Watson?"

"Mm-hmm. They married five years ago. Look. It's in her timeline."

"I thought her privacy was locked down. She hadn't mentioned him."

"This is the only mention. Relationship status."

"It doesn't help," Patty said across the desks. She looked unimpressed.

"What doesn't?" Jade was emerging from the briefing room. Petra was back in the room she'd used to watch the video evidence. Mo wondered if that was going to end up being her office.

Stuart turned to look at the DI, his hand still resting on his computer screen. "Maria Watson and Angus Robertson are married."

Jade stopped in her tracks. "That's good."

"Why?" Stuart looked like he might explode. *Calm down*, Mo thought.

"If they're married, then it affects the strength of any alibi they give each other."

"How?" Mo asked.

"A jury..." She shook her head.

"Surely we haven't got to the stage of thinking about a jury yet," he said. "We haven't even spoken to them."

She stood behind Stuart's chair, looking over his shoulder at the screen. He'd dropped his hand and was resting it on his coffee mug. Mo realised it was fresh. How many had he drunk?

"A jury's going to think worse of them," he said. "What with them being married. Makes them look like a right evil pair."

"I don't know." Jade lifted the cuff of her blouse and scratched the skin of her arm. Mo noticed it was red. "I really don't know."

"It doesn't matter," he added. "We still need to talk to him."

"Fifteen minutes to showtime," Patty said, looking up from her desk.

"Do we have anything else concrete before we go? Anything from the interviews?"

"No." Petra emerged from her office. "I've scanned the

videos again and there's nothing I missed. Certainly nothing indicating a link between the two of them."

"They're married," Stuart said.

Petra arched a finely made-up eyebrow. "Really?"

"Does that make a difference?" Jade asked her.

"It could do. The attachment between them is deeper than we thought. More permanent. In conspiracy cases where couples are involved, the proportion of married couples is fifty per cent higher than in the general population."

Mo nodded. "And if either of them stood to gain financially from either Severini or Montague's deaths, then they both would."

"Which gives both of them a motive," Stuart said.

"Come on, people," said Jade. "Let's calm down. I want facts. Not speculation. We go to see them both, and we find out what they've got to say. We don't tell them we've discovered the link, but we give them an opportunity to mention it themselves." She squared her shoulders. "Patty, Stuart, put everything we have in an email to me and the sarge. We can run through it en route, have a chat when we get there." She looked at Mo. "Good with you?"

"Good with me."

CHAPTER FORTY-EIGHT

"You DRIVE," Jade told Stuart. She slid into the passenger seat of her car and handed him the keys.

"You sure, boss?"

"It's police issue," she told him. "You're covered on the insurance."

"I didn't mean that."

"I know you didn't. But I want to talk to the Super." *And I don't want to use hands-free*, she didn't add.

Stuart slid his hands around the steering wheel, adjusted the seat, then gave her a questioning look, checking she was OK with him doing that. She nodded approval. She was used to letting other people drive her car, and had given up on the idea of ever getting the seat and mirrors into the perfect position.

"Loch Lomond," she told him. "At this time of day, you don't want the motorway. Take the A81 then the A809 up to Drymen."

"I can use the satnav."

"Stuart, I live just across the loch. Trust me."

"OK." He started the car and left the near-empty car park. Jade turned to see Mo and Patty behind them, Mo driving his pool car. It wasn't long before they parted company, Mo heading for the M8 towards Edinburgh. She hoped Patty knew where they were going, as it was clear Mo's knowledge of the Scottish road system was nonexistent.

As they reached the A81 and crossed the river near Maryhill Locks, she dialled Fraser's mobile.

"DI Tanner," he said. "How are your two shootings coming along?"

"I'm not on hands-free," she told him. "And we've found a link."

"That's good, Jade. What kind of link?"

"Phineas Montague's groundsman and Steve Severini's executive assistant are married."

"That's a link."

"I'm not sure yet if it's more than coincidence, but we're on our way to interview them both now."

"Both together?"

"I'm with DC Burns en route to Angus Robertson up at Loch Lomond. DS Uddin and DC Henderson are going to Edinburgh, where Maria Watson works now."

"Good. And the pair know nothing about this, I assume?"

"Nothing. We're coordinating so we knock on both doors at the same time. We don't want them conferring."

"Of course not. What do you need from me?"

"DS Uddin has suggested digital surveillance."

"I assume you've already looked at their public social media, online presence, that kind of thing?"

"Yes, Sir."

"You don't have to *sir* me."

"I have DC Burns with me, Sir."

Jade and Fraser had known each other for years, and were friends. He'd never married, and had occasionally joined her and Dan for dinner at their house. But she wasn't about to call the superintendent by his first name when she was with Stuart.

"Got it," he said. "So you need a warrant to delve deeper. And I assume you'll be bringing the digital forensics team in to assist."

"If we decide it's needed."

"Jade, you're SIO on this. There's no *we* about it. If you decide it's necessary, then that's the direction the investigation will go."

"Of course."

"So you want me to sign off on it, get you that warrant?"

"Patty can organise that, Sir. But I need your approval."

"You have it. Good luck with the interview, Jade. Keep me posted, won't you?"

"Of course, Sir." She allowed herself a smile.

CHAPTER FORTY-NINE

ANTHONY PRICE WORKED out of an office just north of Princes Street. This was the smart part of Edinburgh, known as the New Town, but still old by the standards of most cities.

"Where the hell do we park?" Mo asked as they crawled along the wide streets. They seemed to be dominated by residents-only parking.

"Hang on," said Patty. She was in the back seat, Petra in the front. She waved her phone in Mo's direction.

"There's a multi-storey. Up toward Calton Hill."

That meant nothing to Mo. "Direct me."

"Here." Petra grabbed the phone. "Maybe we should have got you to drive, Patty. Seeing as you're the only one with the first clue."

Patty grinned. "I'm fine in the back, Dr McBride."

Petra let out a sharp laugh. "You don't have to call me that. I'm Petra."

Patty shrugged. "Turn right."

"Shit." Mo cut across the traffic and took a right turn.

The car park wasn't far ahead. "Patty, can you call the DI? Find out if they're at Loch Lomond."

"It'll have taken them longer than it has us. Montague's place is in the middle of nowhere."

"Still. Check, will you?"

He turned into the car park and found a space. The three of them sat in silence while Patty waited for the call to be picked up.

"Boss," she said at last. "We're in Edinburgh, five minutes' walk from Price's office. What do you—" She nodded. "Uh-huh. Right."

She hung up. "They're still twenty minutes away."

Mo took the keys from the ignition and pocketed them. "So we sit here."

"Or we could walk in the general direction. It's nice around here."

"No," Mo replied. "We don't want to risk Maria Watson seeing you."

"Good thinking, Sarge." Patty leaned back in her seat. "I'll carry on with the files." She held up her phone.

"You've got access, on there?"

"Stuart set me up with it. He's quite the nerd."

Mo smiled. The resident nerd in his old team was DC Connie Williams. He wondered how she was getting on with the new DS. He should call her, check in. Maybe Rhodri, too.

"I assume you want me to sit quietly and observe?" Petra asked, inspecting her nails. The polish was still as immaculate as it had been yesterday. Mo wondered if she touched it up each day.

"Is that what the DI had you doing, when you've been in on her interviews?"

A shrug. "It is. But this is your interview, so it's your shout."

"Do the same. I'll lead the questions. Patty, you can come in when there's anything linked to the first investigation. You'll know things about the case that I don't."

"You've read the files though, Sarge?"

"Of course I have." He'd sat up in his hotel room last night, trying to drown his loneliness with work. "But you've spoken to the woman before."

"I watched the interview," Petra said. "What was your impression of her, Patty?"

Patty put down her phone and leaned forward, wedged between the front seats like a child on a long trip, eager to get there quicker. "Didn't get much, really. She didn't like her boss, that was sure enough."

"She complained about him treating her like a dogsbody."

"That was the word she used, yes. Especially after his separation."

"Did you speak to his ex-wife at all?" Petra looked at Patty in the rear-view mirror. Mo checked his phone, wondering how long Jade would be.

"Yeah," Patty replied. "She was upset. Just goes to show that even after you hate someone enough to dump them, it can still hit you when they die."

"And you think that was a genuine response? She wasn't just putting it on for public consumption?"

Patty shook her head. "It was real, alright. She was a mess."

"A mess." Petra scratched her cheek with one of those long fingernails. "Did she dump him, or was it the other way around?"

"She dumped him. Unreasonable behaviour was what she cited on the divorce application. Doesn't mean she didn't still love him, I guess."

Petra licked her lips, her expression sad. Mo wondered if she had a partner, or any family. She seemed so independent.

Mo's phone buzzed: the DI.

Approaching Montague's house. Will be with Robertson in five minutes.

"Time to go," he said.

Patty leaned back and opened her door. "Let's get on with it."

CHAPTER FIFTY

"OK, STUART," Jade said as they approached the house. "I'll lead on this. You take notes. OK?"

"With respect, boss, I'd li—"

Jade turned to him. "Just let me do my job, Stuart."

His face fell. "Sorry. I didn't mean to—"

She softened. "It's fine. I shouldn't have snapped at you. Look, if I need your backup for something, I'll scratch my nose. OK?"

He grinned. "Got it."

Jade turned back towards the house and pulled on the doorbell. The housekeeper, Mrs Carrick, opened the door.

"Oh," she said. "Your forensics fellas have all gone. I didn't think you'd be back."

Jade gave her a reassuring smile. "We just wanted to speak with Angus Robertson. Can you tell me where I'll find him?"

The housekeeper frowned. "He's still working on the High Copse." She pointed away from the loch. "Take the right-hand path as you leave the house, walk for about a quarter of a mile. You'll probably hear him, he's got the power tools out today."

Jade exchanged glances with Stuart. It meant that Mo would be starting with Maria Watson before they began their interview with Robertson. But, she imagined, there still wouldn't be time for the couple to confer.

Stop worrying, she told herself.

"Thank you," she said to the housekeeper, and turned away from the house. She took the path up the hill, into the woods.

"Boss, it's this one." Stuart had taken an alternative turning, to the right.

She looked at him. "You're right. Thanks."

They hurried along the path. There was the chance that Mrs Carrick had phoned Robertson and warned him they were heading this way. But Jade was prepared to bank on the fact that none of the staff here seemed to get along, and that the housekeeper was probably quite content to throw Robertson to the wolves.

At last she heard the sound of a chainsaw.

"He's up ahead," Stuart whispered.

She nodded. After a minute or so, they caught sight of Robertson through the trees. He was cutting logs, wearing safety goggles and ear defenders.

Shit. They had to avoid startling him.

She beckoned for Stuart to follow her and walked past Roberston's position, hoping he'd catch movement from the corner of his eye. She walked at an angle so she could watch him as she did so. At last, he straightened up and removed the defenders.

"Can I help you?" he called out.

Jade exchanged glances with Stuart, then turned to walk

towards Robertson.

"Mr Robertson," she called. "We wanted a word."

He placed the saw on the ground and pulled off the goggles. "Again?"

She stopped in front of him. "We have some new evidence we wanted to ask you about."

He cocked his head. "The post-mortem's come in."

"Not that."

"What, then?" He put a hand on his side and kneaded his flesh. She imagined a person would become stiff, bending over like that to cut wood all day.

Jade looked around them. They were in a clearing which had been widened by Robertson's work on the trees. He hadn't cleared the whole area, but instead was thinning it, removing perhaps every third tree. Jade knew from conversations with Dan that this aided the health of a forest, even if it did make it look a mess in the short term.

"Mr Robertson, am I right in thinking that you're married?"

He stared back at her, unblinking. For a moment she wondered whether Maria Watson had got to him first. He seemed so unperturbed.

"I am," he said.

"Your wife is Maria Watson, is that correct?"

"It is. I don't see how that's relevant."

"We have reason to believe that Phineas Montague's death is connected to the death of Steve Severini."

"Ah." Robertson wiped his brow. "I get it now. That's why you looked so suspicious when you interviewed me."

Jade hadn't known about the connection when she'd first spoken to him, but she wasn't about to tell him that. "Your wife worked for Mr Severini, is that correct?"

"It is. I've got nothing to hide, Detective Inspector."

Jade sensed Stuart's unease. He'd been so proud of himself finding that connection, and now Robertson seemed unconcerned by it.

Her phone buzzed in her pocket. She frowned and ignored it.

"What was your relationship like with Mr Montague again, Mr Robertson?"

"He was a bad boss. I've already told your colleague that. I'm not going to pretend otherwise, just to make myself look innocent." He paused, looking into her eyes. "Because I am innocent. And so is Maria."

Jade's phone buzzed again. *Go away.*

She maintained eye contact with Robertson. "And your wife's relationship with Mr Severini. What was that like?"

He blew out a short breath. "Pretty crappy, if you want the truth. The guy was a control freak."

"Boss." Stuart was holding his phone out. She hadn't heard it ring.

"Not now, DC Burns."

"What's going on, Detective? Are you going to arrest me, or what? Surely it's not a crime to be married."

"Boss."

Jade flashed Stuart a look. She hadn't scratched her nose, she was pretty sure of it. Besides, his brief hadn't been to interrupt her if she did so, but to back her up.

"Boss, you're going to want to take this."

Jade held up a finger, indicating for Robertson not to move. "One moment, please." She turned to Stuart. "This had better be good."

"Sorry. But it's important. It's Patty."

CHAPTER FIFTY-ONE

Anthony Price's offices were on the top floor of a Georgian terrace on Heriot Row. Mo, Patty and Petra sat in the waiting room in silence.

A slim receptionist who couldn't have been much older than twenty opened a door and gave them a thin smile. "She'll be with you shortly."

Mo hoped Jade was having similar problems, and that they weren't running too far behind her. If Robertson and Watson had been able to speak to each other, the element of surprise would be lost.

Patty stood up, patting herself down.

"What is it?" he hissed at her.

"Sorry, Sarge. Can't find my... here it is." She took her buzzing phone out of the inside pocket of her jacket. Mo rolled his eyes.

He watched as she took the call then frowned.

"What?" he whispered, glancing at the door where the receptionist had disappeared.

Patty shook her head and turned away from him.

"OK," she said. "Send it to me, will you? You got it when?"

Mo exchanged looks with Petra. The receptionist reappeared, wearing an insincere smile. "She's ready for you."

Patty was still on the phone. She looked at Mo and raised a finger. "Hang on." She pulled the phone away from her ear. "It's DS Donaldson, he was on the original investigation. He's got something he thinks we need to see."

"Can't it wait?"

Patty shook her head. "Apparently not."

Mo swallowed. "OK, then. You stay here, find out what this Donaldson has." He turned to the psychologist. "Looks like it's just you and me."

"Fine by me."

"Just observe, like we agreed."

"Right-o."

He turned to the receptionist. "Sorry about that."

She gave him a shrug and then turned through the doorway, leading them across an open plan room towards a glass-walled corner office where Maria Watson was waiting.

Mo composed himself as he approached. None of this was going how it should. He was even beginning to wonder whether it had been worth haring over here to surprise the woman just because she was married to Robertson.

As they entered the room, Watson stood up. She looked worried.

"Has there been a breakthrough in the investigation? We've all been worried that Mr Severini's killer might never be found."

I bet you have been, he thought, wondering what Petra was making of this. Even he could see through the woman's insincerity.

"It's not that," he said. He gestured towards the chair she'd been sitting in before they'd entered. "Please. We just wanted to ask you a few questions."

"That's fine." She sat down and placed her hands on the table, her fingers laced together. She looked from him to Petra.

"This is Petra McBride. And my name is DS Uddin."

"I know." She cocked her head towards the receptionist, who was making for the door they'd entered by. "Leanne told me. What can I help you with?"

"Ms Watson, we have reason to believe that your former employer's death might be related to another case we're working on."

Her hand went to her mouth. "Phineas Montague. I saw it on the news."

Mo looked at her. "What makes you think that?"

"He was shot, too, wasn't he? And you'll have noticed that my husband works for him. Worked, I suppose."

Mo felt like she'd punched him. All this effort to surprise her, and here she was freely admitting to the connection. He shouldn't have been shocked, he supposed. It was inevitable that they'd have found the connection eventually, and whether Watson and Robertson were innocent or guilty, they'd have realised that themselves.

"I'm sure you'll agree it is quite a coincidence, you and your husband both working for men who are killed in similar circumstances."

"Not all that similar, I'd say."

"No?"

Mo was aware of movement, out of the corner of his eye. Normal in an open plan office. He ignored it. *Concentrate.*

Why was it important that Robertson and Watson were connected, again?

"Well, Mr Severini died in one of his buildings, right in the heart of the city. Your Mr Montague died in a remote spot near Loch Lomond."

"Both were shot." It had been impossible to keep the fact out of the news, much as Jade had wanted to.

"They were." Maria Watson was calm, her face placid.

Mo felt a hand on his arm. It was Petra, indicating something outside the office.

He looked past her to see Patty heading their way. She looked perturbed, her grey-brown hair bobbing as she walked.

He frowned. What now?

The door to the glass-walled office opened.

"Sorry, Sarge."

"DC Henderson. Come in. We were just getting started."

"Sorry, Sarge. I've just been talking to the DI, and she wants to confer before we go any further."

CHAPTER FIFTY-TWO

"I'M SORRY, Mo." Jade was in her car, outside Phineas Montague's house. "Have you seen it?"

"It's not conclusive. If they hired someone..."

"I know. But when Patty showed it to me, I wanted you to see it. Are you still with her?"

"Petra and Patty are in there. Patty's asking her some follow-up questions to her original interview. I think we should carry on."

Jade leaned back in the driver's seat. "You're right." All the panic over the CCTV Patty had been sent, and it could be irrelevant. And, meanwhile, they'd lost their momentum. "I'm going back up there. We'll talk later."

"Good." Mo hung up.

She passed her phone from one hand to the other. Patty had emailed her a CCTV recording that DS Donaldson had sent her. Angus Robertson and Maria Watson, out together in Glasgow on the night of Steve Severini's death. Each of them would provide an alibi for the other, and this would corroborate it. But what if they'd hired someone?

And there was still the possibility that one of them had gone from the nightclub they'd been seen outside to the spot from where Severini had been shot.

The timings made that close to impossible, though. She knew it, and Robertson and Watson would know it, too.

She left the car and trudged back up the hill to the copse. Stuart was still keeping an eye on Angus Robertson, who'd gone back to chopping wood.

"Mr Robertson," she called out, not caring about the ear defenders.

He looked up. "You're back."

"I am. Can we talk?"

"I thought we were about to do that twenty minutes ago."

"I'm sorry for the interruption."

"You were asking me about Maria. You want to know if she had any motive to kill Severini, and if I had any motive to kill Montague."

Or if the pair of you had any motive to kill them both, Jade thought.

She nodded.

"I suppose if hating your boss is a motive, then yes, we did. But that's all. Neither of us stood to gain from their deaths. Neither Steve Severini nor Phineas Montague was the type of man to leave money to lowly employees. And besides, we can account for our whereabouts at the time of both deaths." He cocked his head. "I think you should be looking at Carla Severini, to be frank."

"She's got no connection to Phineas Montague."

Robertson raised an eyebrow. "No?"

Jade folded her arms. "Is there something you know about Carla Severini?"

Robertson smiled. "You haven't looked into her, have you?"

Jade pursed her lips. "Just tell me, Mr Robertson. Does Carla Severini have a connection to Phineas Montague?"

"Her sister. Check out her sister."

Jade glared at him. "Give me the name of her sister, please."

Another smile. He was enjoying this. Bastard. "Carla Severini's sister was Emily Fogarty. You'll find that she was planning to marry Phineas Montague. Until he broke it off, shortly after his business blossomed."

CHAPTER FIFTY-THREE

Petra sat in the back of Mo's car, listening to the frustration in her new colleagues' voices. They'd thought they'd identified their prime suspects. They'd been about to get digital surveillance authorised. And now, it seemed things had been thrown up in the air once again.

She'd watched Maria Watson while they'd waited for Mo to return from his call to Jade. Patty had gone with him, leaving her alone with Steve Severini's former assistant. The woman had been calm, but her eyes had not left the door through which Mo and Patty had disappeared.

Petra still wasn't convinced they didn't need to keep an eye on Maria Watson, alibi or no alibi.

But it wasn't her job to lead the direction of the investigation. She needed to work on what they referred to as the profile, and for that, she should go back to the office.

They were on their way there now. And now they had another lead, she would probably have the time to develop her thoughts while they conducted background research on Emily Fogarty.

Jade was on speaker through Mo's phone, which Patty held out while he drove. Petra was in the back seat this time, nursing a headache. She had painkillers in her bag but hadn't thought to bring a bottle of water. And there was no way they were going to stop off for her to buy one.

It could wait. In the meantime, she'd watch and listen. And then, hopefully, she'd be of assistance.

"What do we know about Carla Severini?" Mo asked, looking between the road, the phone, and Patty.

"DS Donaldson interviewed her at her home during the initial investigation," Jade said. "She was badly affected by her ex-husband's death. And once we established that the will had been changed..."

"Yes, but did she know that?" Mo glanced at the phone, then shifted his gaze back to the road ahead. They were on the M8, which was slow, but at least it was moving. Petra preferred to take the train between Glasgow and Edinburgh, but she didn't imagine that was the norm during a police investigation.

"She claimed that she did," Patty said. "But we have no way of knowing."

"The contents of a will are confidential," Mo said. "There's no way she would have known unless her ex-husband decided to tell her."

"And we have no way of knowing if he did."

"Did you ask her the question?"

"We've already told you that," Patty said, her voice laced with irritation. "We asked her, she said she knew."

"Did you speak to the solicitors?"

"They wouldn't have been party to any conversations between the couple," Jade said. "I don't think whether or not she knew that she didn't stand to inherit is going to get us anywhere. What about the sister? It gives us another link."

Patty shook her head. "Stuart is going to be so pissed off."

Mo gave her a look. "He'll be fine."

"Sorry, Sarge, I didn't mean it like that."

"We're all frustrated, Patty. But let's not make assumptions about other members of the team."

Patty looked at him as if she was about to argue, then thought better of it. Petra wondered if they'd forgotten she was still there, taking all this in.

"I'm right here, you know," came Stuart's voice over the phone. "We're on hands-free too, remember?"

Patty reddened. "Sorry, Stu."

"It's OK."

"Let's focus," said Jade. "I want to get what background we can on Emily Fogarty as soon as we're back in the office. When was she involved with Phineas Montague, why didn't they marry, was it really him who broke it off?"

"She could have been out for revenge," Patty suggested.

"This isn't a Miss Marple mystery, Pat," said Stuart.

Patty stuck her tongue out at the phone. Mo suppressed a laugh, then adopted a stern expression.

"I want to know where she lives now," Jade continued. "When she was with Montague, whether they kept in touch. Everything we can about their relationship. Surely with him being one of the wealthiest men on the planet, we'll be able to find press coverage."

"Also one of the most private men on the planet," Mo pointed out.

"True. How far out are you from the office?"

Mo looked at Patty.

"About half an hour, boss," Patty said. "Traffic willing."

"We'll be longer. There's been an accident on the A809."

"That's not the best way," said Patty. "At this time of day, you need to take the—"

"Patty, I know," Jade interrupted, "but it's not much use reminding me now. Just get back to the office and do some digging. I'll see you when we get there."

CHAPTER FIFTY-FOUR

THE OFFICE FELT like a haven of tranquillity after the disruption of the previous few hours. Mo slung his jacket over the back of a chair and looked at Patti and Petra.

"Who wants a brew?"

"Do we have time?" Patty asked.

"It's OK, Patty. We don't need to panic. Let's all get our breath back."

She sank into her chair. "Yes, Sarge. You're right." She gazed at her computer screen, her body language loose.

"Petra?" he asked.

"Coffee, please." She frowned and then shook her head. "No, make it tea. Two sugars."

"Coming right up."

"And I'm going to do some work on my suspect analysis, if you don't need me for anything else."

He glanced towards the office she'd requisitioned. "In there, or are you heading off?"

She smiled. "In there. I'd rather not bugger off until the DI gets here."

"OK." Mo opened the door to the kitchen.

Five minutes later, he returned. Standing in the kitchen staring at the kettle, trying not to will it to boil, had calmed his jangled nerves. Patty was calmly looking at her screen and Petra was in her corner office hunched over her personal laptop. This was more like it.

He placed a mug in front of Patty and went to the office to take Petra's in.

"Anything you need from us?" he asked her.

"No thanks."

"Does the fact we have a new lead affect your work?"

"My analysis stems from information about the crime itself, and the possible mindset of someone who might have committed it. Who you're investigating has no bearing on that. In fact, until I've finished this, I'd rather you kept me out of your discussions. Although, of course, if you want me to look at specific individuals in due course, I will need to know who they are."

He nodded. "I'll let Jade know."

"Good."

As Mo returned to his desk, the main door opened and Jade and Stuart entered. Stuart was looking sheepish. Mo wondered what he'd said in the car, whether there'd been more harsh words from the DI.

"Everything OK?" he asked.

"Fine," Jade replied. "Just frustrated, that's all. Have you made a start?"

"You were back quicker than I expected. But yes, Patty's working on background checks for Emily Fogarty."

"Good." Jade eyed his mug. "Any chance of one of those? I'm parched."

He put his mug down on the desk. "Of course. Stu?"

"Er, yeah. Cup of tea for me, please."

"Me too," said Jade. She looked at her watch. Mo had noticed that Jade had a sixth sense for the time, and started checking her watch from early afternoon on. The glances would become more frequent as she realised she might be late for her childcare.

It couldn't be easy.

"Boss?" he said, her watch-checking jolting his memory.

"Mm-hmm?"

"I still need to get over to the lab. Stuart was coming with me."

Stuart's expression perked up. "I don't need the cuppa."

"And you can have mine, boss." Mo gestured towards his own cup, which he hadn't started on.

Jade frowned at it. "Oh. OK. Yes. You get over to Jamie. Tell me what you get, yes?"

Mo grabbed his jacket. Stuart was already at the door. "Will do."

CHAPTER FIFTY-FIVE

PETRA GLANCED out of her office. Mo and Stuart had gone out again, and Jade stood behind Patty's desk, looking over the other woman's shoulder at her computer screen.

Petra knew she should go out there. Tell Jade what she was doing, check there was nothing they needed her for.

But she wanted to focus. She wondered briefly if it might be better to go back to the flat and work there, away from the distraction of the investigation, but then she remembered the boxes of books everywhere and decided against it.

She stood up from her spot facing outwards and shifted to the chair opposite. Her neck prickled briefly at the thought that the two women behind her might be watching, but she told herself not to be daft. She didn't want the distraction of seeing them moving around.

She'd left her laptop here while they'd been out, confident that an office belonging to Police Scotland was one of the most secure places it could be, and it was right where she'd deposited it on the desk. She opened it up and brought up the file she'd been working on.

She didn't like her work being referred to as *profiling*. A profile focused on describing one individual. An imaginary person who might have committed the crime. Petra's files dealt with a range of possibilities and probabilities. She tried to highlight when she was dealing with the one, or the other.

So far, she'd come to a number of conclusions.

Firstly, the murders had been premeditated. These were not hot-blooded killings committed in an emotional moment. It didn't take a forensic psychologist to work that out, though. If that was all she could give them, Fraser Murdo was wasting his money.

Her second conclusion was that whoever had committed these crimes had murdered before. If Severini's death had been the first time the killer had killed in this way, she'd have expected the original investigation to have got further. They'd worked out where the bullets had come from – an office building across the road – but when they'd visited it there had been no forensics to help them. Nothing. The killer knew how to cover his (or her) tracks.

The Montague killing was similar. By choosing a spot in the open but sheltered by the combination of greenery and seclusion, the killer had shown a level of planning that was unlikely for someone with no experience.

She knew that these conclusions guided her in the direction of a professional assassin, but she wasn't ready to go there yet. First, she wanted to identify what frame of mind a person would have been in to want each of Severini and Montague dead. That would help her get closer to understanding whether it had indeed been the same person who had either committed both killings, or hired whoever had.

Despite the connections between the cases, she wasn't jumping to conclusions. She had to start from first principles.

Begin with the crime, and work her way backwards. It wasn't dissimilar to what Jamie Douglas and his team of CSIs did, except in her case she had to rely on what she could infer from the scene of the crime, instead of being able to work with tangible evidence.

To work out the frame of mind of a killer or killers, she had to understand what the motive might be.

She could immediately rule out anger, or any kind of psychopathy. The person behind these deaths was calm and intelligent. A hired killer might display some psychopathic traits, but that wasn't helpful when it came to identifying who had hired them.

No, the motive here stemmed from something cold. Which usually meant one of two things: material gain, or revenge.

Her thoughts strayed to Maria Watson and Angus Robertson. They'd spoken ill of their employers, but had their dislike been sufficient to lead them towards revenge?

No. She had to take a different route. Start with the crime, not the suspects.

She created two columns in a Word document. In the first one, she typed *Money* at the top. In the second column, she typed *Revenge*.

She leaned back and surveyed the words. *Think back to the crime itself.*

Assuming the killer had been hired, that would have cost money. A tick in the financial gain column. The killing could be seen as an investment against future income.

Despite herself, she was struck by the parallels between the two crimes. If the killer simply wanted both Severini and Montague dead, then why go to the trouble of using almost identical techniques? The men hadn't died of the same cause, but they'd both been shot from a distance.

She placed the cursor in the *Revenge* column. There was something theatrical about the way the murders had been staged. The high-rise block on a cold March night. The remote beach on the banks of Loch Lomond. These were more than just practical killings. The killer wanted to draw attention to them.

Would a professional killer think like that? If her source material had been movies and TV shows, she'd have been inclined to think yes. But in reality, what she'd learned about contract killers was that they kept things simple and low-key. Draw as little attention to yourself as possible, and only do what's necessary to achieve the objective.

Which meant that whoever had hired the killer had specified the means of death.

She stood up, mulling over what that meant about the psychology of the person who'd choreographed the killings. They'd been angry. With both Severini and Montague. They'd wanted the police, and maybe people close to the two men, to understand that these killings were linked. It was almost a performance.

She typed a few more notes into the table, then went back to her main file. Did she have enough for Jade? She was getting closer to it.

CHAPTER FIFTY-SIX

THE CSI LAB was in a Victorian building just north of Glasgow city centre. Mo parked where Stuart directed him, and they walked in silence to the offices. There was an anonymous buzzer on the door, which Mo pressed, and to which he then introduced himself. The door clicked and Stuart pushed it open.

There was a moment's awkwardness while both men indicated for the other to go first until Mo decided to break it by going ahead. Stuart had been confident and creative in the office, but it seemed he was wary of his new sergeant.

The lab was on the first floor, an open space with large draughty windows and long desks with technicians working at them. Mo thought of Adi Hanson's lab in Birmingham, which was modern but much darker than this, without the wide windows.

Jamie emerged from a door and gave them both a smile and a handshake. "Thanks for coming over here," he said. "Normally I'm required to go schlepping over to whichever CID offices I'm working for."

Mo shrugged. "Not a problem, this way we can see what you're working on properly."

"And our offices are horrible," Stuart added.

"So I've heard," Jamie replied. "You not settled in yet?"

"We'll need to add about twenty more people to the team if we're going to properly settle into that place."

Jamie nodded. "We've prepared some things for you. Follow me."

The two detectives followed him to a corner desk where a young woman was waiting for them.

"Have you met Heather?"

"Heya, Heather," Stuart said.

"Stu." The woman gave him a nod.

"Pleased to meet you," Mo said. "I'm Mo Uddin."

"Your reputation has preceded you."

"Oh?" He was surprised.

She smiled. "I used to work with Adi Hanson."

Even more surprised. "Adi's a good guy."

"He is."

"So, Heather," Jamie said. "Can you show DS Uddin and DC Burns what we've found so far?"

"Just use Mo," Mo said.

"And Stu," Stuart grinned.

"Yeah," Jamie grunted. "Heather?"

"Yeah, sorry. So I've been looking at the trajectory of the bullets, mapping it with 3D software."

"Bullets?"

"We've found another one. Buried in the pebbles along the beach."

"Does that change things?" Mo asked.

"We've examined the bullets themselves, made some assumptions about the gun they were fired from."

"Calculated assumptions," Jamie interrupted.

"Yeah. Sorry. We've made some calculations. We've got more data to feed into the software now. And we've worked out exactly where the shooter was."

Mo nodded. He could hear Stuart's breathing next to him; it sounded like the DC was coming down with a cold.

"And?" he said.

"Heather, have you got a map?" Jamie asked.

"I have that. A proper one." She opened a drawer and brought out an Ordnance Survey map. Mo smiled. Sometimes paper was better than the fancy mapping technology they used.

She unfolded it on the desk and pointed to the spot where they'd found Montague.

"So he was there, right? We found him at that spot," she pointed, "and worked out that he was standing further south, near the edge of the trees, when he was shot."

"There was evidence of him moving from the one location to the other. Bloody footmarks, indistinct and blurred, but it was his blood," Jamie said.

Heather pointed again to the spot where they believed Montague had died, then traced her finger across the map to the southwest. She stopped on a tiny island.

"Eilean nan Deargannan," she said.

Mo squinted. "Pardon?"

She turned to him. "Yeah, it's a mouthful. Eilean nan Deargennan. Uninhabited island, about quarter of a mile out from the Eastern shore of the loch. It means Island of Fleas."

Stuart scratched his arm. "Lovely."

"I thought the shooter was on the mainland?" Mo asked.

Jamie shook his head. "That's what we originally thought, but the new bullet makes this definite."

Mo frowned. "No one lives there, you say?"

"It's way too small. Nothing on it except trees and birds," Heather replied. "And fleas, I guess."

"And you know this how?"

Jamie nodded at Heather, who bent to a computer and fired up the monitor. She opened up the 3D modelling software and flew around it for a moment, showing the angle of fire from the point of view of the bullets themselves. It made Mo feel seasick.

"If he moved after being shot, how do we know the shots came from that direction?"

"We're fairly confident about his original position and the direction he was facing, so we can extrapolate to this with a good degree of certainty. And this island, it's actually a segment of a circle we're looking at," Jamie said. "But that's the only land within it. And there's no way you could take a shot as accurate as that from a boat."

"Even an experienced shooter?"

"The distance is significant and it hit him in the knee, which isn't exactly a large part of the anatomy."

"Maybe they were aiming higher?" Stuart suggested.

"Steve Severini was shot in the exact same place."

"You're right," Mo said. It was yet another indication that the two killings were linked. That, and the fact that they now had four people with a connection to both.

"So whoever shot Montague had access to a boat, and spent time on that island," he said.

"They did," Jamie replied. "We're looking for any camera footage of people using boats in that part of the loch on Monday night. CCTV from nearby car parks and properties, tourist snaps."

"And you'll be examining the island itself?"

"We certainly will. It means a decent sized operation, logistically, some planning involved. But we'll be there in the morning."

"Good." Mo indicated Stuart. "We'll be joining you."

CHAPTER FIFTY-SEVEN

Jade held up her ID. "Mrs Severini, I'm so sorry to bother you. My name's DI Tanner and this is Petra McBride. We have a few questions in relation to your husband's death."

The woman at the door, who had worn a puzzled look, let her face fall. Jade had the feeling she was doing it for effect.

"Stevie," she said. "I'm still..." Her lip quivered. "It's so hard. Viola is distraught."

"Viola?"

Carla Severini gave Jade a 'you should know that' look. "My daughter."

"Of course. I'm sorry to hear that. Can we come in, please?"

Carla gave Petra a wary look, flicked another look at Jade, then pulled the door back to let them in. They followed her into a narrow but tall hallway decorated in a shade of blue-green paint that Jade imagined was expensive.

Carla waved towards a set of doors. "Come into the sitting room."

"Thank you." Jade waited for the woman to lead the way. She exchanged glances with Petra as they followed her through a set of double glass doors into a broad living room painted in a slightly bluer shade of greeny-blue. Two mustard yellow sofas faced each other, perfectly plumped cushions placed at regular intervals. There was no TV and very little in the way of personalisation. The paintings coordinated with the walls and sofa, as if they'd been picked out by an interior designer, and there was no sign of family photos on any surface.

Carla perched at one end of the closest sofa and looked up at Jade and Petra. She brought a small white handkerchief out from the pocket of her jeans – crisply ironed, deep blue – and wiped under her eyes.

Jade took the seat beside her and turned to face the woman. Petra sat opposite them. Carla gave Petra another wary look then turned to Jade, arranging her face into a sad smile.

"We met during the initial investigation," Jade reminded her. "I came here with DS Donaldson."

"You did. You were nice." A sniff.

Jade took a breath. She'd never warmed to Carla Severini, but felt she'd failed this woman by not finding whoever had killed her ex-husband.

"I wanted to let you know that we're working on a second investigation that we believe might be linked to your husband's death."

"Phineas Montague."

Jade swallowed. "You were expecting that?"

"Well, as soon as I heard, I knew you'd be round here."

Carla's vowels were flattening. The careful Home Counties tones she'd adopted as she'd opened the door were reverting to the South London accent Jade remembered.

"You'll know why we believe there might be a link between the two cases?"

"Both millionaires, both shot."

"And..."

Carla brushed her hair out of her face. "And both in relationships with Fogarty sisters." She fixed Jade with a challenging stare.

"Your sister Emily was engaged to Phineas Montague, is that correct?"

A snort. "I warned her off him."

"Why?"

"He was bad news."

Jade waited, but Carla didn't elaborate. "How did they meet?"

"No idea."

"And he broke it off with her."

"Two weeks before the planned wedding day. Nice man."

"How long ago did the relationship break up?"

Carla's body was very still. She looked across the room at a point somewhere beyond Petra's head, blinking. "Six months. No. Five months and three weeks." She shifted her gaze to Jade's face, but her eyes were dull. "I can tell you the exact date he dumped her, if you like. The shit."

Jade nodded. She wondered what Petra made of all this. Since arriving, they'd had mock grief, irritation, and now what looked a lot like numbness.

"What was the date?" Jade's voice was low.

Carla's nostrils flared. "September. September tenth."

She looked away from Jade, her jaw tightening. "Exactly a week before my sister killed herself."

CHAPTER FIFTY-EIGHT

PETRA SETTLED herself in the passenger seat as Jade started the car and prowled along Carla Severini's road. The lights in the front room they'd sat in were still on, but Petra couldn't see Carla in there.

"Did you not know about that?" Petra asked her.

Jade shook her head, not turning to meet Petra's eye. "We were in too much of a hurry."

"We?"

Jade glanced at her, irritation furrowing her brow. "*I* was in too much of a hurry. I should have stopped to do background checks first."

"Not particularly deep background checks, to find out that a woman you were considering as a suspect had killed herself before the crime took place."

"Don't rub it in." Jade's voice was tight. "You're right, that's why I'm pissed off. I'm annoyed with myself." She raised her wrist to check her watch.

"You need to get back to your son."

"I do. You think I'm unprofessional."

"Whatever gave you that impression?"

"I leave early because of my family, I fail to check if a suspect is even alive, I—"

Petra put a hand on Jade's arm. "You're under pressure. This is your first investigation as SIO for a while, yes?"

Jade shrugged the hand off. "It is."

"Well, then."

"Well, nothing. Carla Severini didn't deserve to be put through that."

Petra turned to look out of the window. "Och, I don't think she was put through anything."

They joined the M74, heading east towards the office. Petra wasn't familiar with the junction but the signs pointed to Edinburgh, so she knew they were going the right way.

"She was putting it on about her husband," Jade said. "That wasn't exactly hard to spot. But she was clearly devastated by her sister's death."

"Perhaps."

Jade tightened her grip on the wheel, her knuckles pale. "Perhaps? She's going to make a complaint about me. She hinted at it, as we were leaving."

Petra eyed Jade. "That's what you care about?"

Jade's posture softened. "It's not. I'm angry that my lack of thoroughness might have impacted the investigation. I'm angry that I've failed Carla Severini twice now."

"How so?"

"I failed to find the bastard who shot her husband first time round. Now I'm doing it again."

"OK." Petra started counting on her fingers. The Clyde snaked out on their left, bounded by industrial estates and waste ground. "First off, you weren't the only person on that investigation."

"I was the—"

"Shush, lassie."

Petra spotted a smirk spreading across Jade's face before she could hide it. That was better.

"Second off, the investigation is still open, isn't it? By spotting the connection the way you did, you've increased the chances of finding her ex-husband's killer. And don't forget she was in the process of divorcing the man. She could still be a suspect, couldn't she?"

"She could. Even more, with the potential for revenge after Emily's death."

"There you go then." Petra clasped her hands in her lap. It was starting to rain and she hadn't brought a brolly. She'd have to stump up for a cab home, she couldn't face the Clockwork Orange.

Jade glanced at her. "What do you think? Do you think she might have been after revenge?"

"She was upset. Who wouldn't be? And yes, it's a possibility. But she gave you an alibi."

"For Montague's death, yes. A good one." Carla had been at a meeting with her daughter's head teacher on the morning of Montague's death, and there was no way she'd have been able to get back from Loch Lomond in time. "But that's irrelevant, if she hired someone to do it."

Petra grunted. "You want to know if she fits my analysis of the person who might have killed Montague?"

"Please." Jade sat up straighter. The rain had intensified and the windscreen wipers all but drowned out their conversation. The traffic slowed, brake lights blurring through the wet windscreen.

"Well, I certainly think we're looking at an extremely cold crime. If it was a professional hit, then someone would have had to take the trouble to hire a paid assassin, not just once but twice. And even if they pulled the trigger themselves, it took planning. The locations, the bullets..."

"What does this mean for Carla?"

Petra leaned her head against the car window. It was cold. "I just can't see her fitting. If she was angry with her husband, or wanted his money, then she would have killed him without divorcing him. And her feelings about Montague... they're too hot. Too passionate."

"So you don't think she did it?"

"I'm just the psychologist, doll. I imagine there's plenty of evidence that will outweigh mine."

"There could be."

Jade's phone rang. She checked it, then shoved it into the cradle. "Mo. I've got Petra with me, on hands-free."

"Boss. We've had a development, on the forensics."

"Which is?"

"Jamie and Heather reckon the shooter was on an island. Eilean nan Dear-something."

"Eilean nan Deargannan," Jade replied. "Isle of Fleas."

Petra lifted her head, alert. She went over her report mentally. Was this relevant?

"You know it?" Mo asked.

"I live on the other side of the loch." Jade's eyebrow twitched. "Just tell me, Mo."

"Yeah. Well, Jamie and his team are heading over there first thing in the morning. I'm going to take Stuart, if that's OK?"

"It's fine. Tell me if you uncover anything useful, yeah?"

"How did you get on with Mrs Severini?"

"Long story."

"Oh?"

Jade dragged her hand through her hair, uncovering a red mark on her forehead. Petra thought it looked like a fingernail scratch.

"I'll tell you later," Jade said. "I just want to fight through this traffic and get home."

"Of course, boss." Mo hung up, his voice small.

CHAPTER FIFTY-NINE

The Isle of Fleas didn't have too many fleas on it, as far as Mo could tell. It did, however, seem to be home to Scotland's entire population of angry swans.

He shrank back in the boat as yet another of the white menaces advanced on them, mouth wide and wings raised. The hissing was spectacular, especially when three others joined in.

"Maybe we should have brought a wildlife specialist," he suggested.

"Tell me about it," Jamie replied. "Normally we'd have got Dan Tanner along, but..."

"Jade's husband?"

Jamie's face darkened. "That's the fella."

"Can you tell me what happened to him? There seems to be something she's not talking about."

Jamie exchanged glances with his colleague, Heather. "Not sure that's my news to share with you, pal."

"I know, and I'm sorry." Mo took a breath just as the boat lurched to the right, a swan crashing into it from behind.

"Shit. Look, don't tell me any more than you need to, but I think it would help me to work with her more effectively. Did he die?"

"He did. Road accident, on the A82. That's all I'm saying."

Mo felt his stomach dip. The A82 was the main road running alongside the other bank of the loch. From what he'd gathered, it was where Jade lived.

No wonder she was behaving oddly.

"Thanks, I won't tell her you told me."

"Ta." Jamie grabbed a pole from the bottom of the boat and jabbed at a swan. Mo wondered if they were allowed to do that. But by this time, it was the swans, or them.

The swan hissed and made off across the water, its wings lifting and its body rising from the surface. It was beautiful, if you ignored the sheer evil of the bloody thing.

The uniformed officer steering the boat found a gap between the trees and moored up. The trees seemed to rise straight up from the water, with no visible evidence of land. The island was tiny but entirely covered by them. Mo looked back to see what view the shooter would have had. There was a clear view of Montague's house and of the beach where he'd been found dead. They'd already circled the island once and got video of the shore, giving them a good idea of what the killer would have been able to see.

This made a suitable place to carry out the crime, alright.

Jamie raised a hand just as the uniformed officer was about to step off the boat. "Hang on. This entire island is a crime scene. We video it first, make visual observations. Then we go ashore."

Mo smiled at the use of the word ashore. This wasn't exactly an ocean-going liner disembarking at Greenock.

Jamie and Heather drew equipment from their bags. They spent a few minutes on the boat, recording video, taking photographs and making notes. Mo watched, intrigued. He couldn't see anything of relevance, just a clump of trees and dozens of nests. The swans had buggered off for the time being, thank God.

"Anything useful?" he asked as Jamie shifted in the boat and put his notepad away.

Jamie wrinkled up his nose. "Trees have been disturbed, over there." He pointed. "Could be animal damage, but it could be our shooter."

"You'll be looking for traces of human presence."

"Aye, that we will. In a place like this it would have been impossible for him not to leave fibres at least. DNA, if we're really lucky."

Mo wasn't convinced. So far, their shooter had shown all the hallmarks of a professional. Glasgow CID had identified the spot from which he'd shot Steve Severini and found no forensics there. He didn't see why this location should be any different. Tougher, in fact, given the killer had at least one shooting's more experience under his belt.

"Anything else?"

"Not yet. Hang on a minute and we'll get out of the boat. Heather and I will go first, check for traces. I don't think you need to leave the boat."

"I'd rather." Mo wanted to get a good look at the scene.

Jamie turned to him. "The more of us step off this boat, the more contaminated this scene becomes. It's already bad enough with the damage the boats will have done."

Mo looked back. Stuart was in the second boat, cocking his head at his senior officer, presumably wondering if there was any news. Mo shook his.

"OK," he told Jamie. He sighed. It had been worth coming out here to look at the place, he'd been convinced of it the whole way here. But given that it had entailed leaving his hotel bed at 5am and driving all the way up here in the half-dark, right now he wasn't so sure.

CHAPTER SIXTY

Jade yawned. Rory had woken early and climbed into her bed before dawn. He'd been whispering to her about the kitten, in the loudest stage whisper she'd ever heard. They were planning on visiting his friend's house later to pick one out. He was so excited she wouldn't have been surprised to get a call from school telling her he'd exploded.

Patty was at her desk, trawling social media for any photos or video taken on Loch Lomond on the evening Phineas Montague had died. Stuart had explained how to override Facebook's settings so you could map posts from a given time window. Jade had nodded approval and decided she didn't need to know any more about it than that. But Patty's instincts were to take the old-fashioned route. Before Stuart had phoned in en route to the island, she'd been calling boat clubs, fishing groups and any other organisations connected to the loch that might have hired or loaned out a boat, or seen someone using one. She'd already trawled HOLMES for reports of stolen or missing boats and drawn a blank. But it was early, and most of the clubs weren't open yet.

Jade knew she should be helping but instead she was gazing out of the window, clutching a cup of coffee with two sugars in it, despite the fact she didn't take sugar. Her conversation with Petra in the car yesterday was playing on her mind. Petra had tried to reassure her about her ability to lead the investigation and find whoever had killed Severini and Montague, but she wasn't quite so confident herself. Carla Severini might be a suspect, but Jade felt in her bones that she wasn't.

Still, they had to pursue it.

She shuffled back towards Patty's desk, rubbing her eyes. The office felt even more empty today, with just two of them in and a fog descending outside. She wondered if Petra would be in later, and whether she had the authority to call and ask where she was.

"You alright, boss?" Patty asked, pausing her work to give Jade her full attention. "You look like you might be coming down with something."

"I'm fine. Just tired." Jade put a hand on Patty's shoulder and Patty returned to her work. "Rory's giving me trouble at night, that's all."

"Can't be easy."

"It's not. But you don't need to know about my woes. How are you getting on with the search for this boat?" She slurped her coffee.

"It's alright you know, boss," Patty said. "If you need someone to talk to..." She cocked her head and gave Jade that pitying look she'd come to dread.

Jade removed her hand. "I'm fine. Besides, I've got the police shrink to chat with, haven't I?" She gave a mock laugh.

"Tell me if you're making any headway, or if I should move you onto doing background on Carla Severini."

"I'm on the page of a birdwatcher who was out on the loch on Monday evening." Patty put a finger on her screen, indicating the name of the page.

"And?" Jade downed the last of her coffee. She'd need more.

"He's got video. Photos, too. Lots of them. If anyone'll have seen a boat, it'll have been him."

"Dennis Clifford," Jade said, reading the name on the page. "Where does he live?"

"That's not on his page."

"Can we get it?"

"I can try. Stuart might need to help."

"He can work on that with you when they get back from the island."

"Any news?" Patty was still scrolling through photos, her gaze intent on her screen.

"Nothing yet," Jade said. "Jamie's securing the scene."

"It'll be a mess."

"I'd be very surprised if it gives us anything. But you never know."

"Hang on." Patty scrolled back up and stopped on a photo. She zoomed in. "What's that?"

Jade grabbed a chair from one of the empty desks and scooted it over so she could sit at the same level as Patty. "A boat."

"And it's heading for the island." Jade nodded. She could feel her skin prickling. "Any more?"

"I'll check." Patty turned to Jade. "But maybe we should pay this Dennis Clifford a visit."

CHAPTER SIXTY-ONE

"Can we get off this bloody boat yet?" Stuart called from the second of the two boats.

Mo turned to him. "Sorry, mate. Jamie says CSIs only."

"What? Why did we come, then?"

Mo shuffled towards the back of his boat. It was just him and the uniformed PC on board now. He leaned towards Stuart, whose boat contained another PC, a third CSI and cases full of equipment.

"To observe," he said. "I want to see what Jamie uncovers, if anything."

"He won't find anything. The killer's a pro, we've established that."

"Have you looked at those trees? Even a seasoned professional stands a decent chance of getting something snagged in there."

"It's a jungle. We'll never find anything."

Mo snorted. "First off, this isn't exactly the Amazonian basin. It's a tiny island in Loch Lomond that can't be much more than a hundred feet across. If there's something to be found, we'll find it."

Stuart folded his arms and sat back in the boat, causing it to shift. The PC who was sharing the boat with him put out a hand for support.

"Mo!"

Mo turned to see Jamie waving at him from the depths of the trees. He was holding something up.

"What is it?" Mo called in return.

"Hang on."

Mo waited, shifting closer and closer to the front of his boat while trying not to make it capsize. He watched Jamie as the CSM approached, trying to make out what was in his hand. It was an evidence bag, but what was inside?

Jamie held the bag aloft as he reached the boat, clambering over a branch. "Found something," he panted.

"What?"

He waved the bag. "Fibres. Fleece, by the looks of it. And it's not been bleached by the elements, so I reckon it's new."

CHAPTER SIXTY-TWO

"Mo, tell me what you've got." Jade was in the office with Patty, her phone on the desk, speaker turned up loud. She could hear the screeching of swans in the background. She tried to ignore it.

"Jamie's found fibres. Looks like a fleece top, just traces of it on a branch."

"How long will it be before he can get it to the lab?"

"He and Heather are still scouring the island. But they're sending Imani back with it in a squad car."

"Imani?"

"She's on the CSI team. She was looking after the kit but they've decided she's best deployed making a start on this."

"You think she'll be able to get DNA from it?"

"We can but hope."

"Good. We've had a development, too."

"The boat?"

"Patty found a photographer's Facebook page with images of a boat approaching the island at around eight o'clock on Monday night."

"Who's the photographer? Is he up this way?"

Jade looked at Patty. She'd been intending to find the photographer's address and head there herself once they were finished with this call, but if he lived near Loch Lomond, it would be better for Mo or Stuart to go.

"We don't know yet. Patty, can you...?"

"Boss." Patty rose from her seat and headed out to her desk.

"Is Dr McBride there?" Mo asked.

Jade shook her head. "You think she'd have an insight based on what you've seen at the island?"

"I doubt it. I've been videoing it on my phone, the CSIs will get better quality footage but I wanted to have something I can send her."

"She likes to visit a scene, get a feel for it."

"Yeah."

Jade glanced towards the door. She still hadn't phoned Petra. "To be honest, I'm not sure where she is. She hasn't arrived yet." She checked her watch. "It isn't ten yet, though."

"No. OK, shall I send her this video footage?"

"Have you got her email address?"

"I have."

"OK." Jade hesitated. "Wait, is it a personal email address or has she been issued with a Police Scotland one?"

"Ummm... personal."

"In that case send it to me. I'll share it with her when she comes in."

Jade spotted movement from the corner of her eye: Patty leaving her desk and heading for the office.

"Don't hang up just yet, Mo." She watched Patty

approach, waving a sheet of paper. "I think we've got an address."

Patty opened the door to the office. "Got it, boss. Address in Balloch."

"Right. Mo, did you hear that?"

"I did."

"Do you know where Balloch is?"

"No, but I've got satnav."

Jade considered for a moment. "OK, you go there. Patty, text him the full address."

Patty nodded and left the room.

"Find out if he's got more photos," she told Mo. "Video, anything. Something we can enhance."

"Don't worry, boss."

"That's Jade."

"Don't worry, Jade. I've done this before."

CHAPTER SIXTY-THREE

PETRA FLICKED open the curtain in the living room at the front of her flat. Along the street, a dark figure moved to one side, attempting to hide behind a car.

She felt her body slump. *How did you find me, you bastard?*

She dropped the curtain and turned away from the window, leaning against the wall. Her aunt's flat wasn't her aunt's any more, was it? The property had been transferred into her name.

Still, it would take a pretty tenacious individual to find the records if you were starting with the name of the owner and not the address.

He *was* tenacious. At least, she thought it was him. It might just as easily be his wife, but the shape she'd spotted had looked male.

She grabbed her phone from the kitchen counter. She had the number of her local police station in Dundee. Her mobile number was in their system so she would be prioritised if she had an emergency.

Was that necessary? Was she imagining things?

No.

There'd been the phone calls. Her doorbell had rung ten minutes ago and when she'd checked the camera entry system, no one had been outside.

And there was definitely someone along the street, watching her.

Stop it, you bampot. She was imagining things. Someone had probably pressed all the buzzers and been let in by one of her neighbours.

The thought made the breath catch in her throat.

She had three neighbours, any of whom might let a stranger into the building. If someone told them they were an old friend of Dr McBride...

The two of them looked respectable. Trustworthy.

Her breathing was shallow, her face hot. She needed to make a decision. Piss or get off the pot.

She tweaked the curtain open again. There was nobody there.

You're imagining things.

Her phone rang, making her jolt. She flung a hand out towards it and it clattered onto the floor.

Calm down, woman. Get a hold of yourself.

She picked it up, not looking at the display.

"Petra?"

"Hello?"

"Petra, it's Jade."

"Jade."

"DI Tanner. Are you OK? You sound... odd."

Petra turned to face the mirror beside the door. Her hair was in disarray and her cheeks red. "I'm fine. What do you need?"

"We've had some developments. The island, near where Montague died. There's fibres there. Fabric. And we've got photographs of a boat."

Petra frowned. "What's any of that got to do with the psychology?"

"Sorry. I thought you'd want to know. How's the profile coming?"

Petra turned away from the mirror. She was frazzled, but she didn't need to take it out on Jade Tanner.

"Sorry. I'll be right there."

She'd have to get a cab. How long would that take?

"Give me half an hour."

"Thanks. Only if you're not busy?"

Petra looked towards the window. She'd been imagining things. She wouldn't call the police. Not yet.

"It's fine. I'll see you shortly."

CHAPTER SIXTY-FOUR

Mo PRESSED a random assortment of buttons on the satnav and cursed it for the tenth time. Using it to find your way around a city was one thing, but out here, where the houses seemed to be half a mile away from each other and a postcode covered an entire village, it was an entirely different matter.

He'd approached three houses looking for Dennis Clifford and been turned away from all of them. How could it be so difficult? At each house, the owner had provided directions, waving in the general direction of where he should be and describing the correct route in terms that made very little sense. It would have helped if he could at least understand the accent, but people here seemed to speak an even less decipherable dialect than what he'd been confronted with in Glasgow.

He'd have to get used to this. Catriona's mum wasn't getting any better, and it was likely that the move would be permanent. His kids would be talking like this in a few months.

He knew that wasn't a problem. He was looking forward to the move, to being able to relieve the stress for Cat of being so far away from her parents, and to give the girls a chance to grow up somewhere with a less frenetic pace of life and a lot less pollution.

But today, working this case, he was frustrated.

He slammed the car door shut, aware that he needed to cool down, and approached the next house. It sat at the end of a long gravel driveway – at least, long by the standards of the modern housing estates in and around Birmingham, with their compact houses and postage stamp gardens. Here this was a short driveway, given that he could still see the house from the road.

He rang the bell and stood back, preparing to be told he'd found yet another wrong address. After a few moments, a balding middle-aged man wearing a blue polo shirt and hiking trousers opened the door.

Thank God for that. Mo recognised the man from his profile picture. It was Dennis Clifford.

He held up his ID. "Mr Clifford?"

"Aye, that's me, son." The man looked him up and down. "Do I need to be worried?"

"No. Sorry to disturb you. I'm working on the investigation of a murder a few miles up Loch Lomond and I have reason to believe you might have photographic evidence that could be of use."

"Me?"

"You run a Facebook page for your photography."

The man beamed. "You found it? That's smashing. I didn't know anyone was looking."

Mo hadn't seen the page himself. Stuart had forwarded

him two photos: one showing the boat approaching the island, and another of the man standing in front of him now.

Mo opened up his phone and held up the first of the two photos. "Did you take this?"

The man bent to get closer to the screen. His smile widened. "I did. How did you find that?"

Mo gritted his teeth. "Your Facebook page, Mr Clifford. You posted it on Monday night."

"Ah, that I did. What d'ye need it for?"

"The boat in this image, we're trying to discover who was in it."

"In it?"

"Can I come in, please?"

"Of course, where are my manners?" The man stood back, waving an arm for Mo to come inside. "Can I offer you a tot of whisky?"

"No thanks. I'm on duty."

"Never stopped PC McLeish down in Balloch. By the sound of your voice, you're not from around these parts, son, but it doesn't mean you can't drink the local product."

Mo smiled. "I'm fine. Do you have any other photos from around the same time? Or video, maybe?"

"I reckon so. I always take millions, then scrap the ones I don't need."

"You scrap them?"

They were standing in the man's hallway. Mo could smell something burning from behind a door to his left. "Do you need to check that?"

Clifford's eyes widened. "Ah, shit. Gi' me a minute, will you?"

Mo stayed put as the man hurried into the kitchen,

cursed a few times and made banging noises, then re-emerged.

"Thanks for warning me. That was a pan of soup, about to go dry."

Mo could only hope this man had kept his photographs. He wasn't sure how reliable he'd be as an eye witness.

"Like I say, do you have any other photos?"

A nod. "I do so. They're in the recycle bin now but they're still on my computer for another thirty days, so you're in luck."

"Thank you. Can you show me where your computer is?"

The man's expression hardened. "You're not going to have to requisition it, are you? I need that machine for my editing."

"If you can show me where the photos are stored, I can transfer them on to a USB stick."

"Good. I'd hate to be without the clunky old thing. It's ancient, and it freezes more often than the top of Beinn Eich. But it's my hobby. I..." The man frowned. "But you don't want to hear about me. Let me show you the photos."

He turned and led Mo into a dark room that was full of photography paraphernalia. SLRs, compacts. Video cameras, spare lenses, photography magazines. Safe to say Dennis Clifford was obsessed.

On a desk to one side was a PC. It did indeed look ancient: the screen was the cathode ray tube type and the PC itself sat directly beneath the screen instead of under the desk. Mo approached it, relieved to see there was at least a USB port he could access.

"D'you want to take a look now, or will you just load them onto your stick?"

"I'll take a look now, if you don't mind."

"Course." Clifford squeezed past Mo and sat in the chair, which creaked under his weight. "Gi' me a few ticks." He stuck his tongue out, licking his lips in a circular motion as he brought up the file manager. He clicked through to the recycle bin and found a long list of jpeg files. The date against them all was Monday's.

"Can you open them up and let me work through them, please?" Mo asked

Clifford glanced at him. "I can do it."

"Sir, I'm looking for evidence in a murder enquiry. I'd rather do it myself."

A cough. "Very well, if that's what you think. It'd be quicker if I did it."

No, it wouldn't.

Mo took a step forward. "Thank you. Is there any chance of getting that tot of whisky after all?" He had no intention of drinking it, but it would get the man out of the room.

Clifford's face brightened. "Of course. Good to see a Muslim taking a dram."

Mo said nothing. It occurred to him that he might get into trouble for accepting alcohol from a witness, but he thought it was worth the risk.

"Thanks."

The man nodded and left the room. Mo scrolled through the photos one by one, heading backwards from the last photo of the day, until he came to the one they'd spotted on the Facebook page. He continued, hoping for something clearer.

He stopped scrolling, his hand still on the mouse.

"Shit."

Clifford had not only captured the boat going towards

the island. He'd photographed the moment at which it was launched into the loch.

He'd caught the face of its occupant on camera.

And it was someone Mo recognised.

CHAPTER SIXTY-FIVE

"You've had developments," Petra said.

"We have," Jade replied. "But I don't want them clouding your thinking."

Petra nodded. The psychologist had dark circles under her eyes and her makeup wasn't as neatly applied as it had been yesterday. Jetlag still taking its toll, Jade thought. She knew from her own limited experience – a weekend in New York with Dan before Rory had been born – that sometimes it got worse on the second or third day.

"OK," Jade said. "In that case, can you tell me what you've got so far? I wasn't planning on rushing you, but I want to hear this before we get any more forensics."

"Putting the cart before the horse," Petra commented.

Jade sipped her coffee. She'd had a rare good night's sleep last night, Rory not waking till six. But one good night didn't make a dent in the caffeine cravings of a woman routinely deprived of them.

"I just want to hear your analysis of the psychology behind this while I've still got a relatively open mind."

"You've got how many potential suspects now?" Petra asked.

"Let's not talk about suspects. I want you to tell me what kind of person you think might have done this, and then I'll see if that could apply to any of our suspects." She hesitated, taking another slurp of her coffee. She was going to need another one before they got much further. "Bearing in mind that we both know none of this will wash with the Procurator Fiscal."

"I know," Petra said. "All I can give you is background, some ideas that'll help you understand the nature of the crime better and so direct the questions you ask your potential suspects more effectively."

Jade nodded. Her coffee was empty. "And I want you to help me formulate those questions, when we do have grounds for an arrest."

"Of course. In fact, that's where I can probably be of most help. If you frame the questions right, you're more likely to get the answers you want."

"I don't want to lead a suspect into a confession just because that would be convenient."

Petra sighed. "Jade, do you think I'm some kind of quack? Because if you do, I'll bugger off now and you can just hire one of those bloody psychics that are always putting themselves for—"

Jade put a hand on the table. "I don't think you're a quack, and I don't expect you to help me get any information that isn't the cold hard truth. But I'm not stupid, Petra. I know that if you approach an interview in the right way, you can encourage a suspect to open up more. If nothing else, you can help me avoid no comment interviews."

"Ah, no comment. I love those."

Jade snorted. "Yeah, me too."

Petra shook her head. Jade felt a wave of tiredness wash over her. She gazed at her coffee mug. Was she seeing double?

"No comment videos can tell you a few things about a suspect," Petra said. "They're also great for nonverbals. When people have decided they aren't going to use words to tell you what's going on inside their heads, their bodies go into overdrive. It's fascinating."

Fascinating wasn't really the word Jade would use for what she wanted to get out of this. It was a murder investigation, not a psychology experiment.

"OK," she said. "I need another coffee. Give me a minute." She rose from her chair.

"White, two sugars, please," Petra said as Jade put a hand on the doorknob.

"Yeah. Sorry." Jade reached out for Petra's mug. "I'll get you one too."

Petra smiled. "You're under stress. I'm not surprised you forget your manners."

Stop analysing me. Just as Jade was getting to a point where she could feel comfortable around Petra, the woman went and did it again. It was like having your mum in the room with you at every turn, constantly understanding what you were about to do better than you did yourself.

And with Jade's head in the state it had been in for the last few months, that was the last thing she needed.

Five minutes later she was back, two cups of coffee in hand. She placed Petra's on the desk and kept hold of her own.

"OK," she said. "Tell me about the kind of person who might have committed this crime."

Petra raised a perfectly manicured eyebrow. "There's no might about it, lassie."

Jade felt her cheek twitch. She was only a year younger than Petra. No lassie. "Just tell me." She gulped down a mouthful of coffee – too hot – and sat back, wishing there was somewhere in this office she could have a lie down.

"Very well," Petra said. "So, we have two murders. All the evidence leads me to believe they have the same perpetrator."

"Why?"

"I was coming to that."

Jade took another sip of her coffee, tentatively this time, and willed herself to be patient. She was aware of Patty outside the door hunting for the boat, and Mo up at Loch Lomond tracking down the photographer. Last time she'd heard from him he'd knocked on two doors already, and got the wrong address both times. She hoped it was just bad luck, and not the sign of a city copper who would never cope up here.

"The psychology behind the crimes is almost identical," Petra said. "Of course you have the fact that the same or similar weapons were used. The same locus of the shot, on the lower knee. But there's also the locations. Both were places where there could be people around, but only at specific times. The killer chose times when the scenes would be deserted. He – and I'm going to say he for now, although I'm not ruling out a woman – he needed time. He needed to be undisturbed. This was a crime, or a pair of crimes, that took some time in the planning, but also some time in the execution."

"So you think the killer was at the scene for some time before and after firing the shot?"

"Before, yes. After, probably not. I believe that he would have quietly and efficiently packed up his equipment and left the scene. He wouldn't have been in a hurry, not showing any outward signs of haste or stress. If a passer-by happened to see him, maybe someone out for a walk at Loch Lomond or anyone on the nearby streets in Glasgow, they wouldn't have noticed anything unusual."

"Except he would have been carrying a large bag or case with the gun and ammunition."

"The shooter was skilled," Petra replied. "He was organised. He would have taken what he needed, and nothing more. If the gun could be dismantled, then it might not have needed much more than a small rucksack to be carried away from the scene. And I'm considering the possibility that he might not have even taken any ammunition with him."

Jade pushed her empty mug away. She was starting to feel more human now. Maybe even capable of running a murder investigation.

"Hang on," she said. "He had to take ammo."

Petra shook her head, a wry smile on her face. "If you're good at what you do, all you need is the bullet or bullets that are already in your gun."

"Seriously? He would have loaded the thing up before travelling there, and just relied on that?" Jade remembered what Petra had already said. "But if the gun was dismantled, that meant it had to be put together at the scene. And you can't load a gun that hasn't been assembled."

"Fair point. But chances are the man had pockets."

"Wow."

Jade looked toward the outer office. Patty was looking back at her. She raised her eyebrows in a question and Patty shook her head and turned away. Maybe she should invite the DC in here, get another head on this. But she needed Patty following up on the boat.

"So you're telling me that our shooter was so cool that he strolled to the scene, put his gun together, loaded it from his pocket, took the shot knowing he'd get it right first time, then dismantled the gun and strolled away. I almost have an image of him whistling."

"He wouldn't have done that. Draws attention. It's important to note that your killer is confident, but not cocky. It's a confidence born of certainty. He knows what he does, and he knows he does it well. In both scenes you found two bullets, yes?"

"Yes."

"And no other bullets in the vicinity. No more that missed?"

"No." Jade ran over the potential suspects in her mind. Carla Severini, still giving the impression of grieving a man she'd filed divorce against, but not hiding her disdain for the man she blamed for her sister's suicide. Maria Watson, angry at the way Severini had treated her and her colleagues. Angus Robertson, forced to work for an employer who treated him like an object.

They were all angry. All fuelled by emotion. The killer Petra had described to her was cold and competent.

"You think we're looking at a hired assassin then?" she asked.

"Assassin. That's a big word, isn't it? Makes me feel like I'm in a James Bond movie."

"Sorry to disappoint."

"Ach no. He's not my type." Petra smiled.

"But you think it was a professional? The confidence, the speed of execution?"

"Well, no." Petra stood up. "I did, but now I'm no' so sure."

Jade watched as she circled the desk, her hands clasped behind her back. For someone who always wore high heels, she had a confident gait, almost laid back. She never walked like someone struggling to balance.

"You're not?" Jade asked.

Petra stopped at the board. She eyed it for a moment. "A professional wouldn't have deliberately made the crimes so similar. A professional wouldn't have gone to the trouble of going out to that island. There were plenty of spots where you could have taken that shot from the mainland, and then just disappeared into the trees."

"OK. But your report says this was done by someone who's got experience with guns."

"That's exactly it. We're in Scotland. Maybe not the Highlands, but still..."

"Hunting?"

Petra nodded, her back still to Jade.

Jade looked at her. "So you think that one of our suspects actually fired the bullets that killed Severini and Montague?"

Petra turned away from the board to face Jade. "I do. Sorry, not much help is it?"

CHAPTER SIXTY-SIX

PATTY WAS WONDERING what the DI and the psychologist were talking about. Dr McBride had been pacing the room, doing most of the talking. Could she really work out who had committed the murders, just from understanding how the killer's mind worked?

It made no sense. As far as Patty could see, there was no way they could charge someone on the basis of a psychological profile. They needed evidence. Forensics, interviews, post-mortem. That was how Patty had always worked cases, and that was how she'd continue.

She was coming up blank on the boat. Only two of the boatyards she'd called had been open, and neither of those hired out the kind of boat they were looking for. It was frustrating. Finding that Facebook account had felt like a breakthrough. Stuart could come up with all his fancy theories and get himself into trouble overstepping the mark. And yes, he was useful with the IT stuff. But Patty believed in good old-fashioned coppering. And today it was failing her.

She sighed and checked her emails. Some files had come

in from the court, documents from the Severini divorce that hadn't been available when Steve Severini had died. Maybe a quick glance through these would get her head out of the funk it was in.

She opened up the first file and was interrupted by a buzzing from across the desks. The boss's phone.

She looked over towards the briefing room. The DI and Dr McBride were deep in conversation. The psychologist was waving her arms around, and the boss was shaking her head.

She'd check who it was.

She got up and hurried across to the phone, anxious now not to miss the call.

It was DS Uddin. That was fine.

She picked up. "Sarge. It's Patty."

"Oh, Patty. Er, is the DI there?"

Patty glanced again at the office. "She's in a meeting with Dr McBride. Can I help?"

"Dennis Clifford has got more photos. One of them... well, I've already put it on an email to the investigation inbox."

"Hang on." Patty returned to her desk, wary now about the fact she had the boss's phone to her ear.

It would be fine. She'd worked with Jade Tanner in the past, and she was a fair boss. A bit flakey lately, but not the sort who'd go off on one just because someone took a call for her. And flakey was understandable.

She opened up the inbox and clicked on the email from the sarge.

"Is that who I think it is?"

"You're looking at the photo of the boat being launched?" he replied.

"Yep."

"In which case, yes. That's him."

Patty stared at the photo. "I need to get the DI."

"Yes."

"Wait." She remembered something she'd spotted in the brief moment she'd had with the court files. "Hang on a minute."

"What is it?"

"We've just had documents from the Severini divorce."

"But this is—"

"It might be relevant."

She switched to the PDF of Carla Severini's bank account. She scanned the document then stopped.

"There's a transaction," she said. "A payment."

"Who from?"

"Carla Severini. To A Robertson."

"You need to talk to the DI. Keep me on the line."

"Yes." Patty didn't hang up, but left the phone on the desk. She hurried to the office and yanked open the door.

"It was Carla Severini and Angus Robertson, boss. We've got evidence."

The DI and the psychologist exchanged looks. The DI looked puzzled.

"I told you," Dr McBride said.

CHAPTER SIXTY-SEVEN

"ALRIGHT." Jade grabbed her coat. "Who's at the Montague estate, right now?"

"Stuart's still on site, boss. And the sarge isn't too far away."

"OK. I'll call Mo, let him know what we've found. And I'm going to call in on Carla Severini."

"Have you got enough?" Patty asked. "You can't arrest her, surely?"

Jade stopped in her tracks. "Keep digging through those divorce files, see if you can find anything else suspicious. Any other transactions between her and Angus Robertson. Any more evidence that the two of them are connected. Take a look at her social media accounts as well."

"No problem, boss."

"What about me?" Petra stood in the doorway to the office. "What do you need from me?"

Jade looked at her. "Your profile, can you send me a copy?"

"It's not a profile. And it's by no means finished."

Jade sighed. "I don't care if you haven't dotted the I's and crossed the T's. I just need what you've got right now. I want to corroborate it against Carla's behaviour when I go and knock on her door."

"You think that's wise?" Patty asked. "Shouldn't we wait until we've got enough to at least caution her?"

Jade shook her head. "If she and Robertson worked together to kill Severini and Montague, what's to say they won't target somebody else too?"

"But there's a personal connection," Petra said. "Robertson is connected to Montague. Carla is connected to her ex-husband."

"So is Maria Watson," Patty added.

Jade nodded. "We need to work out if she was part of it."

The other two women looked back at her. Most of the evidence they had so far was circumstantial. But there was the photo of Angus Robertson on the boat. That placed him at the spot where the shots had been fired, not long beforehand. And it wasn't as if many people went out on that island.

"OK," she said. "Patty, keep digging. Petra, make any final changes you need to that profile – analysis, whatever – and send it to me."

"Right." Petra disappeared into the office.

Jade looked at Patty. "I want to speak to Carla Severini. See if she can explain away that transaction. Meanwhile, call me if you find anything else."

"Your call, boss." Patty sat down at her desk.

Jade stared at her for a moment then hurried down the steps towards her car.

CHAPTER SIXTY-EIGHT

Mo was still in Dennis Clifford's study, trawling through his files. Clifford had told him there was a video somewhere in the trash, but he was having problems finding it. Still, there were less than thirty days' worth of deleted photos and videos in there; even Mo's dodgy IT skills should be enough to unearth what he was looking for.

He kept scrolling, clicking on any file that looked likely, opening them up, and then frowning when he came up blank.

His phone rang. He glanced at the display and picked it up.

"Boss," he said. "Jade, I mean. I'm going through Clifford's files, trying to find a video. He says there's one that shows the boat, but it's in the trash."

"We've got more evidence," she replied. "Linking Angus Robertson and Carla Severini."

Mo straightened in his chair. "What kind of evidence?"

"Financials. There's a bank transaction from Carla to Angus."

"When?"

"Last October."

"That was after Steve Severini died."

"It was."

"How did it not come up first time round?"

"It's from the divorce papers," Jade replied. "We didn't have those when we originally investigated the case."

"What's your thinking?"

"Maybe Carla paid Angus Robertson to do it. He's a groundsman, he'll know his way around guns."

"He would."

"It fits," she said. "The photo of him going to the lake, the bank transfer. The way he behaved when we spoke to him."

"So she hired Robertson to kill her husband, and then hired him again seven months later to take out the man who jilted her sister?"

"I'm not sure," she replied. "She could have met Robertson through her husband, via Maria. Or through her sister. Maybe she realised he had access to guns, and..." she hesitated. "We don't have to worry about that right now. The important thing is she had motive, he had means, and we've got evidence placing him at the scene and linking her to him."

"OK."

"I'm on my way to speak to her. I want to see what she says when I confront her with the evidence of her connection to Angus Robertson."

Mo considered. "She's got a legitimate reason to know him. She would have known Maria Watson through her husband, and Maria was married to Angus."

"It doesn't give her a reason to transfer ten thousand pounds to him."

"Ten thousand? No." Mo stared at Clifford's computer screen. His eyes were beginning to blur. "What about Watson?" he asked. "That could explain it."

"She worked for Carla's husband."

"They could argue it was a business transaction."

"It was after he died," Jade said.

He could hear her breathing down the line. "Boss, where are you?"

"In my car, outside the office."

"You're on your way to see Carla?"

"I was. I can't figure out whether we need more before I speak to her."

"What do you want me to do?"

"I want you to get Jamie's team in, they can take over with hunting down that video."

"I can do it."

"I know you can," she told him. "But you're more use to me elsewhere. Call Jamie, and then head back up to Montague's estate. I want you ready to arrest Robertson."

Mo gave the files a final quick scroll then pursed his lips. The boss was right. "OK. I'll call you when I'm up there."

"Get Jamie to send one of his people to you, they can't be far away."

Mo smiled. "Truth is, I've got no bloody idea where I am."

"You'll get used to it. I'll call you if we get anything more from the divorce paperwork. And I want to know as soon as that video shows up."

CHAPTER SIXTY-NINE

Stuart was getting off the boat from the island when his phone rang.

"Sarge," he said, "are you on your way back here?"

"Kind of. I need eyes on Angus Robertson. Have you seen him?"

"Sorry, Sarge. It's just me and the CSIs now. Couple of Uniform guys were here but they've gone back to Balloch."

"OK," replied Mo. "I need to speak to Jamie, get him to go through some computer files for me. Is he still on the island?"

"He's back now. I can ask him."

"I'm at Dennis Clifford's. He says there's a video but it's in the trash and I haven't been able to find it."

Stuart felt his skin prickle. This was where he could demonstrate his worth. "You want my help, Sarge? I'm kind of good at that sort of thing."

"It's fine. I need you to find Angus Robertson for me. Tell Jamie to call me about this computer, and then head over to where we last saw Angus Robertson. Don't draw attention to yourself, just watch him. I need to make sure he doesn't go anywhere."

Stuart cupped his hands over the phone. "Is Robertson our suspect now?"

"Perhaps. He was on that boat. And the boss is on her way to have a chat with Carla Severini, too."

Stuart turned back towards the loch. Jamie and Heather were unloading the contents of the boats into plastic crates, ready for transporting back to the lab. They hadn't found any more fibres, but they'd taken samples of the trees and undergrowth. Specialists in botanical forensics might be able to do something with them.

"Carla Severini?" he asked. "What's she got to do with Angus Robertson?"

"She transferred a large sum of money to him after her husband died."

"D'you think she paid him to kill her husband?"

"Let's not jump to conclusions. Just find him. Keep an eye on him. And tell me if he goes anywhere."

"Will do."

"I'm heading back your way, but I won't speak to him until the boss has spoken to Carla. When she has, you and I can interview Robertson again. Maybe under caution."

"No problem, Sarge. I'll keep you posted."

CHAPTER SEVENTY

JADE PARKED her car round the corner from the Severini house and paused to catch her breath. She'd dashed out of the office and not stopped to consider what she was going to say to Carla Severini.

Whatever happened, she needed an update before she went in there.

She dialled Patty first.

"Boss, where are you?"

"Outside Carla Severini's house. Have you found anything else?"

"Two more transactions, going back to before her husband died. The first is four months before his death, the second a month before."

"And then the one you found first?"

"Yes."

"Any more?"

"That's all I've got. It doesn't mean nothing else has gone in since those documents were passed to the courts, though."

"How much does it add up to?"

"They're each for ten grand."

"Thirty grand in total. OK, I think we have grounds to request access to Angus Robertson's bank records now. Does it say which bank he's with on the documents you've got?"

"Bank of Scotland."

"Good. I'll speak to the Super, get a warrant for financial oversight."

"Anything particular you're looking for?"

"I want to know what he did with the money. Has he hung onto it, or has it changed hands again? And for anything involving Maria Watson. I assume there's nothing going out to her in the records you've seen?"

"Nothing."

"A shame." Jade leaned back in her seat, stretching out her neck. She yawned.

"Right, I'll speak to the sarge too, then I'm going in. Text me if you get anything else."

"Boss."

Jade hung up and redialled.

"Jade, good to hear from you. Any progress on the Severini and Montague investigation?"

"Yes, Sir. We've got records of three large bank transfers from Carla Severini to Angus Robertson. That's Steve Severini's ex-wife. Her sister was Phineas Montague's girlfriend until he dumped her and she killed herself. She paid Robertson, Montague's groundskeeper, whose own wife worked for Severini. And we have photos of Robertson taking a boat out on the loch not long before Montague was shot."

"And you still think he was shot from Eilean nan Deargannan?"

"We do. DS Uddin and Jamie Douglas have found fragments of a fleece on the island, the CSIs are analysing it now."

"You need a warrant?"

"For Angus Robertson. With the photo of him on the boat, and the bank transactions, I believe that's enough."

"I'd rather wait until we know more about this fleece top. And what about the bullets?"

"With respect, Sir—"

"Fraser."

Jade took a breath. In the context, she preferred to keep things professional. "With respect. We don't have a match for the bullets yet, but the psychologist believes that the shooter may not have taken any extra ammunition with him."

"Why not?"

"Confidence. Lack of baggage. The less he took with him, the smaller his bag would have been. He could have slipped away unnoticed."

"Which he clearly thought he had. Unless your photo of the man in the boat is pertinent."

"I believe it is."

Silence.

"Fraser?"

"OK. I think you're right, but the truth is, we won't get an arrest warrant until that fleece has been analysed. The new procurator fiscal has been anxious to demonstrate probity."

"How about financial records? I want to see Robertson's bank statements."

"That we can do."

"And I'd like to interview him under caution."

"That's your call. Her as well?"

"I want to keep things informal with Carla. She still thinks we're on her side."

"And if she's innocent, then indeed we are. She's the widow."

"They were divorcing."

"Not yet divorced. Speak to Robertson under caution. Have your friendly chat with Mrs Severini. And call me if you get anything useful from the forensics."

"Sir." Jade hung up. Her phone was vibrating.

"Mo?"

"Jade, I'm back at the Montague estate. Stuart has been keeping an eye on Angus Robertson, he's in his cabin."

"Good. We can't get an arrest warrant until we've analysed that fleece, but in the meantime, I want him interviewed under caution."

"You want me to bring him in?"

"Yes. Take Stuart with you. Just in case."

"Of course."

"Sorry. You don't need me to tell me how to do your job."

Mo's voice was flat. "I understand. You don't know me, and you have no idea how I'll handle this."

"You're doing OK so far."

"Glad to hear it. I'll call you when we're in the car en route to Glasgow."

CHAPTER SEVENTY-ONE

JADE STROLLED around Carla Severini's living room, taking in the photographs and knick-knacks on the mantelpiece and dotted around the various side tables. This was a different room from the one Jade had been in last time. She wondered if it was deliberate, bringing her in here where the echoes of Steve Severini were so strong.

The photos on the surfaces were family shots. Some from studios, others taken on holiday. Carla, Steve and their daughter. A few with other adults, grandparents perhaps. Over the mantelpiece hung a vast studio photograph of the three of them that had been printed in a style that made it look like a painting. It wasn't exactly Jade's thing, but she could see the attraction. Olivia looked to be about twelve in it, so it must have been taken a couple of years earlier. When the marriage was still intact.

Jade wondered if Carla had left these pictures here when her husband moved out, or if she'd reinstated them after his death. Was this room a shrine to a man who'd been rejected in life but was missed in death?

The door opened and Carla Severini entered carrying two white china mugs of coffee. Jade took one and sat on one of the two white leather sofas. This wasn't the formal sitting room where she and Petra had spoken to Carla before, but it was far from relaxed. She wondered where the daughter was. Upstairs doing homework or whatever teenagers did in the evening, or out with friends?

"Is your daughter at home?"

Carla frowned. "She's in her room. She's been... quiet since her father died."

"Was she close to him?"

A half-laugh. "I wouldn't say that. He hardly saw her." Carla fixed Jade with a stare. "Too busy working."

"Your husband was a workaholic."

"We've gone over this before, Detective. You don't need to come here and rake through the coals of my marriage. What's this about?"

Jade placed her mug on a coaster on the glass-topped coffee table. She leaned back. Carla sat on the sofa opposite her, her mug balanced on her knee. She was perfectly still, no sign of nerves.

"Have you heard of a man called Angus Robertson?"

Jade watched Carla's face, wishing she'd brought Petra with her. Carla's brow furrowed for the briefest moment, then returned to smooth perfection.

She shook her head. "I'm afraid I haven't. Is he a suspect?"

"We've been provided with copies of your bank statements by the court. They were submitted as part of the divorce process."

"Steve and I weren't divorced."

Only because he died before the process could be

concluded, thought Jade. "You filed for divorce. In October of last year."

"There was a cooling off period. We had to wait."

"And amongst the papers were your bank accounts. We found a series of payments to Angus Robertson."

Carla pouted and shook her head again. She held Jade's gaze for a moment, then reached out to place her mug on the table. She leaned back, smoothed the fabric of her pale trousers over her knees, and smiled. "I've never heard of him. Who is he?"

Jade held Carla's gaze. "He's the groundsman on the Montague estate, up at Loch Lomond."

A nod. "Phineas Montague. You think his death is related to my husband's."

"We do. You have to admit, it was... surprising for us to find that you'd been paying Angus Robertson large sums of money."

"How large?"

"Ten thousand pounds, three times. And those are just the tran—"

Carla raised a hand. "I can explain it."

"Go on."

Carla swallowed. She ran her hand over her trousers again. "I didn't talk about this before, for reasons that will shortly be obvious, but Steve was in the habit of occasionally running payments through my bank account."

"Hiding them from the tax authorities," Jade suggested.

"Exactly. I hope—"

"We don't care about your tax dealings, Mrs Severini. This is a murder enquiry, which is significantly more serious. Were you aware that your husband had made these payments through your account?"

"I was aware he made payments, but not of any individual ones."

"At the time the final transaction was made, the two of you had separated. Did he ask if he could carry on using your accounts like this, despite the two of you not being together?"

"He never took money from me. He would move money in, then move it out again. Always in different quantities, but if you look through, you'll find money coming in that matches the amount going out. It'll probably be spread over four to six transactions."

"Did you consider getting your own bank account that your husband couldn't access, after you split?"

Carla picked up her coffee, drained it, then set it down on her knee, one hand loosely holding it upright. "You think I'm stupid, don't you?"

Jade said nothing.

"Yes, of course I set up a separate bank account. I had one all along. Didn't tell the divorce lawyers, though."

Jade didn't care a whit about the divorce lawyers. "So you're saying you know nothing about these transactions and you've never heard of Angus Robertson."

"You can polygraph me, if you want." Carla moved her mug onto the table. She frowned. "I can hear my daughter calling me."

Jade glanced towards the door. She'd heard no such thing.

"If there's nothing else?" Carla stood up. "If you need me to, I can find more transactions of a similar nature. They go back years."

Jade twisted her lips. "Can you tell me more about your sister's relationship with Phineas Montague?"

"No."

"No?"

Carla was near the door. "I never met him. She didn't talk about it. So, no."

"Were you close to your sister?"

"I didn't kill Montague because he dumped her, if that's what you're thinking. Now if you don't mind, my daughter needs me. I can hear her again."

The rest of the house was silent, as far as Jade could tell. But she had no further grounds to keep Carla Severini from her daughter, or wherever it was Carla was actually going.

"Thank you, Mrs Severini. I'd be grateful for whatever you can provide to evidence your assertion that your husband made regular transactions through your bank account. And if we think of anything else, I'll be in touch."

CHAPTER SEVENTY-TWO

At least this time Mo knew where he was going.

He pulled up at the Montague house, got out and opened the gate leading through the grounds toward Angus Robertson's cabin. Uniform had soon established that it was possible to bring a car up here, even a sluggish two-wheel-drive like Mo's pool car.

He swung the gate open and returned to his car.

"I got that." A woman appeared from the house and hurried to hold the gate open. Taylor Gannon, the PA.

Mo stopped. "You're still here?"

"My flight's not till the day after tomorrow. Are you here to speak to staff?"

"Just Angus Robertson."

"Uh-huh. What's happened?"

Mo hesitated. He approached the young woman. "How long have you worked with Angus Robertson?"

"Six months or so. Since Phineas took over here."

"What was your impression of him?"

"Why? D'you think he did it?"

"Did you ever see Mr Robertson using a boat to go out on the loch?"

"Sorry, no. That doesn't mean he never did, though."

Mo looked around them. "Is there a boat house in the grounds?"

Taylor nodded. "It's the other way from where Phineas was found."

"Is there a boat?"

"I guess so. I never checked."

"Whose job would it be to manage that boat?"

"It's not part of the house, so it's grounds. Which means Angus, I guess."

"Can you hold the gate for a few minutes? I need to make a call."

She glanced back towards the house, anxiety in her face, then her expression relaxed. "Course. Sorry, those old habits die hard."

Mo smiled, imagining how the atmosphere in this house must have changed since Montague had died. "Thanks."

He hurried back to his car and picked up his phone. Voicemail.

"Boss, it's Mo. I've just been talking to Taylor Gannon and she tells me there's a boat house on the estate, and a boat. Stuart's going to investigate it while I go up to Angus Robertson's cabin." He hung up and dialled Stuart.

"I want you down at the boat house," he told the DC. "We need to know if there's a boat there, and if it matches the one in that photo."

"But you'll be going after Robertson on your own."

"I can handle that."

A pause. What was Stuart doing, was he about to question an order?

At last Stuart replied. "I'm in the woods. Where do I need to go?"

"Opposite direction away from the house from the crime scene. Head south for about quarter of a mile."

"How come we didn't know about this?"

"Hopefully you'll find out when you get there."

"It'll be hidden in trees or something."

"That's what I'm guessing," Mo agreed.

"No problem. I'll come up to Robertson's cabin when I'm done."

"Cheers." Mo got in his car, aware that Taylor Gannon was still waiting for him, and drove through.

CHAPTER SEVENTY-THREE

JADE'S PHONE buzzed as she left Carla Severini's house. She picked it up as she walked along the street to her car: a message from Mo.

She slowed her pace and clutched her phone tighter as she listened. She wasn't at all happy about this. They were investigating a double murder, and they had a possible suspect. Mo and Stuart shouldn't be splitting up like this.

She dialled Mo as she picked up pace: voicemail.

Damn. Reception up there was patchy.

"Mo, it's Jade. I don't like the idea of you and Stuart splitting up. I want you both at Robertson's cabin. Call me when you get this."

She hung up and dialled the office.

"Boss?"

"Patty, I want Uniform up at the Montague estate, asap. The sarge has learned that there's a boat house, and a boat. Stu's investigating it while the sarge goes to speak to Angus Robertson."

"They're not doing it together?"

Jade knew Mo wanted to prove himself, but this was foolish. Stu... well, Stu was ambitious, and not always sensible. Mo's job was to rein him in, not to encourage his more reckless side.

"Shit."

"What's up?" Patty asked.

"Sorry. Nothing new. I'm just annoyed. It's... it's fine." She might have known Patty for years, but it wasn't appropriate to badmouth the new sergeant to her. "Just get some more officers up there. I don't care who it is, we just need bodies."

"Boss."

"And have you managed to find anything else in the divorce records?"

"No. But I've been digging into the NDA that we found for Taylor Gannon."

"And?"

"Nothing yet. But I feel like I'm close. There are some letters that Jamie's team took from Montague's study. Apparently he kept a diary. If it's anywhere, it could be in that."

"A personal diary?"

"Kind of a cross between a blog and a diary. Online, but private."

Jade was standing next to her car. She gave the roof a light punch. "We need that diary."

"I know, boss. I could really do with Stu to help with the tech side of this. I'm out of my depth, truth be told."

"Patty, I want you to bring Digital Forensics in. If this private blog is encrypted or behind a firewall, they're the best people to unearth it."

"Yeah. Leave me to make the calls. Uniform, then Digital Forensics."

"Good." Jade was glad as ever for Patty's cool head. The digital forensics might be the key to the case. But Patty knew as well as she did that uniformed backup for Mo and Stuart was the highest priority right now.

"I'm on my way back in," she said. "Call me when Uniform are at the scene."

CHAPTER SEVENTY-FOUR

Mo PARKED a short way from the cabin, behind some trees that he hoped would disguise his car. He knew it was pointless; Robertson would have heard the car approach. And if he was indeed the killer, he would be on alert.

He sat in the car for a moment, planning his approach. He knew he should have discussed this with the boss beforehand, but he'd been up at Dennis Clifford's house, and then she'd been unavailable, straight to voicemail.

No point creeping around. Robertson knew he was here, and he had every right to be. Better not to raise the man's suspicions.

He got out of the car, closed the door without any attempt at gentleness, and strode along the path leading to the front door of the cabin. He walked in the centre of the path, his pace brisk and his expression neutral.

He reached the house and rapped the knocker. He leaned back on his heels and waited.

No one appeared.

Mo rapped the knocker again, then shifted sideways to

stand in front of a window. He cupped his hands around his face to peer inside. Net curtains obscured the view.

There could be anyone in there. Robertson, if he was the killer, could be watching him with a gun in his hand.

Mo slipped back towards the door, anxious to put something solid between himself and Robertson, wherever he might be.

A crack. Not a loud one; no gun or backfiring car. No, that was a twig snapping.

He turned away from the house, his back to the door and his breathing shallow. The car was too far away. If Robertson was already out here...

Stop it, he told himself. He was here to take Robertson in for questioning, under caution. He had every right to be here.

His phone buzzed and he fumbled it out of his pocket. His breaths were coming fast, his heart thumping. There was something about being out here, all this green. He longed for concrete. Graffiti, anything that showed they were in civilisation.

"DS Uddin," he muttered into the phone.

"DS Uddin," came a voice. "Everything OK?"

"Who is this?"

"PS Douglas, Response Unit. My team are on their way to provide backup."

Mo was about to object, but then thought better of it. Of course he needed bloody backup. "OK. Where are you?"

"We're at the Montague house. We'll leave one car here, and bring another to you. Are you at the cabin half a mile east of the main property?"

"I'm outside it right now."

"OK. I suggest you get back inside your vehicle and wait for us to arrive. We'll go in first."

"Don't leave the other car there. My colleague, DC Burns. He needs assistance too."

"I know. Down at the boat house. We've got it covered."

"Thank you."

"Sit tight, DS Uddin. Wait for us."

Mo swallowed and plunged his phone into his pocket. He took two deep breaths then made a run for his car, his muscles tense. He was half expecting to be shot at any moment.

Don't be daft, he told himself. *This is Scotland, not Chicago.*

But still.

He grabbed the remote key fob from his pocket as he ran, held it out to unlock the car door and threw out the other hand to yank the door open. He dived inside, throwing himself down across the front seats and thanking the heavens for PS Douglas, whoever he was and however he'd known to come here.

CHAPTER SEVENTY-FIVE

JADE ALMOST TUMBLED into the office to find Patty not at her desk as expected, but in the briefing room, adding to the board.

She hurried across the outer office and threw open the door, puzzled.

"What's happened? Why do you need to work on the board? I asked you to—"

Patty turned. "It's Emily Fogarty, boss."

"Emily?"

"Carla Severini's sister."

"What about her?"

"She was pregnant."

"Sorry?" Jade looked past Patty at the board. She'd written on it: the word 'pregnant' beneath Fogarty's name, and a line to Taylor Gannon.

"What's Taylor Gannon got to do with it?"

"She organised it all. Kept it quiet, hired the doctor, made sure the press didn't know."

"Didn't know about... oh." Jade looked at the board again. "Emily Fogarty had an abortion?"

Patty nodded. "She and Montague were living in Arizona at the time."

"Where abortion is illegal."

"She travelled out of state. Taylor set the whole thing up. Montague had a house in California, he sent her there."

"Sent her there." Didn't go with her, Jade thought. Nice guy. "How do you know all this?"

"The blog. It was only lightly encrypted. Digital Forensics got into it almost immediately."

"He blogged about this?"

"It was on his hard drive. Not online. I guess he thought no one would ever get at it."

Patty turned back to the board. She wrote 'abortion' under 'pregnant', then drew another line to Taylor Gannon.

"It explains the NDA," Jade says. "But what's it got to do with Steve Severini?"

"I still need to work that one out. But Emily Fogarty was his sister-in-law. It must relate to that somehow." Patty looked at Jade. "What was Carla like, when you spoke to her?"

"Calm. She was totally unfazed by my questions."

"You think she's got nothing to do with it?"

"I'm not sure. But I do know that she gave me nothing that provided grounds to interview her under caution."

"No." Patty turned back to the board.

"How much of this blog have you read?"

"Digital Forensics did a search for specific words."

"OK. We need to search on there for Steve Severini. Glasgow, property development. Carla Severini, too. Anything relevant. Have we got access to an unencrypted copy of the blog?"

"Not yet. I've told them I need one, but they're being funny."

"Bollocks to that." Jade took out her phone and dialled. "Jamie. I need your help."

CHAPTER SEVENTY-SIX

Mo STOOD behind his car as two uniformed PCs approached the cabin. He didn't like doing this. His intention had been to approach the building casually, engage Robertson in conversation, then invite him to come in for questioning. Yes, he was going to caution the man, but he'd been hoping to bring the whole thing off without too much fuss. That wasn't about to happen now.

But PS Douglas had been right. If Robertson had guns, they couldn't be too careful. They'd discussed whether they should wait for an armed unit to arrive, but Mo had refused to sit around that long. They didn't have grounds to arrest Robertson, but they did know he had access to guns.

The shorter of the two PCs knocked on the door. "Mr Robertson, this is the police. Can you open the door, please?"

Nothing.

Another knock. "Mr Robertson. This is the police. Open up, please."

Still nothing.

The PC looked back at PS Douglas. Douglas gestured towards the door handle. The PC put his hand on it.

Mo held his breath as the handle turned and the door opened. He kept himself very still, expecting to see Robertson waiting in the doorway.

The doorway was empty.

The two PCs looked back at their sergeant, who nodded then followed as they made their way inside. Mo listened to their voices, muffled within the cabin. All he could hear was the three officers announcing their presence, asking Robertson to make himself known and communicating with each other.

After a few minutes, PS Douglas emerged. "No one in there, DS Uddin."

Mo let out the breath he'd been holding and walked towards the house, willing his legs not to tremble. "Thanks. Any sign of weapons?"

"Nothing."

Mo's shoulders slumped.

"We'll get out. Leave the place for the CSIs."

Thanks." Mo stood back as the two PCs left the cabin and each in turn gave him a nod. He looked in through the open door.

Jamie and his team would probably be in here at some point, but right now he still didn't have grounds for a search.

He did have reason to knock on the door and call out, though. He could pretend not to know the cabin was empty.

He strode towards the door, pulled on a forensic glove from his pocket and knocked.

"Mr Robertson? It's DS Uddin. From the Complex Crimes Unit. I need to talk to you about the evening that Phineas Montague died."

He leaned in and craned his neck to look round the cabin. A single room downstairs with stairs leading up to what looked like a mezzanine bedroom. The space was compact and unadorned, but clean and tidy. If it hadn't been for the single plate and mug waiting to be washed up next to the sink, Mo would barely have known it was inhabited.

He let his eyes roam the space, searching for somewhere that Robertson could have hidden weapons. There was a rug, which might have been concealing a hidden compartment under the floorboards. But he still didn't have a warrant.

He jumped at the sound of a phone ringing. He swung round to find its source. A landline phone lay on the kitchen worktop, hidden behind the dirty mug.

The phone rang twice more, and then the answerphone kicked in. A voice filled the space: Robertson.

"I'm out, leave a message."

"Angus, it's Taylor. I've been trying to track you down but you're not answering your mobile. Answer the goddamn phone, will you? The police are here, and they want to talk to you. They don't suspect me. One of them is at your cabin, another at the boat house. I can hold one of them off, but not both. Call me as soon as you get this."

CHAPTER SEVENTY-SEVEN

THE BOATHOUSE WAS HIDDEN in a clump of trees near the water's edge. It wasn't all that close to the loch, and there was too much in the way of undergrowth and tangled bushes between it and the water for them to have seen it when they'd gone out with the CSIs.

Stuart raised his arms and fought his way through, following a path that seemed to have been trodden by someone else before him. His senses were on a trigger; if someone had come here before, then they might still be here.

At last he reached the building. It was little more than a shack, and didn't look robust enough to provide shelter for a boat. He wondered if the boat they'd seen in Dennis Clifford's photos was in there.

His heart was pounding and his mouth dry. He looked back towards the house, but could barely see the path he'd followed down here.

Stuart swallowed and turned back towards the water. The boathouse was quiet, its one window dark. He approached it and tried to reach up to see inside, but the ground was too soft. His shoes were already caked in mud; he should have changed them at the car.

He felt in the inside pocket of his suit jacket for his phone. Should he call the sarge, let him know what he was doing?

What was he doing? Did he plan to knock on the door and pretend he was just making a friendly visit? Was he going to scout the place out and approach Robertson by stealth, if the man was inside?

Or should he just watch and wait?

Chances were that Robertson was back at his cabin.

Now wasn't the time to back down. Stuart's job was to check for the boat Robertson had taken out to the island on the night of Montague's death. If they found it here, that could be a vital piece of corroborating evidence.

He edged forward, attempting to ignore the damp seeping into his socks. He shuffled his feet through the wet ground, trying his damnedest not to make a sound.

At last he was within touching distance of the boat house.

He looked round again. Still no sign of anyone approaching from the house. He was invisible from the path now.

That was a good thing, right? If Robertson, or anyone else from Montague's staff, came past, they wouldn't know he was sneaking around.

He put a hand on the wall of the boat house. It was soft to the touch, crumbling from rot in places. He'd have to be careful, or he'd push the bloody thing over.

He edged sideways, coming nearer to the front of the structure, where the boat would access the loch. There was a ramp leading towards the water, the wood giving way to concrete at the base of the walls. If there was a door at the front, would it be open?

Either way, he wasn't getting in through the front. There was too much undergrowth blocking his way, and he'd never keep his footing in the water.

He'd have to find a way in at the back. There had to be one.

He edged away from the water. His socks were soaked; it would be a while before he felt warm again. He turned and moved carefully around the building.

There was a door at the back. A double wooden door, with a worn handle.

Stuart crept up to it, wrapped his fingers around the handle and turned, praying it wouldn't squeak.

It didn't.

Phew.

He pulled in a shallow breath, then turned it further. He pulled and the door opened towards him. He opened it slowly, not sure what he expected to see on the other side.

At last the door was open, but it was blocking his view. He rounded it to enter the structure.

He froze.

A man was inside, standing immediately next to a boat that was half in, half out of the water. The boat looked like the one in the photos.

The man was Angus Robertson.

Robertson gave him a quizzical smile. His gaze flipped downwards, then back up again to meet Stuart's.

The object he'd looked down at, resting in his hands, was a gun.

Stuart backed away. He stumbled and grabbed the door to right himself.

"Stop."

Stuart did as he was told.

"Don't try anything. Come inside and don't call out. If you had anyone with you, I'd have seen them. You're on your own. I watched you walk down here from the house."

Shit.

Stuart glanced back towards the house. Dusk was creeping in.

Shit.

Where was the sarge? Back at the cabin, of course. More than half a mile away.

"Now walk slowly forward and close the door behind you. Don't shout out. Don't take anything out of your pockets."

Stuart rounded the door again, his eyes meeting Robertson's. He stepped inside the boat house and closed the door behind him.

"Good lad. Now if you carry on like that, I won't have to shoot you."

CHAPTER SEVENTY-EIGHT

Jade and Patty were on video link to Jamie in the forensics lab. He had Gus from the Digital Forensics team beside him, and they were working through the blog. The four of them each had it open on their screens. Gus looked deep in concentration, his tongue sweeping around his bottom lip.

"How long?" Jade asked, looking up from her screen.

Jamie looked at Gus, who wrinkled his nose.

"We're going as fast as we can," Jamie said.

"I need any reference to Steve or Carla Severini. Look for Emily Fogarty too, she's the link."

"We do know that," Gus muttered. "It takes a little time. I can't just press control and F. The encryption was light, but it's not non-existent."

Patty was leaning into her screen, trawling through her copy of the blog. "I've scanned through for Severini and all of his businesses, but I can't find anything."

"Can you get locations on some of those entries?" Jade asked Jamie and Gus. "I want to know which of them were made in Scotland."

"We need to know if Montague and Severini were ever in the same place," Patty added.

"And Robertson," Jade said. "Gus, look for him too."

"Angus Robertson, groundskeeper," Jamie told his colleague.

"Already on it," Gus grunted. He was small and round with dark, blinking eyes that made him look like he spent little time away from a computer screen.

Jade punched the desk. They were getting nowhere. Maybe she was wasting all their time.

"Taylor Gannon," Jade said. "I need to know more about her NDA. Did the Severinis have any connection to it?"

"I'm already looking," Gus told her.

She turned to Patty. "This is useless. We've already got everything we're going to get from the blog. Even if Montague and Severini were connected, what'll it have to do with Robertson?"

"If he really is the killer," Patty added.

Jade raised an eyebrow. "You think he isn't?"

"Taylor Gannon clearly hated her boss. Seeing what he did to his fiancée might have tipped her over the edge."

Jade had interviewed Taylor twice. She hadn't come across as a crusading feminist. "I don't know." She shook her head. "It might be the opposite."

"How d'you mean?"

"Maybe she didn't like being asked to arrange an abortion. Maybe she was opposed to it."

Patty shook her head. "She's a young woman."

"She's American. They feel differently about these things."

"Bloody stupid, if you ask me."

"We need to be looking elsewhere," Jade said.

Patty looked at her. "What about society columns?"

"They're just pretty photos of rich people."

Patty shook her head. "Stuart reads them. He thinks it'll help him progress, somehow. I keep telling him the police doesn't work like that any more, but he won't listen. We might be able to find photos of Severini and Montague together. Emily and Carla."

"Can't do any harm."

Patty switched from the blog to her browser. She started googling the Glasgow society websites and blogs. She sniffed as she scrolled through them.

"Blimey," she muttered.

"What?"

"This is a load of old crap. No idea how Stuart can stomach it."

"Keep looking." Jade turned to the screen with the video link. "Anything else from the blog?"

"Sorry," Jamie said.

"Hang on a mo," Patty interrupted.

Jade turned to her. "What?"

"Severini's never pictured with Carla, always some bimbo."

"I'm not sure that's the—"

"They're bimbos, boss. Look at them. But look at this one." She pointed at a photo of Steve Severini with an impossibly tall and thin young woman. She had blonde hair and wore a shimmering dress that was barely decent.

"What am I looking at?" Jade asked.

"Her hands. Her stomach."

The woman had her hands on her stomach. They lay there in just the way Jade had laid her hands on her own stomach when she'd been carrying Rory.

She leaned in. The dress did a good job of disguising it, but the woman's stomach wasn't flat.

"She was pregnant."

"She's holding a glass of orange juice," Patty said. "The rest of them have got Champagne."

"OK. Find out who she is. See if she had the baby."

CHAPTER SEVENTY-NINE

Mo GRABBED his phone and dialled Stuart.

No answer.

"Stuart, it's the sarge. Call me as soon as you get this, and don't go into the boat house. Return to the main house and await further orders."

He hung up and looked at PS Douglas. "I've got a member of my team who's gone to the boat house. He could be in danger."

"We've already sent a vehicle down there. I'll radio them."

"Good."

PS Douglas walked away from the cabin, talking into his radio and scanning their surroundings as he moved. Mo blinked a few times, following the other man's gaze. Where was Robertson? And what about Taylor Gannon?

He ran after Douglas.

"Have you got anyone at the main house?"

Not right now, DS Uddin. You told me to—"

"I know. But we need to go back there, and find Taylor Gannon."

Douglas nodded. "We'll drive."

Mo followed the sergeant to the 4x4 parked on the path that led from the main house to Robertson's cabin. He stared out at the woods as they drove to the house, scanning for Robertson, Gannon and Stuart.

As they pulled up, he called Stuart again. "DC Burns, it's DS Uddin. Repeat, do not enter the boat house. Return to the main house and wait at the door. Call me when you get this."

PS Douglas and the PC who'd driven them here were at the door to the house. They were motionless, waiting for instructions.

Was Taylor Gannon still in there? Would she be out in the woods, looking for Robertson?

Mo thought back to the message on Robertson's phone. *They don't suspect me.* So there was a reason to suspect the PA.

Was this related to the NDA? What had she done for Montague to pay her off?

Mo stopped. Severini! Maybe she was involved in his death, and Montague knew about it.

No. That was the wrong way round. If she'd been paid off, then it meant she knew something about Montague.

Or that she'd been involved in something.

Whatever it was, she considered herself worth being under suspicion. Which was good enough for Mo.

"Quietly," he muttered to Douglas. "She might not know we're coming."

The sergeant nodded. The 4x4 was on the far side of

some shrubs. There was a chance Gannon hadn't heard them, but it was slim.

Douglas nodded and the PC opened the door. He pushed it wide in silence and the two uniformed officers stepped inside. Douglas gestured for Mo to stay behind them.

Mo licked his lips and followed. The house was quiet, no sign of habitation.

The two officers worked their way through the space, silently opening one door after another. This was a modern building, one for which no expense had been spared. The doors opened smoothly, the floors muffled their footsteps. Mo would have been glad of it, except he knew that Gannon and Robertson would have the same advantage.

Douglas's radio crackled. He put a finger on it to silence it and inserted an earpiece into his ear. He listened for a moment, then beckoned Mo closer.

"Your DC is in the boat house," he said. "Robertson is with him."

Mo put a hand out to the wall. "Gun?" he whispered.

"We don't know. But we need more backup."

The PC was in front of them, looking back at his sergeant. The two of them exchanged nods.

"We need to withdraw," Douglas said. "I've requested an armed unit, it's on its way."

"We'll lose them."

"Only safe course of action."

Shit. The sergeant was right.

Mo nodded and turned back towards the door.

He stopped in his tracks.

Standing between them and the door, a wheeled suitcase in her hand, was Taylor Gannon.

CHAPTER EIGHTY

"SHIT."

Jade looked at Patty. She widened her eyes.

"That girl, in the photograph. Her name's Lola Villada, and she's seventeen years old. Or she was. I've found five more images of her with Severini, and there's a record of an NDA in the Severini holdings files."

"She looks older," Jade said.

"Amazing what you can do with makeup."

"She was paid to keep quiet about her pregnancy?"

"Another abortion, I'll bet. The next set of photos are from five months after that one, and look at her."

Jade bent over Patty's screen. If anything, the young woman was skinnier. Definitely not pregnant.

"We don't know if it's relevant," she said. "But I want to know who arranged that abortion."

"There are records of three more NDAs in the files. All with ridiculously young women. Each of them above sixteen, but only just. I bet you if I went through the society pages, I'd find them all hanging off Severini's arm. I've already seen a bunch of him with Montague and Emily. None of Carla, though."

"Bastard."

Patty flashed her eyes at Jade. "You said it."

"OK," Jade said. "I want to know who arranged those abortions. If Taylor set up Emily's, then maybe Severini approached Montague for assistance."

"Guys like that never talk to each other about these things. But he might have known about Emily, through Carla. And he might have known what Taylor did."

"She signed an NDA."

"Emily didn't, though. No record of one anywhere."

Jade tapped her chin with a fingernail. "We need to speak to Taylor Gannon."

"I don't get it though, boss."

"Get what?"

"It's Robertson we saw getting in that boat. He's married to Maria Watson. Severini's assistant. Taylor is Montague's assistant. It's the wrong one."

"The two women might have talked to each other. And Robertson would have been working for Montague when Emily was pregnant."

"In Scotland. Her abortion was in the US."

"Still," Jade said. "I want to talk to Taylor Gannon."

"The sarge will be able to find her, he's up at the Montague estate."

Jade nodded and grabbed her phone.

CHAPTER EIGHTY-ONE

"You can't shoot me, you know." Stuart stared at Robertson, forcing himself to maintain eye contact and not look down at the gun. It rested lightly in the man's hands, almost nonchalant despite its deadliness.

"Why not?"

"I'm a police officer. There's uniformed backup outside. You'll be shot."

"I've been watching you. There's no fucking backup. And who says I'm going to shoot you?"

Stuart's gaze flicked to the gun, and he cursed himself inwardly. Then he frowned. "You're not going to shoot me?"

Robertson laughed. "I've got you well and truly confused, nae? It's fun watching your face."

"If you're not going to shoot me..." Stuart knew he didn't have enough confidence in that idea to challenge the man.

"Then what?"

Stuart took a step forward. "Angus Robertson, I'm arresting you for assault. You don't have to—"

Robertson opened up his hands and waved the gun. Stuart tried not to shrink back.

"Where are the cuffs?" Robertson asked.

Stuart hadn't brought cuffs with him. They didn't have an arrest warrant, and he'd expected the sarge to deal with all that.

Bloody eejit.

"Back pocket," he said, trying to quell the tremor in his voice. "You're not getting away with this."

"Who says I want to?"

Stuart frowned. "You want to get shot?"

He heard a noise from behind him. Outside the boathouse? *Please be the sarge, please be the sarge.*

Or did he want the sarge turning up and putting himself in danger? That could just make things worse.

"I'm a martyr, pal." Robertson smiled. He didn't seem to have heard anything. "Dying for a cause."

"What cause might that be?"

"Life. The sanctity of life."

Stuart had no idea what Robertson was on about, but he did know he had to keep the man talking. Maybe backup was on its way. Maybe that was the sarge he'd heard, coming to find him after he hadn't turned up at the cabin.

That wasn't what they'd agreed. Was it? Stuart's brain felt fuzzy.

"You killed Phineas Montague. That's not exactly respecting the sanctity of life."

"He killed others. Plenty of them."

"Who?"

"You'll find out."

Stuart took a breath. He had to carry on talking, then

force himself to get closer to Robertson. If he could just get him to wave the gun again...

"Police! Don't move!"

Stuart felt his body seize up. The voice had come from behind him. It was Scottish. Not the sarge.

Who?

Robertson looked past Stuart's shoulder, towards the back corner of the boathouse. Stuart wondered if he should duck, or throw himself at the boat.

The voice behind him had given no instructions. Best to stay put.

Robertson's weight shifted just as Stuart heard a gunshot from behind him. Without his brain engaging, he threw himself to the ground, landing crooked against the side of the boat. Robertson fell no more than a foot in front of him. He cried out.

Fuck.

Stuart twisted round to see the source of the voice. Two armed officers stood in the doorway. One of them approached him, gun still raised.

Slowly, Stuart pushed up his arms.

"DC Stuart Burns, Complex Crimes Unit. Don't shoot."

CHAPTER EIGHTY-TWO

Mo's phone rang.

Not now.

He stared at Taylor Gannon, who stood very still. Eventually, she broke the silence.

"Who let you in?"

Mo's phone went quiet, then beeped. He ignored it.

"Police," he said. "Stay right where you are."

Behind him, PS Douglas had his truncheon raised. Gannon looked from Mo to him, seemingly unimpressed.

"That all ya got?" she laughed. "A fucking stick?"

Mo grabbed his phone and scanned the message onscreen. It was from Jade.

Taylor Gannon and Angus Robertson conspired to murder Montague and Severini. Warrant obtained.

He looked up. He didn't know the detail of it, but he trusted his new boss.

He took a step forward. Gannon looked back, her movements jerky. But he knew that between them, he and Douglas could outrun her.

"Taylor Gannon, I'm arresting you for conspiracy to murder."

CHAPTER EIGHTY-THREE

"WELL DONE," Fraser said. He gestured towards the two easy chairs in the corner of his office.

Jade followed his lead and sat down. She smoothed her trousers over her knees. "I didn't make either of the arrests."

"It was your team. And it was the evidence you found that gave us what we needed for a warrant."

"I'm still concerned that the CPS might not have enough."

"Angus Robertson threatened an officer with a gun. That's enough to send him down for some time, injuries or no. And your new DS said in his report that Taylor Gannon confessed to pretty much everything in the car en route to Glasgow."

Jade smiled. Taylor had indeed confessed to everything. She'd also thrown Angus Robertson deep into the shit, in the hope it might earn her a lighter sentence.

Trouble was, she'd done all this without anyone giving her any prior indication that it might work in her favour.

"Mo's written up a detailed report of what she told him in the car. And PC Hines from the armed unit can corroborate it."

"Good. They'll both be standing up in court, and then the defence will have no case."

"I hope so."

"So they were after revenge, were they? For the abortions."

Jade nodded. "Angus Robertson and Taylor Gannon belonged to a fundamentalist church. They were horrified by what Taylor had been required to do for her employer and his friend, and took matters into their own hands."

"Rather drastically."

"Indeed." She crossed her legs. "So, what's the future for the unit?"

"Before I answer that question, I need to know how much impact Dr McBride had."

"Her report pointed to an organised criminal, to it not being a crime of passion."

"It was revenge."

Jade nodded. "Cold revenge though, not hot. And Robertson had experience with guns.

"You think her analysis was useful?"

"She also pointed out that the gunman might have been an experienced hunter. As is Robertson. But it wouldn't have been enough without the blog and the legal documents that DC Henderson discovered."

"Good old-fashioned coppering."

"That's what Patty would say." She smiled. "Sir, I have a question."

"My name's Fraser, as you well know, but go ahead."

"This unit. It has a very grand name. The Complex Crimes Unit. But you have it headed up by a lowly DI. And one who hasn't exactly covered herself in glory in recent years."

"You're bloody good at your job, Jade, and don't try convincing yourself otherwise. And if we brought in a DCI or worse, there would be too much attention paid to the unit. I prefer not to make a big hoo-ha about what we're doing."

"The press has already made plenty of hoo-ha about this case."

"It'll die down. And internally, people will forget you."

Jade frowned. She didn't like where this was going. "Are you saying that some of our cases might be a little closer to home?"

He eyed her. "You know we have Professional Standards for corruption investigations. So, no. But when you're looking into the deaths of high profile individuals like Steve Severini and Phineas Montague... well, things can get awkward."

Jade opened her mouth for a follow-up question, then decided against it. She didn't want to know.

"Keep up the good work," Fraser said. "Petra can work with you on a freelance basis when she's needed, and you have your new DS to assist you."

"He did well at the Montague estate."

"So I heard." Fraser stood up. "Anyway, Jade, this is all much too formal. How have you been?"

Jade thought of Rory. He'd woken in the night and climbed into her bed, drenched in sweat. She was still struggling with the turning off the A82. But her own nightmares had stopped. Maybe one day she would be able to lead a normal life.

"I'm getting there."

He smiled and put a hand on her arm. "I'm glad to hear it. I miss our dinners. I know it's a bit weird just you and me, but I hope we can still be friends."

Jade felt her muscles relax. "Of course. I'd like that."

CHAPTER EIGHTY-FOUR

"Daddy!"

Isla hurtled through the ticket barrier and ran towards Mo. He planted his feet firmly, aware that she was getting bigger, and let her jump into his arms. He dipped for a moment under her weight, almost falling, then managed to correct himself. He buried his face in her hair. He'd almost forgotten what his kids smelt like.

Catriona wasn't far behind, tugging a vast suitcase with Fiona's help. She waited for Isla to disentangle herself, then gave Mo a hug.

"Hey, love," he said.

"Hey," she replied, her lips right by his ear. He felt a shiver run down his neck. He tightened his grip on her. It was good to see them all again.

"Where are we staying?" Fiona asked. She was ten now and beginning to show signs of teenage cynicism.

"I've rented a flat," he replied. "Well, my friend Patty has found one for me."

Cat raised an eyebrow. "Patty?"

He gave her a playful bat on the arm. "DC Patty Henderson. She's in my team."

Cat smiled. "Glad to see you're settling in. Where's this flat, then?"

"Glasgow, somewhere. I don't know."

"Nice?"

"I'm told."

"Good. Don't get too settled though. We've got six house viewings tomorrow."

"Six?"

She laughed. "It'll be fine. They're lovely, I'll show you."

"Let's get ourselves a cuppa first." The girls had gone on ahead, dragging the suitcase between them. Mo grabbed Catriona's arm and pulled her in for a kiss.

"I've missed you."

"It's only been a week."

"Still."

"You'll see plenty of me once I've moved up. All the more reason to find ourselves a lovely house."

"Or six of them."

She winked at him. "Or six of them."

CHAPTER EIGHTY-FIVE

Petra closed the door to her kitchen cabinet. She'd finally offloaded all the food that her aunt had left behind and gone shopping for her own. It wasn't exactly healthy: most of it was in tins. But this was Glasgow's West End and Petra was expecting to live mainly on takeaways. And now the case was closed, she was planning a brief trip to New York to see Ursula. She felt bad about the fact she'd been ignoring her girlfriend's messages while she'd been focused on the case and on settling into her new flat.

She looked out of the window, checking for movement along the street. No sign. Maybe she'd been imagining it.

But there had been calls, as well as the ring on the doorbell.

She shuddered. She could only hope they would give up.

Sighing, she went to the fridge and pulled out a bottle of Picpoul, her favourite. She'd found an independent wine shop a five-minute walk away and could see herself becoming a regular customer. She poured a glass then walked through to the living room and slumped on the sofa.

Her phone was on the coffee table. Its surface was clear now, none of her aunt's junk cluttering the place. She'd gone into a branch of Age Concern and told them they could take all the books for their shop. The flat felt twice as big without them.

She hesitated, calculating the time in New York. Nine pm here, so four in the afternoon there. It would be fine.

"Ursula Morris speaking."

"Hey, honey."

"Petra." A pause. "Hey."

"Is it a good time? You're not working?"

"Well..."

"I can call back." Petra took a swig of the wine.

"No. I've been meaning to call you."

Petra felt her stomach dip. "I know. I've been useless. I'll make it up to you. I can get a cheap flight to JFK next Tuesday."

"It's alright."

"Sorry?" Petra clutched the glass.

"I mean, don't put yourself out."

"I'm not... I'm not putting myself out." Petra bristled. "What's that supposed to mean?"

"I've been calling you and messaging you, and this is the first contact I've had from you since you left New York."

"It's only been eight days."

"Eight days, and a lot of unanswered calls. I was worried about you."

Petra sat up straight. "I didn't mean to... Look. My job is important to me. I was focused on helping with a murder inquiry. I can't just drop that to answer a personal call."

A sigh. "I know. But..."

"But what, Ursula?"

Petra tried to imagine Ursula on the other end of the line. She would be in her art gallery, winding up for the day. Her blonde hair tied up, perhaps, or flowing over her shoulders. Looking hot, either way.

"Ursula, I'm sorry. I'll come to New York, and we'll spend time together. It'll be great."

"Yeah, I know it will. But then what?"

"Well..."

"You'll go back to Glasgow, and you'll forget about me."

"I won't." Petra's voice was low. She knew she wasn't being entirely honest. Truth was, Petra was dreadful at giving people the attention they needed when she was focused on work. It was why she was still single.

Single.

She was about to become single again, she could feel it.

"Ursula, I love you. I want to make this work. Please, let me try."

"But that's just it, honey. You shouldn't have to try. It should just come easily."

It didn't. Petra had never found relationships easy and she wasn't about to start doing so in her forties. "All I can say is I'm sorry."

"I know, honey. I believe you. But..." A sigh. "But I'm afraid this just isn't going to work."

Petra said nothing. It was pointless.

"Petra? Aren't you going to say something?"

"What am I supposed to say? This is me. It's what I do. I'm sorry, Ursula. I really am."

"I know. Maybe we can be friends."

Petra shook her head, spilling wine on the rug. "I don't do that."

"OK. Then I guess this is goodbye."

CHAPTER EIGHTY-SIX

Jade's headlights swept across the front of the house, illuminating two silhouettes in the front window. One of them, the smaller one, jumped up and waved. She felt her heart fill up.

She sat for a few seconds to get her breath, then opened the car door just as the house's front door opened. Her mum stood in the doorway, Rory in front of her.

Rory ran towards the car and grabbed Jade's hand.

"It's here!"

"What is?"

She looked over him to see her mum had an eyebrow raised. Jade shrugged her shoulders in question and her mum responded with a quiet miaow.

Jade's eyes widened. She looked at Rory. "The kitten! Is it cute?"

"It's awesome, Mummy!"

"I bet it is!" She let Rory pull her inside. Her mum closed the door behind them.

She scanned the living room. "Where is it?"

"Shut in the bathroom," her mum replied. "Where it can do the least damage."

"Damage."

"It pees everywhere."

Rory laughed. "It hasn't been litter trained!"

"Then that'll be your job."

He looked horrified. "Ew."

She ran her hand through his hair. "It's OK. We'll do it together."

Rory adopted a solemn expression. "That's a job for a grown-up."

Jade looked back at the living room. A vase of flowers she hadn't seen before was on the side table. "Where did those come from?"

Her mum raised an eyebrow. "There's an envelope. I didn't open it."

"Give me just a second, Rory." Jade went to the flowers and grabbed the envelope from the table beside them. She had a sudden memory of Dan sending her flowers the day after their first date, and her chest hollowed out.

She put a hand on her stomach. *Breathe*. Her mum's hand was on her shoulder.

"You OK, love?"

Jade blinked. "Fine." She opened the envelope. "Shit." She turned to Rory. "I didn't say that, sweetie."

"Say what?"

"Nothing."

"Who are they from?" her mum asked.

"A colleague. Thanking me for cleaning up a case."

"That's quite a thank you."

Jade nodded. The flowers were from Fraser. It made her feel uneasy, and grateful at the same time.

She grabbed Rory's hand. "Come on. Show me this cute wee kitten."

He dragged her up the stairs. She pretended to resist, tugging on his hand and making out that she was being forced up there against her will. At the bathroom door, he stopped.

"You have to be very quiet."

"I will." Jade put a finger on her lips and her son nodded.

"Shall I?" she said, her hand on the doorknob. He nodded, his eyes bright. It was so good to see uncomplicated delight in his face, untainted by the memory of the last six months.

She opened the door. Peering out from the back of the toilet, its eyes wide and its ears so big Jade could barely believe it, was a kitten.

"I'm calling him Hamish."

"Hamish. That's a grand name." She put an arm around her son. "Welcome to the family, Hamish."

I hope you enjoyed *Blood and Money*. Do you want to get a taste of my bestselling Dorset Crime series, featuring Petra McBride? The series prequel, *The Ballard Down Murder*, is free from my book club at rachelmclean.com/ballard. *Thanks, Rachel McLean.*

READ A FREE NOVELLA, THE BALLARD DOWN MURDER

The Ballard Down Murder - the FREE prequel to the award-winning Dorset Crime series

DS Dennis Frampton is getting used to life without his old boss DCI Mackie, and managing to hide how much he hates being in charge of Dorset's Major Crimes Investigation Team. Above all, he must ensure no one knows he's still seeking Mackie's advice on cases.

But then Mackie doesn't show up to a meeting, and a body is found below the cliffs a few miles away.

When Dennis discovers the body is his old friend and mentor, his world is thrown upside down. Did Mackie kill himself, or was he pushed? Is Dennis's new boss trying to hush things up? And can Dennis and the CSIs trust the evidence?

Find out by reading *The Ballard Down Murder* for FREE at rachelmclean.com/ballard.

ALSO BY RACHEL MCLEAN - THE DORSET CRIME SERIES

The Corfe Castle Murders, Dorset Crime Book 1

The Clifftop Murders, Dorset Crime Book 2

The Island Murders, Dorset Crime Book 3

The Monument Murders, Dorset Crime Book 4

The Millionaire Murders, Dorset Crime Book 5

The Fossil Beach Murders, Dorset Crime Book 6

The Blue Pool Murders, Dorset Crime Book 7

...and more to come!

Buy now in ebook, paperback or audiobook

ALSO BY RACHEL MCLEAN - THE DI ZOE FINCH SERIES

Deadly Wishes, DI Zoe Finch Book 1

Deadly Choices, DI Zoe Finch Book 2

Deadly Desires, DI Zoe Finch Book 3

Deadly Terror, DI Zoe Finch Book 4

Deadly Reprisal, DI Zoe Finch Book 5

Deadly Fallout, DI Zoe Finch Book 6

Deadly Christmas, DI Zoe Finch Book 7, coming late 2022

Deadly Origins, the FREE Zoe Finch prequel

Buy now in ebook, paperback and audiobook

Made in the USA
Las Vegas, NV
31 July 2022

52458525R00204